D0312467

NEVER EVER

Sara Saedi

VIKING

VIKING
An imprint of Penguin Random House LLC
375 Hudson Street
New York, New York 10014

First published in the United States of America by Viking,
an imprint of Penguin Random House LLC, 2016

Copyright © 2016 by Sara Saedi

LIBRARY OF CONGRESS CATALOGING-IN-PUBLICATION DATA IS AVAILABLE
ISBN: 978-0-451-47576-3

Printed in U.S.A.   Set in Fournier MT   Book design by Kate Renner

10 9 8 7 6 5 4 3 2 1

To my parents, Ali and Shoreh Saedi.
For all of your sacrifices, encouragement, and love.

CHAPTER ONE

last day

wylie Dalton didn't know it yet, but in precisely two hours, sixteen minutes, and thirty-two seconds, her life would change forever. All that she once thought was real and true about the world would quickly fade away. Even the laws of gravity would no longer apply. Unlike every other detail of her life, the particulars of that day were something she wouldn't be allowed to share on any of her social media accounts. They would have to be kept a secret till the day she died.

Years from now, when Wylie relived the events of the day in her head, she would remember the weather was strangely warm for February in New York City. It was the kind of day when everyone strips off their winter coats and secretly admits that maybe climate change isn't so bad after all—minus the hurricanes and tornadoes and drowning polar bears. She'd also remember it was her seventeenth birthday. The first birthday when her mom forgot to make pancakes for breakfast and stick candles in them like she did every other year. These days it was a miracle if her mother even got out of bed. And anyway, the tradition felt childish and Wylie wasn't a child anymore. She hadn't been one for a long time. By the end of the night, she would no longer be a normal teenager either.

If she had known what was coming, Wylie might've done more with her last hours of normalcy than melt chocolate over a hot stove while trying to ignore the fact that her parents were berating each other upstairs. As her dad's voice got a touch louder, Wylie poured scalding batter into a ramekin dish, smiled brightly into her webcam, and silently prayed the audio from the fight wasn't loud enough to be recorded. It was so typical of her parents to strike up an argument just when she needed the house to be quiet. Plus, the bickering was currently at its most annoying decibel level: loud enough to be disruptive, but too quiet to make out exactly what was being said.

"Just place your ramekin in the oven for twenty minutes and you've got yourself a hot, gooey, chocolate soufflé. Or, as I prefer to call it, a chocolate volcano."

Wylie spoke the words into her webcam, but before she could get them out completely, her mom sobbed and her dad yelled out several choice expletives she could now decipher perfectly. Wylie barely flinched as she deleted the video. She couldn't teach anyone to cook with her parents dropping F-bombs in the background. Maybe a better upload would be *How to Deal with Your Insanely Dysfunctional Mom and Dad*. Wylie shut her laptop, stuck a spoon in the batter, and trekked upstairs to the disaster area known as her bedroom.

Every inch of Wylie's desk was covered with homework assignments and textbooks. The bed hadn't been made in weeks. The hamper was filled to the brim with dirty clothes, including her sweaty basketball uniform. But keeping a clean bedroom was low on her priority list. Who had the time, with school, basketball practice, piano lessons, SAT prep classes, and her cooking channel?

"You're too scheduled," her guidance counselor at school lectured her. "You're a teenager. You have the rest of your life to feel overextended and stressed out. At this rate, you'll get wrinkles before you turn eighteen. You have to give something up."

School, Wylie wanted to respond. *I'll give up school.*

At least now that her cooking video was a bust, Wylie had the rare window of opportunity to take a nap. She curled up under her flannel sheets and closed her eyes just as she heard her dad yell, "I will not stand here and let you blame me for your mistakes!"

You're both to blame! Wylie wanted to yell back.

Most people wouldn't be able to fall asleep with their parents in the middle of a shouting match, but it was white noise to Wylie—sort of like those machines that make the sound of waves crashing to help lull you to sleep.

That hadn't always been the case. When she was a kid, the fights had knocked the wind right out of her. Wylie's younger brothers, Joshua and Micah, would tap on her door and seek shelter in her room. They were little then, but it was still a tight squeeze for all three of them to sleep in her twin bed together. Even when they were children, she knew to lie and tell them everything would be okay: *Sometimes grown-ups fight.*

But as the years went on, the arguments became so frequent that the Dalton siblings stayed in their separate bedrooms, no longer fazed by the emotional confessions, the empty threats, or the varying degrees of passive-aggression. Wylie became so good at falling asleep to the timbre of their fights, she dreaded evenings when her dad had to work late and their Upper East Side brownstone became eerily quiet. Those were the nights Wylie lay in bed awake, her thoughts drowning out the other sounds of the city she'd become accustomed to: car alarms, fire trucks, muffled jazz music coming from the home of their next-door neighbors.

What kept her tossing and turning was the nagging fear that one day she would be old, just like her parents. She would grow up to be just as damaged and bitter as they were. The thought of looking in the mirror years from now and seeing her mom or dad staring back at her was enough to keep Wylie up all night.

A knock on the door put an untimely end to Wylie's nap.

"Wylie, can I come in?" her dad asked.

"Am I allowed to say no?" she answered.

"No."

"Fine, door's open."

Her dad walked in, looking different to Wylie from the last time she'd seen him, a few days before. There was more gray in his hair, and his eyes looked red and puffy from what she guessed were some sleepless nights. He held a perfectly wrapped present in his hand. Wylie was tempted to ask if his assistant had picked it out.

"Happy birthday, sweet pea," he said, handing her the gift.

"I'm too old to be called that, but thanks," Wylie said as she placed the present on her bedside table.

"Aren't you going to open it?" her dad asked.

"Maybe later."

Wylie wasn't sure if it was a birthday gift or a bribe, but either way, she preferred to open it in private. If she liked it too much, then it might absolve her father of some of his guilt.

"Wylie, you know . . . if there's anything you want to talk about, I'm here for you."

"Actually," Wylie said, "you're not here. You're living in a hotel room."

Two weeks before, her mom had called for a Dalton family meeting, and as they all gathered in the living room, she announced (somewhat melodramatically, Wylie thought) that their dad would be moving out of the house, because *he* wanted a divorce. Wylie's mom openly wept, as though she were an innocent bystander in her failed marriage, but Wylie knew that wasn't the case. Over the years, she had witnessed her mom slowly inch away from her dad. The occasional "I love you" would go unreturned or her hand would pull away as soon as her dad reached for it. That was why she couldn't muster any sympathy or words of comfort for either of her parents. It wasn't until Wylie was alone in her room that she collapsed on her bed and cried her eyes out. And then she promptly wiped away the tears and buried her face in her SAT workbook.

As if that wasn't enough, all this came in the weeks leading up to her brother Joshua's sentencing. But even with their family in turmoil, they still planned to celebrate Wylie's birthday together with dinner at Le Bernardin followed by frozen hot chocolates at Serendipity. According to her mom, it was just a case of "unfortunate timing" that this would be their last night together before Joshua got shipped off to juvie.

Wylie and her brothers had always been a package deal. Wherever one Dalton sibling went, the others followed. But this time, that would be impossible. And it was all Wylie's fault.

"How's Joshua really holding up?" her dad asked, glancing at Wylie's bulletin board covered with photos of her friends.

"Okay, I guess."

"I know you love this house and your room and that there are a million reasons to stay with your mom. But just so you know, I've signed a lease on an apartment with enough space for you and your brothers. It's close to your school—oh and here's the best part: it's got a big kitchen with a brand-new Viking stove and plenty of counter space. Perfect for us to cook together. Think about it."

If the same opportunity had been posed to Wylie a year before, she would have agreed to live with her dad without hesitation. He attempted a smile.

"Great sound system, too—I can just see us making

some homemade pizza, singing along to a little Simon and Garfunkel—"

She cut him off. "Is your girlfriend going to be living there, too?"

"I don't know what your mom's been telling you, but—"

"She hasn't told me anything. It's amazing what you can find out about a person with one Google search."

Her dad loosened his tie as beads of sweat formed on his brow. He cleared his throat.

"Look, Wylie. I've made some mistakes as a husband, but I don't want it to change how you feel about me as a dad. I wish I could explain things better, but there's a lot you won't understand about marriage until you're older."

She hated when adults said stuff like that. If they were so wise and evolved, then why did they always seem to make a mess of everything?

"I should get ready for dinner," Wylie said. "Thanks again for the gift. I'll see you downstairs."

As soon as her dad left, Wylie jumped out of bed, examined her face in the mirror, and wiped the sleep from her eyes. Her normally olive complexion had turned a pale yellow from the months of dreary winter weather. She quickly applied a generous amount of blush to her cheekbones and covered her lips with a coat of coconut-flavored gloss. Now for an outfit change. She threw the doors to her closet open, gave the pile of clothes a once-over and opted for a navy dress to throw over the leggings she was already wearing. It wasn't her favorite dress, but she knew it was clean. She finished the outfit off with a pair of brown leather booties.

Heels weren't an option. They were far too impractical for climbing down a rickety fire escape.

Wylie knocked on the wall three times, and Joshua and Micah tiptoed into her room. Micah was in his regular uniform: combat boots, black cut-offs, and a skull-and-bones T-shirt. Joshua wore jeans, a Henley, and a knitted cardigan with suede elbow pads. Wylie smiled at her brothers and tried to shake off the anger she was still feeling from the conversation with her dad.

"This is it," Wylie announced mournfully. "Our last night together for who knows how long."

"Stop," Joshua insisted. "I don't want a pity party. It's your birthday, and all we're going to do is celebrate. And anyway, I'll be in good company. A lot of great men have served time, so don't waste any energy feeling bad for me."

It was so like Joshua to worry about everyone else. Wylie liked to think that one day the accident would no longer be part of his legacy and that her brother would still fulfill his childhood aspiration of running for president. His future campaign advisor would find a way to spin things so that Joshua's error in judgment would make him more grounded and relatable. And maybe even the girl they'd put in the coma would wake up tomorrow and forgive them. Years later, they would arrange for her to go on the campaign trail with him. "If I can forgive," she would say from her wheelchair, "America can, too." Joshua's dreams of becoming the leader of the free world would come true. He would single-handedly clean up Washington and change the world.

Wylie quietly opened her bedroom window, and she and her brothers carefully climbed out onto the fire escape.

They sat there for a while, passing around the chocolate batter that had never made it into the oven. Even though it was February, the air felt warm. Wylie fanned herself with her purse, certain that in a few hours the temperature would drop drastically and she would freeze her ass off.

"What did Dad have to say?" Joshua asked.

"Nothing important. Just that I'm too young to understand anything."

"Then what's his excuse?" Micah mumbled. He licked the batter off the spoon. "Why does this taste so spicy?"

"I added a pinch of cayenne pepper," Wylie admitted. "Maybe more than a pinch."

"Would it kill you to actually follow a recipe?" Joshua piped in.

"I always follow the recipes. I just like to experiment, that's all."

"Maybe we should have gotten you a cookbook," Joshua said as he handed her two birthday gifts, wrapped in the finance section from the *New York Times*.

Wylie never understood why some people carefully peeled away at gift wrap. As far as she was concerned, birthday presents were meant to be torn open. She opened Micah's present first. It was a comic book he had created himself. She flipped through it. The Dalton siblings were the heroes, all with unique superpowers. Joshua could literally kill people with kindness, Micah could become invisible, and Wylie could control people's minds. The villains bore a striking resemblance to their parents, of course.

Wylie gave Micah a huge hug. She told him how talented

he was, and he brushed off the compliment like he always did.

Next came Joshua's gift. She ripped it open, only to find another layer of wrapping, then another, and another. She eventually reached the last scrap of newspaper. Inside was a shiny silver compass.

"I found it at a pawnshop near school," Joshua explained. "I thought you could keep it with you while I'm gone."

Wylie slipped the compass into her purse and thanked Joshua. She didn't tell him that regardless of which direction she headed in, she would be absolutely lost without him.

"Kids! The car will be here in five minutes to take us to dinner," Wylie's mom yelled from downstairs.

"We'd better get down there before she has an aneurysm," Joshua said.

Wylie shook her head. "We're not going to dinner."

"You gonna break the news to her? Because there's no way I'm doing it," Joshua replied. "It's already bad enough that I'm going to jail. I don't need to get murdered by Mom beforehand."

"No one's going to tell her. We're sneaking out," Wylie said.

"Seriously?" Micah asked.

"Seriously. There's no way we're spending Joshua's last night of freedom at some stuffy French restaurant with Mom and Dad. I'm giving you a night you'll never forget. It's the least I can do."

Her brothers didn't need much convincing. As soon as their feet hit the sidewalk on East 83rd Street, Wylie waved her hand at an off-duty cab, and as usual, its light magically went on. The yellow Prius pulled over and they all piled in.

"Where to, kids?"

"Williamsburg," Wylie replied.

"And if you don't mind, could you take the scenic route?" Joshua added.

Wylie noticed this was the one mention of what waited for him tomorrow that Joshua allowed himself. Tonight might be the last time for a while that he'd get to stare out a car window at the sights of the city he grew up in.

But tomorrow none of them would wake up in Manhattan. Or any of the neighboring boroughs, for that matter.

eye contact

rooftops were the only proper place to throw a party in New York City. Most apartments were small and claustrophobic, and unless you were an heiress or a movie star, you hit capacity at ten guests. Luckily, Wylie's best friend Vanessa and her parents lived in a brand-new building in Williamsburg where the roof offered a view of the Manhattan skyline and the ripples of the East River. Wylie was glad Vanessa had volunteered to throw Joshua's good-bye party, since there was nowhere else they could fit everyone who loved her brother.

As soon as the Daltons arrived, Micah retreated to a corner of the roof and scrolled through his phone. Some of their friends hung back, not entirely sure what form of greeting would be appropriate under such unhappy circumstances. But Joshua's smile instantly put them at ease.

"I am gonna miss you all so much when I'm doing hard time," he called out, "except for you, Evan. Three years of not having to look at that tragic mug is what I like to call a silver lining."

Evan was Joshua's friend and biggest rival. He was the sophomore class vice president and with Joshua going to juvie, he'd get to slide into his position as president.

"What do you say we ditch this party, Dalton, and get you a teardrop tattoo?" Evan replied.

"The night is young," Joshua answered. "Anything could happen."

Wylie was pulled in a million different directions as she moved her way into the party. She stopped to say hello to Kendra and Jess, who were in the middle of discussing a new Broadway show they'd just seen. They were always trying to get Wylie to audition for the school musical, but no one seemed to believe it when she said she couldn't carry a tune unless she was doing karaoke.

"Catch!" One of Wylie's friends from her art class tossed a piece of colored chalk at Wylie, and she caught it with one hand. A few of the artsy kids from Harper Academy were drawing a mural in her brother's honor. Wylie added a quick sketch of their brownstone, then excused herself to say hello to Abigail, Joshua's girlfriend, the Jackie to his JFK.

"How are you holding up?" Wylie asked.

"As well as could be expected," Abigail answered, slurring her words slightly. Abigail hardly ever drank, but right now she smelled like she'd taken a bath in tequila.

"We'll get through it," Wylie said, trying to convince them both. Abigail left to occupy her usual spot by Joshua's side, and Wylie moved off to find Vanessa and the rest of the girls from the basketball team.

"This party sucks," Vanessa said as soon as she saw her.

"No, it doesn't. Everyone's having a blast," Wylie replied.

"But no one's dancing."

Wylie shrugged. "Never fear, bestie. If there's one thing I know how to do, it's get a dance party started."

Wylie grabbed a bottled water from the bar and confidently moved to the center of the rooftop. She started dancing by herself, half expecting Vanessa and the rest of the team to join in. When they didn't budge, Wylie took Vanessa's hand.

"Come on! Dance!" she urged.

"Everyone's going to think we're total weirdos, dancing by ourselves!" Vanessa said, trying to pull out of her grip.

"Who cares?" Wylie did a few ridiculous dance moves and Vanessa finally joined in.

"You're crazy, Wylie."

"That's why you love me!"

Within a few minutes, the dance floor filled up. A few of Wylie's friends abandoned their circle to dance with their boyfriends, but none of the guys from school approached her. A few of them lingered nearby, hoping she'd accidentally dance with them, but that tactic never worked on Wylie.

After at least an hour on the dance floor, Wylie felt a pair of eyes burn into the back of her neck. Someone was staring at her. *Just keep dancing,* she told herself. She never liked the way some people ogled her, like they were trying to decide if her glossy hair, enormous green eyes, and pronounced dimples meant she was a stuck-up bitch. Too many guys stared her down, then never even bothered to walk over to say hello.

"Don't look, but there's some guy checking you out," Vanessa teased, confirming Wylie's suspicion. She didn't look.

"Do we know him? Does he go to our school?"

Vanessa glanced at the guy, then reported her findings.

"I don't think so. He looks older and he's ridiculously hot. He's sitting with Micah."

"My *brother* Micah?"

Vanessa nodded. "He has not taken his eyes off you."

Maybe it was from all the dancing or the bizarre weather, but Wylie felt herself getting hot. Her entire body went still, suddenly too self-conscious to move to the music. No one had ever stared at her so intensely. She could feel her resolve slipping as the desire to turn around started to get the best of her.

"Oh my God. He's coming over here!" Vanessa nearly shrieked.

Now Wylie couldn't help herself. She looked over her shoulder and glanced back at her admirer. He wasn't looking at her body, like most guys did; he was focused purely on her eyes. And he was irrefutably beautiful. Not in a movie-star way. More like a work of art, as though someone had drawn every feature and sculpted every limb. His hair looked brown, but as he came closer, she could see it was more auburn. In the fairy tales her dad used to tell her when she was little, all the princesses had auburn locks. She'd tried to put auburn streaks in her hair with henna once, but it just made her brown waves look even darker.

His eyes, still glued to hers, were nearly the same color as his hair. Or maybe they were more hazel—it was dark and he was still too far away to be certain. He had a small scar above his eyebrow and when he smiled at her, she could see that he needed a little dental work, though she barely noticed his teeth behind his full lips.

Vanessa was right, though. He seemed older, and Wylie had a rule about avoiding college guys. Men who couldn't find someone to date their own age probably had something wrong with them. If he was coming over here to hit on her, she'd ask him where he went to school and once the answer was Columbia or NYU or Fordham, she'd tell him she and her friends were having a girls' night and ignore him for the rest of the party.

After a series of slow, deliberate steps, he stopped right on the periphery of where Wylie and her friends were dancing. He gave her a small wave and she acknowledged the greeting with a polite smile. She expected him to come closer and say hello, but instead he simply nodded his head back, gesturing for her to leave with him. *He's definitely older*, she thought. No guy her age had that kind of confidence. But she didn't like being summoned.

Before she could contemplate her next move, a few of her girlfriends screamed in excitement as the DJ, a junior at Wylie's high school, played what Wylie considered her theme song. She'd heard it a million times, but it was one of those few anthems she never got sick of, and all her friends knew it was her favorite. The DJ leaned into his microphone.

"This one goes out to Wylie Dalton from all your fans

at Harper Academy. Happy seventeenth birthday, girl."

Wylie's friends and the rest of the partygoers drunkenly cheered. A few different male voices yelled, "We love you, Wylie!" She made a face at Vanessa and the rest of her friends. The shout-out was a sweet gesture and normally she would embrace it, but she didn't want anyone making a fuss over her birthday. Tonight was supposed to be a last hurrah for her brother, not a party for her.

Once the cheers subsided, Wylie allowed herself to glance at the guy, but as soon as she looked at him, he took two steps back. It was his way of telling her she was running out of time. If she didn't make a move soon, he would leave and she might kick herself for the rest of her life. She took a long gulp of her water, handed the bottle to Vanessa, and walked over to him. His gaze was still too intense for her, so she focused on his chin. It was perfectly chiseled with little bits of auburn stubble all over it. She figured it was the safest facial feature to keep her eyes fixed on while she steadied her nerves, but even his chin got the best of her. Wylie cleared her throat.

"Didn't your parents teach you it's rude to stare?" she asked him.

"No," he said, smiling. "They never got the chance. They died when I was a little kid."

Crap. Wylie felt her ears burn. She'd thought she was being brave and flirtatious, but she'd said a mere nine words to him and had already put her foot in her mouth. She looked down at the floor.

"I'm sorry."

Wylie quickly turned around to seek refuge back on

the dance floor, but the guy reached for her arm and gently grasped it. His fingertips touched the inside of her wrist.

"Didn't *your* parents teach you it's rude to turn your back on people?" he asked.

Wylie laughed. She couldn't help it.

"No. They turn their backs on everything."

Vanessa and the rest of her friends called for her from the dance floor, but Wylie knew she wouldn't be joining them any time soon. She gave them a small wave, then returned her attention to the boy with the auburn hair.

"Wylie. I'm famished." He said it like they'd known each other all their lives. "What do you say we go get something to eat?"

He must have heard the DJ say her name. Wylie had always liked her name—it was tough and unique and seemed to suit her—but hearing him utter the two syllables made her like it even more. There was nothing but confidence in his voice. Most guys shuffled their feet and kept their hands in their pockets when they spoke to Wylie, but this one was an entirely different creature, and she wasn't sure how to respond.

"I don't even know you," she finally replied.

"Which is exactly why I'd like to have dinner with you. So we can get to know each other."

Wylie hesitated. She was supposed to spend tonight with her brothers. What kind of sister would she be if she ditched them for a hot, mysterious stranger?

"Tell me your name first."

"Phinn," he answered. He extended his hand to her. She

took it. His palms felt a little dry and callused, but his handshake was firm and gentle at the same time.

"Okay, Phinn. Thanks for the invite, but I can't leave my brothers."

"That's very considerate, but I'm sure they'll be fine without you—take a look."

Wylie looked around. Micah was sitting on the ledge of the roof, preoccupied by his phone. He was probably playing a video game, like he always did at parties. She spotted Joshua and Abigail hanging out near the bar, in the thick of an argument. Wylie could tell by the way her brother's girlfriend was leaning against the bar that she was wasted.

"It seems like they need their alone time. Come with me, just for a little while. I promise it'll be an adventure."

"How old are you?" she asked him, suspicious.

"Seventeen. Same age as you."

She wasn't sure she believed him. She knew she was taking a risk by leaving with a stranger, but Brooklyn was still relatively busy at this hour. Wherever they went to eat, it would be well lit, and there would be plenty of people close enough to hear her scream. Plus, if he tried anything, she had a few self-defense moves in her back pocket, and pepper spray in her purse. Wylie wasn't afraid to gouge someone's eyes out if left with no other choice.

"You seem older."

"So do you. What do you know? We already have something in common."

"Hold that thought," Wylie said.

She hurried over to Vanessa. "Hot guy and I are gonna get some food. Text me in two hours if I'm not back."

"Nicely done," Vanessa said. "Be safe."

Wylie turned back toward Phinn, but he was waiting by the stairwell, as though he already knew she was coming with him.

❖ ❖ ❖ ❖ ❖ ❖

SHE ASSUMED HE'D HAVE A FAVORITE THAI PLACE IN the area or a quaint little wine bar; this was the last spot in the world Wylie had expected him to take her. The lights were far too bright and the restaurant was nearly empty, apart from a few homeless people. She was probably five or six years old the last time she'd eaten here. These days, even when she was out late and starving, she opted to go home and whip up a grilled cheese sandwich instead of heading to their neighborhood McDonald's. But apparently, the boy with the auburn hair who went by the name of Phinn had a weakness for fast food.

She sat at a booth, composing a text to her friends that the weirdo from the party had taken her on a hot date to Mickey D's, but before she could hit Send, he returned with five happy meals and a goofy smile on his face. Wylie's decision to quit drinking was turning out to be a big mistake tonight. She wasn't sure how long she could sit across from him, completely sober, under the fluorescent lights of a fast-food franchise.

"I hope you're hungry," Phinn said, still grinning. He opened up each happy meal and carefully placed containers of Chicken McNuggets, sweet-and-sour sauce, and French fries and several cheeseburgers on the table. The smell of the food took Wylie back to simpler times, but she wouldn't allow herself to give way to her hunger. They'd watched a documentary about the meat industry in science class a couple years before, and she was still traumatized by it. Phinn, on the other hand, had no qualms about indulging in greasy food and clearly wasn't shy about eating in front of strangers. Sloppy eating would normally be a turn-off for Wylie, but on a guy this handsome, the loud chewing and the ketchup dripping from his mouth was oddly humanizing, and felt like a sign that he was comfortable around her.

"Are you nervous?" he asked, talking with his mouth full.

"No," Wylie lied. "Why?"

"You're fidgeting."

Wylie quickly sat on her hands, hoping it would help her keep still.

"And you're not eating." He said it less like an accusation and more like an observation. Wylie tried to respond without sounding judgmental.

"I'm not really into fast food," she answered.

"I know it's not healthy. But you have to admit, it tastes pretty damn good."

Phinn picked up a chicken nugget, dipped it into the sweet-and-sour sauce, and waved it an inch from her face.

"Come on, take a little bite. You know you want to," he said flirtatiously.

"Really, I'm okay."

"You're totally grossed out right now, aren't you? I don't eat this way all the time. They don't have McDonald's where I'm from, so I try to get it every time I'm in the city. It's kind of a tradition."

Wylie stared at him, confused.

"Where could you possibly live that doesn't have a McDonald's? They're everywhere."

"I'm from a very small town." Phinn brought the chicken nugget even closer to her lips. "Come on, one bite. Please. It would mean a lot to me," he teased.

Wylie opened her mouth and let him feed her. He was right: it tasted delicious. The bite reminded her brain and her belly that the only drawback to skipping dinner with her parents was that there was no food in her system. So Wylie helped Phinn polish off every last bite of the feast he'd laid out on the table—the fries, the burgers, even the signature apple pies.

As soon as Phinn had eaten his last pie, he wiped his hands on his pants and leaned close to her.

"Wylie." He spoke her name with such gravity, like he was about to tell her he was dying, and this was his last night on earth.

"Yes?"

"I want to know everything about you."

It was easily the sexiest thing anyone had ever said to her, even if it was some line he'd used on countless girls before tonight.

"Where do you want me to start?" she asked.

"Tell me about your family."

Before she could say a word, the fluorescent lights in the restaurant began to flicker, and one of the homeless guys yelled that he wanted a free refill on his soda.

"You want to get out of here? The present company's not exactly conducive to sharing your life story," Phinn said.

Wylie nodded. Phinn put a hand on the small of her back as they walked through the exit and onto a now-peaceful street in Williamsburg. The cold draft and absence of bright lighting felt like a huge relief once their feet hit the sidewalk.

"All right, start at the beginning," Phinn said. And so she began by telling him about her parents.

"When my parents were young, my dad was this fancy investment banker and my mom was this crazy artist. They kind of met by accident. He was tagging along with a friend to her going-away party. She was supposed to leave New York to study art in California, but they fell in love and she changed all her plans."

"She stayed in New York for him?"

"Yup. They had this whirlwind romance and got married after a few months. And instead of having kids, they decided they would travel the world. My mom got knocked up with me in Paris. It was their first trip together. They've never said it outright, but I'm pretty sure I was an accident," Wylie said, sticking closely to the truth for now.

"A happy accident," Phinn was quick to add.

"Depends on the day. Anyway, my dad always said my brothers owe their lives to me. I was such a sweet and easy baby, they decided to have more kids. So my mom never went to art school and stayed at home with us instead. My whole life, I've never even seen her pick up a paintbrush."

"Does she miss it?" Phinn asked.

"I wouldn't know."

From there, the conversation turned to her brothers.

"They're my best friends," Wylie explained. "I would

do anything for them. Joshua's the smart one. It's actually a little annoying. He's a year younger, but people always think he's the oldest, just because he's the most responsible. He actually wants to be president someday."

Phinn let out a small laugh.

"I know it sounds ridiculous coming from most people," Wylie told him, "but not from Joshua. When he tells people who know him that he's going to run for office, they don't pat him on the head and tell him he's adorable, they say they'll vote for him. He's like a young JFK. And you should meet his girlfriend, Abigail. They've been together since their freshman year in high school and I swear, she'll probably be First Lady someday."

Wylie was tempted to leave out the entire story about the hit-and-run and the fact that her brother was going to be sentenced tomorrow, but it felt like too big of an omission. And she was glad she'd given Phinn the bullet points, because he admitted to reading something about it online. But when he made more inquiries about what had caused the accident, she didn't tell him that the whole thing was her fault. The only other people who knew that part of the story were her brothers.

The clouds began to roll in and a light mist fell. They sought shelter under the awning of a bus stop. Phinn cleared the trash off the bench and they sat down.

"I met your brother Micah when I got to the party," Phinn told her. "He seems like the introspective type."

"He's always been shy, but he's also really talented. I guess he takes after my mom. He loves comic books and he's been working on a graphic novel for a while."

Wylie left out Micah's therapist visits over the years, all the diagnoses he'd been given, and all the Ritalin and anti-depressants he'd consumed. And she didn't breathe a word of that night a couple years ago, when she'd snuck a bottle of whiskey into Micah's room and gotten him drunk while their parents had their worst fight ever. And the fact that since that night, he never left the house without his flask.

"And what about your parents now," Phinn asked. "Are they happily married?"

Wylie laughed. She debated making up a story about how in love they still were, but there was no way she'd get through it with a straight face.

"They're in the process of getting divorced, which means we're in the process of picking which one we want to live with."

"So, who's the chosen one?" Phinn asked.

"I'd rather run away from home than live with either one of them. I wish I was old enough to live by myself."

Wylie made no mention of her dad's affair. It felt wrong to tell Phinn something she'd never had the courage to tell her brothers, especially since she had only found out by accident. She'd gone to her dad's office late one night to surprise him and saw him kissing another woman through the open crack of the door. Wylie had slipped away before they noticed her. She tried not to get lost in the memory.

"What about you? Tell me about your life," she asked.

"What do you want to know?" Phinn responded.

"I don't know—what's your biggest fear?"

Wylie had been trying to come up with a more interesting question than the old standbys of "Where do you go to school?" and "What do you do for fun?" but Phinn answered as if he'd expected this exact line of questioning.

"Getting old."

Wylie nodded. "Yet another thing we have in common."

Phinn's excitement was infectious as the words poured out of him, and Wylie could relate to almost everything he said. Phinn confessed he would rather die young than grow old, because old people were cynical and bitter and couldn't take care of themselves anymore.

"I've never been all that interested in the confines of convention," Phinn continued. "High school, college, job, wife, kids, grandkids, nursing home, death. I could live without all of it."

The buzz of Wylie's phone interrupted their conversation. She checked her texts and found messages from Micah, as well as one from Vanessa, making sure she was okay. *Never been better,* she quickly texted back.

She wanted to stay, but it was getting late and she needed to get back to the party.

"I know that look," Phinn said. "You're about to break my heart by telling me you have to go."

"I am," she responded, and then before she knew the words were coming out, "Do you want to come with me?"

"I can't, Wylie. I was supposed to be home hours ago. But," he continued, "there's one last thing I want to do with you before I go."

Wylie waited for him to lean in or pull her face toward him for a kiss, but instead, he reached into his back pocket and took out a small pouch that looked like it had been woven out of reeds. He tilted it, revealing a bundle of tiny royal blue flowers unlike any she'd ever seen before. Phinn gently took her hand and placed a flower in the center of her palm. Wylie wondered if it was some peculiar parting gift he gave to every female stranger he stumbled across.

"Go ahead. Try it," he told her.

"What do you mean, 'try it'?"

"It's edible."

"There's no way I'm eating this."

"Don't you trust me?"

"Of course not! I just met you."

Phinn took another flower out of the pouch and placed it in his mouth. He chewed it slowly, then swallowed.

"That's too bad. I was hoping we could have an adventure together."

Wylie wasn't about to let all her common sense go out the window just because a cute guy was paying attention to her. The night had been almost perfect, and now he had spoiled it.

"I should go. It was nice to meet you."

Before she could walk away, Phinn suddenly grew several inches right before her eyes. It took her a while to figure out that his body hadn't expanded, but that he was in fact floating above the bench they'd been sitting on. Phinn slowly drifted all the way to the top of the awning and did a backflip in the air. Wylie's eyes widened.

This could not be happening. And if it was, then Wylie was dreaming. She opened her fist and looked at the tiny blue flower, still in the palm of her hand. Phinn must have slipped something in the sweet-and-sour sauce, because she was definitely hallucinating. She closed her eyes, opened them, closed them again, opened them again—but he was still there, floating in front of her, until they heard footsteps and voices, and then he quickly floated back down to the bench.

"Now do you trust me?" he asked.

This time Wylie nodded.

As soon as the voices and the footsteps were no longer audible, Wylie chewed the flower. It tasted like mint and honey. Her stomach plummeted as her entire body floated up into the air. Phinn glided back up to her and took her hands. And then suddenly, the two of them shot straight up into the sky like a rocket ship. Wylie screamed her head off. The adrenaline was more intense than any roller coaster she had ever been on. She closed her eyes tight, not wanting to see how high up in the air they were.

"This is scary! I want to go back down!" she shouted in his ear. Phinn squeezed her hands tighter, but they kept going higher and higher.

"You're panicking because you feel out of control," Phinn told her. "But you're safe with me. I won't let go. The more you fly, the more you'll be in control."

Wylie nodded, but kept her eyes shut.

"Open your eyes. I promise you won't regret it."

Wylie's eyes popped open and she let out a small scream, then succumbed to laughter. They were flying high above the Williamsburg Bridge, so high that no one would ever be able to see them.

"Can I show you the rest of the city like this?" Phinn asked.

Wylie was scared to move, but she managed to whisper

her consent. Phinn held her hand the whole time as they whizzed past the Empire State Building and over Central Park. They swooped above the Upper East Side, and Wylie was able to point out their brownstone to him and the fire escape that was her salvation. Seeing the city, the place she had grown up in, from a bird's-eye view was so incredible that Wylie didn't even have time to wonder whether Phinn was a magical elf or an alien or a robot. She felt safe here.

There was only one thing that made her anxiety bubble. Micah and Joshua weren't with her, and it felt wrong to experience this without them.

the after-party

"wylie!" Micah screamed.

"Where did she say to meet her?" Joshua asked, his patience clearly wearing thin.

"Her text said right here in front of the building. She said it was an emergency."

"Well, she's not here. She made us leave the party for no reason."

Wylie observed the rest of their exchange, hovering just a few feet above them. She bit her bottom lip, trying hard not to laugh as her brothers bitched and moaned about their irresponsible older sister, who was always running off and disappearing.

"I'm right here, jerks," she finally called down. "Look up."

Joshua and Micah tilted their heads up to the sky and locked eyes with Wylie, floating on her stomach. Phinn did a somersault in the air next to her.

"What the hell?" Joshua said.

"Remember how you wanted to take the scenic route to-night?" Wylie asked Joshua. He slowly nodded. "Well, it doesn't get much more scenic than this. You guys feel like taking flight?"

"This is crazy," Micah said, lowering himself to the curb. He took a sip from his flask.

"I don't know what kind of joke you're trying to play on us, but it's not funny. Now get down," Joshua demanded. Wylie knew his tone well. She'd been hearing it a lot recently. Combine one cup of disapproval with a half-cup of indignation and a healthy pinch of pissed-off, and stir.

Phinn grabbed Wylie's hand and slowly brought her back to solid ground. It took her a while to regain her balance, like when she took her ice skates off after gliding in circles at the rink in Central Park. Wylie tried to focus on steadying her legs, but she couldn't ignore the judgment on her brothers' faces. It didn't matter that she'd just defied the laws of gravity in front of them; she'd deserted them at the party.

"I suck," Phinn said to Joshua and Micah. "I dragged your sister out of the party. And then I scared the crap out of you. The whole 'flying in midair' thing usually kills. Anyway, we thought you might want to join us."

His mouth maneuvered into a sweet smile, but Wylie's brothers were immune to his charms. Joshua rolled his eyes and shook his head.

"Who are you?" he asked.

Phinn extended his arm for a handshake. "I probably should have opened with that. My name's Phinn."

"Do you have a last name?" Joshua asked.

"I do, but if I tell you, you'll have all the ammo you need to make fun of me. And I feel like we've already gotten off on the wrong foot."

"Just tell me what it is."

"Joshua," Wylie interrupted. "Back off."

"It's cool," Phinn said. "If you have to know, it's . . . Moonlight."

"Moonlight?" Joshua laughed. "Your last name is *Moonlight*?"

Phinn nodded. "My parents were hippies. I'm as embarrassed about it as you are."

Wylie noticed that Phinn never stuttered or stumbled over his words, which was no small triumph when confronted by Joshua. In the brief time they'd spent together, he'd never said "um" or "like" between sentences, the way she did.

"Where are you from?" Joshua asked.

"A small town, a few hours from here," Phinn answered.

"What are you doing in New York?"

"I needed a change of scenery."

"How did you get our sister to fly?"

"I gave her a *parvaz*."

"What's a *parvaz*?"

Phinn took the bag of tiny blue flowers out of his pocket and showed it to Joshua and Micah. He told them the plant was natural and homegrown, just like marijuana.

"I've been taking it for a while now, and I haven't noticed any negative side effects, except for some fatigue, drowsiness, and a little joint soreness the morning after. Don't take my word for it, though," Phinn said. "Try one. I promise you won't regret it."

Phinn held out the bag, but Joshua didn't budge.

"I think I'll pass. It was nice to meet you, but my brother and sister and I have to go now."

"We're not leaving."

It took Wylie a second to realize who had said it. Micah hardly spoke, and when he did, it was never to disagree—especially with Joshua.

"I want to try one," Micah continued, "A *parvaz*. And so does Joshua. He's just being too much of a pussy to say it himself."

Joshua knew better than to shoot down their brother's rare moment of defiance. He held out his palm. Phinn placed a *parvaz* in his hand, then passed another one to Micah and one to Wylie. The Dalton siblings looked at each other in agreement as they all popped the flowers into their mouths at the same time.

Joshua floated slowly at first, then shot up into the air like he was attached to a jet pack. He let out a scream and then, just like his sister had done earlier, evaporated into a fit of giggles. Wylie was the next to take flight. She whizzed by Joshua, then floated in front of him with her phone, poised to take the world's greatest snapshot. Before she could choose the appropriate filter and upload the picture, Phinn quickly shot up into the sky next to her and took the phone out of her hand.

"No pictures." His tone was kind but stern, and Wylie felt silly for taking her phone out in the first place. Why couldn't she just enjoy herself without having the compulsion to share everything she did on the Internet? Joshua flew above her and did a series of backflips in the air. Wylie yelped with joy. She had been the cause of so much unnecessary pain; it was nice to be able to provide her brother with some happiness.

"Nothing's happening!" Micah yelled up to them from the street.

"Give it another minute," Wylie shouted back.

Wylie looked down to where Micah was standing. Aside from her brother, the street was empty. She could still see the last of the party stragglers on the rooftop, but no one seemed to notice them. Wylie stretched her legs in the air. She wanted to fly over the city again and the longer they idled, the sooner the drug would wear off.

"It's not working!" Micah screamed so loud, it sounded like his lungs might explode.

"Can you give him another flower?" Wylie asked Phinn, concerned.

"I don't have any more. Don't worry. I'll help him."

Wylie watched as Phinn quietly landed on both feet right next to Micah and offered him his hand.

"You just need a little boost. Take my hand," Phinn said.

Micah firmly stuck his hands in his pockets.

"No. It's weird."

"Get over it!" Wylie yelled from above.

Phinn grabbed Micah's arm and before he could squirm out of his grip, they were flying circles around Wylie and Joshua.

"I'm going to let you go now," Phinn told him.

"Please don't!" Micah cried.

"You can trust him," Wylie assured her brother.

"I'm going to let go and you are going to be fine," Phinn told him.

Phinn spoke the words with such conviction that Micah slowly relaxed his grasp. When he let go, he was still in the air. He could fly by himself now. He didn't need anyone holding his hand or protecting him. Wylie watched as he soared above them. For once, he looked free from all the fear and anxiety that weighed him down.

"Thank you," Wylie mouthed to Phinn.

They flew for what felt like hours. Phinn led the way as they circled over all five boroughs. The air was still warm, and the city noises felt like they were on mute. From hundreds of feet in the air, they couldn't hear the horns or fire trucks or the sounds of drunken people crying or singing or fighting. All they had to do to get a clear look at the stars was float on their backs and look up at the night sky, with no tall buildings obstructing their view. Every so often, Phinn would hang back so Wylie could catch up to him. They would fly side by side like they'd done it all their lives.

None of them talked much, mostly because they feared if they acknowledged what was happening, they'd wake up from a dream. They only spoke to point out landmarks and check on each other. When the Daltons were kids on vacation in Montauk, Wylie would take Micah and Joshua on long bike rides. She rode faster than they did and worried they might get hurt or kidnapped if they trailed too far behind. She trained them to periodically yell out her name, so she'd know they were still safely riding behind her. During the silent stretches, she'd look behind her shoulder, just to be sure they were still there. She did the same thing today as they glided past bridges and high rises and subway lines.

"I will never forget this," Wylie whispered to Phinn, tugging gently at his collar. He'd given Wylie and her brothers the perfect last night together, and in the short time they'd known each other, he had helped her see the world through a brighter filter.

As they careened above Jamaica Bay, hand in hand, Phinn checked his watch and broke the news that they were dangerously close to the time when the *parvaz* would wear off and all four of them would plummet through the sky. He said he liked to think of the drug's effects as being like a gas tank, and it was better to pull over and fill up before it hit empty. Wylie and her brothers quickly did backflips above the boats to savor their last few seconds of cheating gravity.

Phinn directed them to their destination, and the Dalton siblings held hands and reluctantly followed him back to ground level. It took them some time to regain their equilibriums once they landed. The effects of the tiny blue flower had nearly worn off, but the euphoria stayed with them. All they wanted to do was scream and shout and giggle till they cried. Phinn grinned as he watched his new friends revel in the gift he'd bestowed on them.

"I propose we have a nightcap on my boat to celebrate an epic evening," he announced.

"Let's do it," Wylie said, not wanting to give her brothers the chance to turn him down.

Phinn led them to his sailboat, which was much larger

than Wylie had anticipated. It looked a little old and dank, but she was impressed that he knew how to operate a boat.

"Who taught you to sail?" she asked him.

"I taught myself."

They followed him down the steps, into the cabin, which was clean and spacious, but looked like it hadn't been redecorated since the sixties. The wallpaper was pea green and adorned with oversized daisies. Brown shag carpet covered the floor, and aqua-blue vinyl lined the seats of a small booth. It smelled like mothballs and mildew.

Phinn filled four cups with water.

"It's important to stay hydrated after flying," he explained.

He passed out the cups, and they each took a long swallow. Micah and Joshua walked off to explore the boat. It was nice to be alone again with Phinn, but Wylie could feel the seconds and minutes slipping away. Soon they would have to say good-bye, and there was no guarantee they would ever see each other again.

"Are you feeling okay?" Phinn asked, concerned.

"I don't want this night to end." She nearly choked on her words. "I don't want my brother to go to jail."

Phinn nodded sympathetically. "I know," he said.

A lightbulb somewhere was buzzing loudly, and the sound, combined with the dim light in the cabin, was making Wylie feel claustrophobic. She moved to reach for a light switch, but her eyes suddenly felt like they weighed a ton. All the flying had made her sleepy.

"If I told you I could take you someplace that would fix all your problems, a place where your brother wouldn't have to go to jail, would you want to go?" Phinn asked.

"Sure. When do we leave?" Wylie heard herself say as she sat down on a vinyl cushion. Phinn placed a blanket around her shoulders.

"Whenever you want."

"How about now?" she asked groggily.

But before she could hear Phinn's answer, Wylie's eyelids grew heavy and she gave in to sleep.

❖ ❖ ❖ ❖ ❖ ❖ ❖

IT WAS BRIGHT—ALMOST BLINDING. WYLIE OPENED her eyes, but the light was so strong, it burned her pupils. She closed her eyes and tried to fall back to sleep, but her mouth was as dry as sand and her head felt like it was splitting wide open. She hadn't drunk an ounce of alcohol the night before, but she still felt massively hungover. Maybe it was the *parvaz*. As the sunlight pierced her windows, she had no recollection of how she'd gotten home last night. *Open your eyes, Wylie*, she told herself. All she needed was a hot shower, a cup of coffee, and a bowl of cereal, and she'd feel better. After much resistance, she let her eyelids drift open and she reached toward her window to pull her curtains closed.

But there were no curtains. And no window facing a fire escape. Wylie wasn't in her room. She quickly took in her surroundings. The shag carpet. The peeling wallpaper. The lightbulb, still buzzing. She was still on Phinn's boat, and it was morning. Her parents were going to kill her.

"Micah! Joshua! We have to go," she tried to call out to her brothers, but her voice sounded hoarse and raspy and nearly inaudible. Micah and Joshua were both on the floor of the cabin, quietly snoring. Wylie stumbled out of the vinyl booth, lowered herself to the floor, and shook her brothers awake with all her strength.

"You guys. Wake up! It's morning. Joshua has to be in court! We are so screwed!"

Micah and Joshua finally came to, but they were slow to react and couldn't even manage to get up. Wylie needed them to move faster. They had to leave here immediately. The sun was already up, and they still needed enough time to go back to the house, face the wrath of their parents, shower, get dressed, look halfway presentable, and make it downtown to the courthouse for an eight a.m. sentencing. Wylie had no idea where Phinn was, but at this point, she didn't care. Leaving in a hurry would just make it easier to say good-bye.

Wylie stood, but the boat lurched, causing her to lose her balance and fall back to the ground.

"Are we *moving*?" Joshua asked.

Wylie bolted up the stairs and ran to the deck, while Micah and Joshua followed. The second Wylie set foot on the deck, her jaw dropped. All she could see was ocean. The New York City skyline was gone. How could this happen? They were only supposed to have a nightcap, and now they were in the middle of nowhere.

"PHINN!" She shouted it so loudly, it made her head throb even more. Micah and Joshua arrived on deck, and both of them nearly buckled at the knees. Wylie could feel her stomach going weak. It was either the seasickness or the flying or just the fact that she had no idea where they were, but she was seconds away from barfing her guts out. She heard Joshua behind her repeating the same words over and over, his tone eerily calm:

"I am so dead. I am so dead. I am so dead."

Wylie tried not to show the dread that was forming in the pit of her stomach. They were in this mess because of her, and she needed to get them home as soon as possible. She spotted Phinn at the bow of the boat, leaning against the tiller, whistling to himself and sipping from a steaming mug of what she assumed was coffee. She was struck by how chipper and relaxed he seemed for someone who had just kidnapped three people.

"You're up!" he said excitedly when he saw her.

"What is going on?" she asked him, her voice trembling.

"We're going on an adventure," he replied, practically bursting at the seams. "Can I get you a cup of coffee? Some tea, perhaps? It's a beautiful day!"

If Wylie knew how to sail a boat or had any idea where they were, she would have thrown him overboard right then and there and hauled ass to get them home.

"Where are we? What happened last night?"

"You and your brothers fell asleep as soon as we got on the boat. It happens the first couple times you take *parvaz*. I should have warned you. I didn't want to wake you, so I just took your advice and set sail. Was that wrong?" Phinn asked, seeming genuinely confused.

Micah and Joshua were slowly making their approach. Joshua had conquered his lethargy, and Wylie could see beads of sweat forming on his forehead.

"You need to take us back to New York," Joshua demanded. His voice was at least two octaves lower than normal.

"I don't get it. I thought this was what you guys wanted," Phinn replied, almost dumbfounded. "I thought we'd all be celebrating right now. I told Wylie last night I could take you someplace to make your problems disappear, someplace where Joshua wouldn't have to go to jail, and she took me up on the offer."

"What? Are you crazy?" Wylie's memories of last night were spotty, but she vaguely remembered the tail end of her conversation with Phinn. "I thought we were speaking in hypotheticals."

"I never speak in hypotheticals," Phinn said. "Either way, it would be a waste to let Joshua rot away in jail. Don't worry. Where I'm taking you is so much better, and we're almost there."

Wylie could tell that Phinn was spontaneous and eccentric, even otherworldly, from the brief time they had spent together, but she'd never thought he might actually be a psychopath. How could he do this to them? She grabbed Phinn by the collar and pushed him against the tiller. Phinn's coffee spilled everywhere, but it would take more than first-degree burns to stop her.

"You have to get us home!" Wylie begged. "What is wrong with you? You can't play with people's lives like this!"

Joshua quickly pulled Wylie off Phinn and held her arms back as she tried to break free. Phinn, shocked, examined his formerly white T-shirt, now covered in coffee, and stripped it off. It was hard not to notice the many scars and cuts on his chest and back. His body had more wear and tear than you'd expect on a seventeen-year-old. Phinn caught Wylie looking at the scars, then quickly grabbed another shirt out of a nearby knapsack and pulled it on. She could see a plastic alarm tag hanging off the hem, which meant he'd stolen it. Phinn straightened out his hair with his hands, then cleared his throat and addressed them calmly.

"This hasn't gone the way I'd hoped, but I can understand why you might be pissed off or confused. It must feel like a huge shock, and I'll explain everything soon. I brought the three of you here because I like you."

Phinn probably meant to say it to all of them, but he was staring right at Wylie when the words came out. He pointed in the distance, where Wylie was now able to make out a small island. Good. Dry land. Maybe even civilization. Hopefully that ruled out Phinn killing them on the boat and dumping their bodies into the middle of the ocean.

"I didn't tell you that I was taking you here, because until you were on my boat last night, I didn't know I would. But after our evening together, I realized I couldn't in good conscience leave you in New York. I'm bringing you to a place you have to see to believe. If I had told you about it while we were docked in Jamaica Bay, you would have thought I was a lunatic. I admit my methods are a bit unorthodox, but believe me when I say you're going to thank me."

The island was getting closer and closer. Wylie could make out a small dock with several other boats tied to it. Wherever they were going, there were clearly other inhabitants, unless Phinn was some sort of boat aficionado. The island itself was small and full of greenery, while the water surrounding it was a paler shade of blue than the rest of the ocean. Oversized palm trees swayed in the wind and lined what looked like a path into the heart of the island. The sand seemed untouched, and the sky was full of puffy cumulus clouds that resembled heaps of cotton balls.

Wylie looked at her brothers' faces to see if they were also on the verge of a nervous breakdown. Micah's features were unmoved. He hadn't said anything all morning, but Wylie didn't blame him. Joshua looked like a vein might break through the center of his forehead. His jaw was clenched, and sweat was now dripping down his face.

"Phinn, please take us home. Joshua has to be in court. He'll be in a lot of trouble if we don't get him there on time," Wylie pleaded.

"It's too late. Even if I turned around now, we'd never make it on time. But I swear, I'm going to make it up to you. I really need the three of you to calm down and put a little trust in me, just like you did last night."

Wylie could only imagine the fight her parents were having right now back at their house. They would undoubtedly blame each other for their kids not coming home. At least it was one argument she didn't have to bear witness to. Once the boat approached the dock, Phinn, nearly giddy, turned to Micah and Joshua and asked them to help him anchor it, but neither of them budged.

"It's okay," Phinn said, "I'm good on my own."

He moved deftly around the boat as he maneuvered into the empty spot in the dock and tied the line to a wooden pole. Wylie was afraid if she opened her mouth, she'd start to cry.

"This is not your fault," Joshua said to Wylie, placing a hand on her shoulder. "We all got on the boat with him."

"I don't have a good feeling about this," Micah finally said, "We don't know anything about this guy. I'm not going to hang out on some deserted island with him. He could be a serial killer."

"He's not a serial killer." Wylie said it with total certainty, but she wouldn't put anything past Phinn at this point. Just as she began to internally weigh his potential as a murderer, he returned to the deck of the boat and pulled a machete out of his backpack. *Great,* Wylie thought. The one guy she'd found remotely interesting in years had kidnapped them and was going to chop them into little pieces.

"No need to be alarmed," Phinn said, swinging the machete. "This is just to help us clear the trail—it gets overgrown quickly. In fact, Joshua can hold on to it." He passed the knife toward Joshua, but Wylie grabbed it by the tip of the blade. She wasn't sure if she was worried that Joshua didn't have the guts to use it on Phinn or that he did.

"I'll hold it," Wylie said.

Phinn paused as they reached the end of the dock. "All I'm asking for is twenty-four hours of your time. That's it. Once those twenty-four hours are up, we can all get back on my boat and I'll have you home in no time. But I want you to be prepared. If you follow me onto the island, everything you know to be real and true about the world will change forever. Can you handle that?"

"We don't really have any other choice, do we?" Wylie asked.

Phinn grinned. "Welcome to Minor Island."

Joshua was the first to step off the dock and onto the island. Wylie quickly tied her hair back in a ponytail, applied a coat of lip gloss from a tube she had in her purse, tightened her grip on the machete, and followed him onto the sand. Micah took a small sip from his flask and stepped into the shadows of his brother and sister. Wylie was right: they had no choice but to follow Phinn.

CHAPTER FOUR

minor island

the trail was not as arduous as Wylie had anticipated. When she stepped off the boat and onto the island, she felt like they were setting off on a journey straight out of an Indiana Jones movie, her dad's favorite franchise. It had never occurred to Wylie that all the years of rewatching *Raiders of the Lost Ark* would help prepare her for an excursion onto a mystery island. So far, there were no signs of snakes or rats or any of the things Indy had to overcome. She used the machete sparingly on the few plants and branches obstructing their path. They hardly needed it, and she wondered if Phinn had thought they'd feel safer if they were wielding a weapon.

Wylie checked her phone to see how much time had passed since they'd stepped off the boat, but the battery was dead. She had no idea whether they'd been walking for an hour or ten minutes. She snuck the compass Joshua had given her from her purse and it showed they were moving east. The trail was peaceful and beautiful, and despite her tension, Wylie couldn't help enjoying their unique surroundings. Bright green sticks of bamboo lined the corridor of rich, white sand that from a distance looked like freshly fallen snow.

The sun was warm on Wylie's back, but there was no trace of humidity and when she felt herself start to perspire, a cool breeze would blow just long enough to prevent her from sweating. Certainly not the kind of weather one would expect in the Northeast in February, even with global warming. Wylie had always been prone to bug bites, but there were no insects or gnats to swat away. They'd been walking for at least a mile in complete silence and the only creatures they'd crossed paths with were monarch butterflies and bright yellow ladybugs.

Even if Phinn didn't have any more surprises in store, Wylie couldn't get around the fact that he'd brought them here in the middle of the night without their consent. It took a special kind of person to pull off a kidnapping the way he did. The kind of person who couldn't, under any circumstances, be trusted. But every so often, he'd turn back with a reassuring smile, perhaps to make sure Wylie was still walking behind him or to gauge where they stood with each other since last night. His tendency to check in gave Wylie hope that he wouldn't let anything bad happen to them. He had to have good reason to bring them here.

"Phinn." She meant to say his name quietly, but it came out angry and forceful. Phinn stopped walking and turned to face her.

"How much longer do we have to go?" she asked.

"Come on. You're New Yorkers. You're used to walking," he said, bouncing with excitement.

"That doesn't answer my question. How much longer?" Wylie asked again.

"Not too far. A few more minutes."

"Why is it so warm here? It's winter in Manhattan. We couldn't possibly be that far away from the city."

"Isn't this weather a nice change of pace? I don't know how you guys do it. The temperature in New York is brutal this time of year."

"Yeah, the winters suck. Now answer the question," Wylie said.

"I can't. I'm not a meteorologist. As long as I've lived here, the weather has been mild."

"Where exactly are we?"

"We're on the west side of Minor Island, heading east, but to be honest, we've never named this trail."

We. So there *were* more people on this island.

"How many people live here?"

"You'll see. Like I said, you'll have all your answers soon."

If Phinn kept up with the vague responses, then it was only a matter of time before Wylie took the machete to his throat.

"Do you think for one minute you could stop being so mysterious?" she said. "I'll ask you again. How many people are on this island?"

Phinn scratched the back of his neck. Something about the way he looked off into the distance made it clear he wasn't used to being questioned and he wasn't sure how to handle it. But he was the one who'd dragged them here. They were supposed to be in a courtroom in downtown Manhattan right now.

"There are about fifty people who live here. I can't guarantee that you'll like them all, but I can tell you that I do, and I'm a very good judge of character."

Wylie's heart rate suddenly sped up. She normally got along with all types of people, but the idea of meeting fifty strangers at once unleashed the butterflies in her stomach. If she was feeling anxious, then she could only imagine how terrified Micah felt at this point. There wasn't enough Xanax in the world to get him through this, and she was pretty sure he'd left his anxiety meds at home.

"I know I haven't given you any reason to trust me. In hindsight, my methods were . . . inexcusable. I messed up," Phinn continued, sounding remorseful. "But the sooner we reach our destination, the sooner you'll understand why I did what I did. If you can muster up a little patience, then we can keep moving."

In about another half a mile, the path they'd been on widened and forked. Phinn's legs started to pick up speed as he veered to the left and gestured to the Daltons to follow quickly. Wylie could see him tense up as he hurried around the corner. And when she and her brothers looked in the direction opposite the path they'd taken, it was impossible to miss what Phinn was rushing away from.

Barbed wire and an oversized wooden fence blocked off the other trail. Yellow caution tape was strung between two palm trees a few feet ahead along with signs that said KEEP OUT. It looked like a crime scene. Scrawled in large letters on the fence in red spray paint were the words HOPPER WAS HERE.

"Who's Hopper?" Wylie asked.

"No one of consequence. Don't let all that freak you out," Phinn said. "The fence is just a safety precaution."

Right. A safety precaution for an entire section of this strange, unknown, mystery island that was apparently off limits. *That doesn't seem ominous at all*, Wylie thought. Before she could demand that Phinn elaborate, her eyes landed on a row of bungalows perched in the distance. From where the Daltons were standing, it looked like there were at least a dozen. Phinn gestured toward them.

"And those would be our crash pads. They're made from wood and bamboo. The roofs are stucco and they keep the rain out."

Abigail had once told Wylie that her grandparents met each other on a commune in the sixties. It was a farm in upstate New York where a bunch of hippies lived in a barn together without running water or electricity, and they slept on hay. These bungalows were charming and a step above sleeping in a barn, but Wylie worried they were a preview of what was to come.

As Phinn walked faster down the path and they moved twice as fast to keep up with him, she was sure she heard the faint drumbeat of what sounded like a hip-hop song. Eventually she could hear a girl's voice rhyming over the beat. It was still too distant for Wylie to make out the lyrics, but it wasn't exactly the kind of song you'd expect a bunch of hippies to have on rotation. Wylie and her brothers looked at each other.

A huge goofy grin took shape on Phinn's face, and without giving them any warning, he started running toward the music. They practically had to sprint to catch up to him, and as soon as they followed him around a corner, they found themselves standing at the edge of a vast clearing. Wylie's eyes went wide as the loud drumbeats shook the ground under her feet.

At one side of the clearing lay a lagoon with water the color of turquoise. The surface sparkled so much, it looked like there were a thousand tiny diamonds floating in it. A waterfall spilled perfectly frothy water from a small cliff that stood at least a hundred feet high.

Wylie felt like her head was spinning and her vision was getting blurry. She tried to slow down the adrenaline with quiet breaths, but every direction she turned, there were pockets of teenagers partying as if it were their last day on Earth. A steady line formed at the top of the waterfall as people dived off the cliff and into the water. A small dance circle gathered in the lagoon. The music they'd heard wasn't a recording: a live band played on a stage near the lagoon and a young girl fronting the group rapped along flawlessly. When she arrived at the hook of the song, every person at the party sang along at the top of their lungs as though it was their national anthem.

All of Wylie's senses were working overtime as the smell of salt and grilled vegetables lingered in her nose. She looked to her left and spotted two chickens cooking on a spit above a massive fire pit. Not far from the pit was a charming tiki bar, where people sipped drinks out of coconuts and pineapples. It wasn't until Joshua tapped her on the

shoulder and pointed to the sky that she noticed a handful
of teenagers flying in the air.

This was definitely not your typical high school party.
At the get-togethers Wylie attended, there was always at
least one drunk girl crying over a guy, or a dramatic lov-
ers' quarrel bringing everything to a halt, or a few wasted
football players letting their 'roid rage take over. This party
was tension-free. Happy was too weak a word to describe
the teenagers in its midst. Whatever these kids were smok-
ing, Wylie wanted some immediately. There were no signs
of any adults, but at this point it was safe to assume they
were either very progressive or out of town for an extended
vacation.

It took a while for anyone at the party to notice them,
but as soon as one person caught a glimpse of Phinn, the
band stopped playing. Everyone stood perfectly still, except for the kids in the air who hovered over the lagoon. It
was like they'd been caught doing something they weren't
supposed to be doing. Wylie waited for Phinn to confront
them, but instead he simply took a bow, and they all broke
into loud cheers, as though they were in the presence of a
rock star.

"Phinn's home!" Wylie heard a guy's voice shout. An or-
derly line instantly formed in front of them as various kids
greeted him warmly with hugs and high fives, without so
much as glancing in the direction of the Daltons. Wylie
watched and listened as Phinn enthusiastically said hello to
each person like he or she was the only human being in the
world who mattered to him.

"Bailey, how's that ankle? Still swollen?" he asked

the girl who'd been rapping onstage. "It definitely hasn't messed with your stage presence.

"Bandit, I got you the contraband you asked for." Phinn unzipped a pocket in his knapsack, took out a bag of bite-sized Kit Kats, and tossed it in the air. A kid floating right above the lagoon caught it and shouted an enthusiastic thank-you.

The longer the greetings continued, the more Wylie felt invisible. No one acknowledged their presence or even glanced in their direction. Before she could say anything, a girl dived down from the sky and gracefully landed inches away from Phinn. She jumped up and wrapped her legs around his waist.

Wylie felt her stomach tie up in knots while the girl clung to Phinn tightly and showered his face with kisses. It shouldn't matter if he had a girlfriend. Nothing romantic had gone on between them in Brooklyn. He'd just conveniently forgotten to mention he was already dating someone before he kidnapped her.

Phinn peeled the girl off him and slowly lowered her to the ground. She had pale pink skin, enormous blue eyes, and a short blonde pixie cut. Her body was tiny and compact, and Wylie couldn't help noticing how small and perky her breasts were. It was hard not to look at her chest, since she was clearly not wearing a bra underneath her cotton summer dress. She was barefoot and couldn't have been taller than five feet, which officially made her Wylie's physical opposite.

"I missed you," the girl whispered.

"I was only gone for a day," Phinn responded casually.

"One day too long." Then the girl turned her attention to Wylie. "Who's this?" she asked, her eyes taking full inventory. The island went from ignoring the Daltons to staring at them suspiciously. The girl circled around her and sniffed her like a dog.

"She smells awful." She announced it loudly so everyone could hear. A few people laughed. Wylie's face turned crimson. She hadn't showered or brushed her teeth since the day before. She'd been sweating last night from all the dancing and flying. She'd slept on Phinn's boat, which smelled of mothballs and mold, and then she'd hiked through a trail onto the island. The pixie girl was right. But Wylie didn't appreciate being publicly humiliated.

Wylie leaned down so her face was level with the girl's and held up the machete. She inhaled deeply, then confidently exhaled with her mouth wide open right in the girl's face: morning breath. It was the perfect revenge. The girl nearly gagged as most of the crowd, including Phinn, erupted into laughter. Wylie stood up straight, smiled, and winked at her brothers, who were visibly mortified.

Phinn raised his voice, addressing everyone.

"This is Wylie. And these are her younger brothers, Joshua and Micah. Wylie, this is my *friend* Tinka."

He put special emphasis on the word "friend" and Wylie could see the girl, Tinka, bite her lower lip.

"They are our honored guests for the day. I want everyone to treat them the way you would treat anyone who lives here: with love, respect, and everything in between. We're gonna show them a good time. They've been on a really long journey and I dragged them away from some important obligations back home."

The faces staring back at them seemed to soften with Phinn's orders. Phinn turned to Wylie.

"I have a few things I need to deal with right now," he told her. "But I'm leaving you in good hands. Tinka, please do me a favor and give them a tour of the island."

Tinka rolled her eyes and mumbled something under her breath.

"I mean it. Be nice," Phinn scolded. He turned back to Wylie and her brothers. "The three of you will be my guests for dinner this evening, and then we'll discuss the possibility of extending your visit, if you want to—"

"We're not going to stay longer," Joshua said, cutting him off. "You're taking us home."

Phinn simply shrugged. "I'll go along with whatever you decide after twenty-four hours. I promise." Phinn gestured to two people among the crowd. "Maz, Bandit, let's catch up."

The two guys obediently followed him as he ventured off. The taller one looked to Wylie like he might be foreign. He had jet-black hair, tan olive skin, and eyelashes that seemed to go on for miles. He smiled warmly at Wylie, and for the first time since they'd arrived at the clearing, she felt welcome. The other guy, Bandit, was the recipient of the bag of contraband. He ripped open a Kit Kat and took a bite as he passed Wylie and her brothers. He had a shaved head and his skin was a deep sepia hue. He was on the shorter side, but his body was muscular and fit. Wylie gave him a smile and he nodded in return.

"I'll take that off your hands," he said, glancing at the knife. Wylie dutifully handed it over, though she wasn't entirely convinced she wouldn't need it.

"Okay," Tinka said, "I guess I'm supposed to give you a tour or something."

Wylie checked to see if her brothers were as appalled by the pixie as she was, but Joshua seemed lost in his own thoughts, and Micah was shuffling his feet and smiling timidly at Tinka. They'd known this girl for five minutes and she'd spent most of that time humiliating Wylie, and now Micah was into her? Wylie gently punched him in the shoulder to get him to snap out of it, but he just glared at her.

"Let's start where we're standing, shall we?" Tinka waved her hand around at the clearing and the waterfall like a jaded Vanna White.

"We call this place the Clearing. We don't get any points on creativity for that one. It's where we always hang out, party, swim, barbeque, fly. It's sort of the community area. It's where you go when you don't feel like being alone."

Wylie dipped her hand into the lagoon. The water was so warm and inviting, Wylie had to resist the urge to jump in with her clothes on. She had done a decent job of pretending Tinka's comments about the way she smelled didn't faze her, but she was desperate to rinse off all the dirt and grime from her body. Tinka led them to a nearby palm tree with a wooden cupboard built into its trunk. She opened the small door a crack, took out a small chalkboard and a stub of chalk, and drew an X on the board.

"This is where we are now," she explained. She drew a staircase that led to the bungalows, then gestured to the Daltons to follow her. "Ugh, this is so bridal," Tinka complained to herself as she led them up the stairs.

The wooden steps were rickety. There were no handrails, so the Daltons had to be careful to keep their balance. Tinka seemed to still have *parvaz* in her system, because she floated up the staircase. If Wylie could take a stash of tiny blue flowers home with her, maybe she could use them as her secret weapon on the basketball court. She imagined the whole school watching her as she flew in the air and dunked the winning shot in the playoffs.

They stepped onto the deck and walked toward the huts. All the structures on Minor Island had clearly been built to surround the Clearing. On the north side of the deck, where they were now standing, the row of bungalows was numbered one through thirty. Tinka mumbled that the tropical houses were powered by solar panels. Some of them were shared, while some residents lived alone. One bungalow stood larger than the rest. Wylie pointed to it.

"Who lives there?" Wylie asked.

"Who do you think?" Tinka answered.

Tinka dragged them to her bungalow next and reluctantly invited them inside. The interior was not unlike a summer camp bunk or a dorm room. A bed. A desk. A bay window facing the Clearing. The sheets on the bed were tangled up in a heap. The floor was covered with various articles of clothing, but the walls of the bungalow helped detract attention from all the crap on the floor. They were decked out in large vibrant watercolors that were so well done, they could have easily fit in at the Whitney Museum. Most of the paintings were abstracts, along with a few self-portraits. Micah seemed especially drawn to one of the pictures: a painting of Tinka flying in the nude. *Awesome*, Wylie thought. *My little brother's falling in love with the she-devil, and now they have art in common.*

"None of the bungalows have their own bathrooms," Tinka informed them. "We all use communal restrooms. They're all built with showers, toilets, and running water. And we do have shower curtains, so if you're modest, you can keep them closed. Friendly warning: I'm not the modest type," she added, winking at Micah.

"I have to admit," Joshua piped up, "I'm really impressed by the infrastructure here." Wylie stifled a laugh. If Micah got off on naked paintings, then Joshua was hot for efficiency.

"Thank you," Tinka said. "We give all the credit to Phinn."

As they made their way around to the south side of the deck, Tinka directed their attention toward the island's common areas. She drew a series of larger huts on the chalkboard and marked them as the kitchen, dining area, clinic, and a boutique where she told them residents were fitted for custom-made clothing. Joshua asked if the island had its own currency, and Tinka explained that they didn't believe in money or bartering. Everything on the island came free of charge. Money, she said, was the downfall of every society. Wylie could tell her brother wanted to argue the benefits of capitalism, but it wasn't easy to debate those points in a place where things like food and lodging came at zero cost.

The Daltons followed Tinka through the hut that contained the dining room, which was surprisingly roomy. Phinn had told them there were only fifty people on the island, but this space could comfortably seat twice that amount. It was filled with long picnic benches decorated with wildflowers in vases carved out of driftwood. The room smelled of oatmeal and cinnamon and had a log-cabin feel. Wylie noticed a poem, hand-printed on parchment paper, hanging off the wall:

> *Never forget to live life to the fullest.*
> *Do it for the troubled; do it for the lost.*
> *The days may feel shorter; the nights may*
>   *feel long.*
> *But when we remember, our memories*
>   *grow strong.*

"Who wrote that?" Wylie asked.

"Phinn," Tinka answered. "He fancies himself a poet."

"Who are the troubled and the lost?"

"Everyone who doesn't live here."

Wylie read the poem again.

"Come on, let's keep moving," Tinka whined. "We don't have all day."

Tinka walked them through the kitchen, and now it was Wylie's turn to be impressed. Their brownstone was spacious by New York City standards, but it had a small galley kitchen that wasn't always easy to maneuver in. The kitchen here was industrial-sized. The appliances were old and shabby, but there was plenty of counter space, an array of pots and pans hanging from the ceiling, and a wood-burning stove.

A girl stood at the counter, effortlessly gutting a scaly green fish with violet colored fins. She was so focused on the task at hand, she didn't even notice they'd entered the room.

"This is Lola," Tinka said.

The girl, startled, dropped her knife on the floor, nearly cutting herself in the process.

"Tinka! Are you trying to kill me?" Lola blurted. "Give me a little warning next time you're in here. You know I don't like any distractions when I'm cooking."

"Take it up with Phinn. He's the one who told me to give them a tour. Lola's the chef here. Lola, these are Phinn's latest souvenirs from New York."

Wylie gave Lola a smile, but received a tentative one in return.

"I heard there were strangers among us. News spreads fast here. Welcome to my castle. I'd shake your hands, but I'm covered in fish guts."

Lola had golden skin with small freckles covering her cheekbones. Her hair, a deep umber color, was long and tied into a side braid. The Daltons introduced themselves one by one.

"Tinka may have told you already, but we grow all our own vegetables and catch fish and raise chickens. Please tell me none of you has any dietary restrictions for dinner tonight. It's fine if you do, it's just that I've already planned the menu and might have to throw myself in the woodburning oven. I'm only half kidding."

"We eat everything," Wylie assured her, tracing her fingers along the wooden countertops. "This is my dream kitchen, by the way."

"Do you cook?" Lola asked.

Wylie nodded. "I dabble."

"Well, if you think the kitchen is tropic, you should see our garden."

Lola led them through the back doors, and they stepped out into a vast fruit and vegetable garden. There was almost a wider selection here than in the Daltons' neighborhood grocery store. Wylie spotted basil, thyme, and oregano plants, along with colorful herbs labeled with names she'd never heard of: chipney, pame, and woodmeg. There were cucumbers, glossy red tomatoes, and bushes with every type of berry. The sound of chickens squawking in a nearby coop disrupted the otherwise peaceful setting.

Wylie was officially in heaven. She'd begged her parents to clear out the furniture on their roof-deck to grow a vegetable garden, but they didn't think it was worth it if all the plants would just die in the winter anyway.

"These are my babies," Lola said. "Every plant, every vegetable, every root. I love them all."

"It's . . . incredible," Wylie replied. "I don't know anything about growing a garden."

"You don't grow your own food?" Lola asked, confused.

"No, Lola," Tinka jumped in. "They have grocery stores where they're from, remember?"

"Right. Such a strange concept. Anyway, I hate to kick you guys out, but I've still got fish to prep."

As they made their way out of the garden and back

through the kitchen, Wylie waved good-bye to Lola and wondered if they were around the same age. Lola had the face of a teenager, but how many seventeen-year-olds would have the stamina or the drive to maintain a garden and serve three meals a day to fifty people? It struck her then that they hadn't come across any discernible adults since they'd arrived on the island. Maybe they took residence on the part of the island that was off limits, or maybe they didn't live here at all.

"Everyone here seems really young," Wylie said, watching Tinka for a reaction. "Where are all the adults?"

Tinka stopped in her tracks. Wylie thought maybe she'd asked the million-dollar question and they'd all be showered with confetti, but then Tinka's smile gave way to a giggle that quickly evolved into one of those uncontrollable cackles. She kept apologizing between breaths, but she could not stop her body from shaking with laughter. Once her episode finally subsided, she mumbled to herself, "Where are all the adults?" then started to giggle all over again.

"It's not a weird question," Wylie said. "I don't get why you think it's so funny."

"Sorry," Tinka apologized, still howling. And then she declared, "I'm going to pee in my dress!"

With that, Tinka ran off to the nearest bathroom.

"What was that about?" Wylie asked her brothers.

"No clue," Joshua said. "These people are weird."

"It was just a giggle fit—what's the big deal? I thought it was kind of cute," Micah said.

Wylie shook her head in disbelief. "How can you be into

that girl after how rude she's been to me? You're supposed to be on my side."

"I'm with Wylie on that one, buddy," Joshua added.

"I'm not into her," Micah fumed. "And Wylie, I'm always on your side. I cover for you all the time, and you know it."

"Really?" Wylie responded. "Name one time."

"You know what? You're being a real bitch right now."

As soon as the words came out of Micah's mouth, Tinka fluttered back from the bathroom.

"What's going on, kids? Family squabble?"

Tinka moved them quickly through the rest of the tour. The next stop was the clinic. Wylie was surprised to find it stocked with medical equipment and hospital beds. Two doctors, who had to be teenage prodigies based on their youthful appearance, were tending to a patient they said was recovering from a bout of appendicitis. The place looked a little like those old-school war hospitals Wylie had seen in movies. There were a handful of beds laid out in one room, all of them unoccupied except for the one where the appendicitis kid rested.

The last stop they made was at what looked like a storefront just a few feet away from the clinic. Tinka led them inside, where three very stylish girls happily chatted away as they sewed. The room was chock-full of fabrics and swatches and mannequins. There was a rack of summer dresses next to another rack of linen pants and button-downs.

"This is where we get most of our clothes, aside from the stuff we bring back from the mainland," Tinka explained.

"The mainland?" Joshua asked.

"Otherwise known as the United States of America. Or New York City. It's the closest city to us. Around these parts we call it the mainland, so if you're sticking around, you might want to get used to that."

"We're not sticking around," Joshua replied. Wylie tried not to go to pieces every time Joshua mentioned leaving. At some point along the tour, she had started falling in love with the island. They'd already missed Joshua's court date. What was the harm in staying for a few more days? She hated her brother's recent tendency to speak for all of them, but didn't want to fight with him in front of Tinka.

Just as they were leaving the boutique, one of the girls behind the sewing machine pulled a long pale blue maxi dress off a rack and placed it next to Wylie.

"This is exactly your size. You should wear it to dinner tonight," the girl gushed. "You'll look porcelain in it. We'll make sure it's waiting for you in the guest bungalow." Wylie didn't know what she meant by "porcelain" but hoped it was a compliment. She smiled and thanked her. The girl threw a smug smile in Tinka's direction, and Wylie could swear that on their way out, she caught Tinka flipping the girl off.

"That's it. You've seen everything," Tinka announced.

"*Everything?* You're entirely positive about that?" Wylie asked.

"That's what I just said," Tinka replied, irritated.

"What about that part of the island that's fenced off? What's behind there?"

"Ah, yes," Tinka said. She drew a line on the map from

the Clearing and marked it in large capital letters with the words THE FORBIDDEN SIDE.

"Why is it forbidden?" Joshua questioned.

"That information is classified," Tinka replied.

"Who's Hopper? Or is that classified, too?" Wylie asked.

"He's a homicidal maniac." Tinka said it matter-of-factly, then let out a laugh. "Look, you're *visitors*," she went on. "I'm not going to answer all your questions. I've shown you where we sleep, where we eat, where we drink, how we get clothes and medicine. I've gone above and beyond."

"What about the fact that as far as I can tell, there are no phones here or computers, no Internet or television? Do you guys have some sort of weird law against technology?" Joshua pressed on.

It wasn't until Joshua asked the question that Wylie realized aside from some kitchen appliances, the medical equipment, and the sewing machines, there was a serious lack of electronics on the island.

"We don't have any of that crap. Phinn believes, and so do the rest of us, that being plugged in all the time takes away from human interaction. Phones don't work out here. We don't have the Internet either. We don't want it, and we don't need it."

"Then how do you find out what's going on in the world?" Wylie asked.

"*This* is our world. As long as we know about what's happening here, that's all that matters. But don't sweat it if you need to run back to New York to—what do you call it?—update your statuses."

Micah stuck his hands in his pockets and tilted his head as he looked in Tinka's direction, still too shy to look at her directly.

"I think it's really cool that you guys don't let technology consume you," he said.

So much for being on her side, Wylie thought. Of all the Dalton kids, Micah was the one who was glued to his iPhone at all times. She was surprised he hadn't broken out into hives by now, considering he hadn't been able to use it all day.

"So, what are we supposed to do until this dinner we're invited to?" Joshua asked.

Tinka was clearly done answering questions. She just shook her head and gestured to them to follow her. They stopped at a bungalow and waited for Tinka to fish a set of keys out of her pocket and unlock the door. The bungalow had three beds, with a towel laid out on top of each one. There was a large carafe of water on a table, and a giant spread of fresh fruit and crudités. The maxi dress Wylie had been presented with was already hanging outside the closet door, along with two pairs of linen pants and soft cotton T-shirts for Micah and Joshua. Tinka pointed to the snacks.

"In case you get hungry before dinner. There's a bathroom next door. I'll come get you when dinner's ready."

Tinka grabbed a couple slices of fruit and pranced out of their bungalow without so much as a good-bye.

"What do we do now?" Joshua asked them.

Wylie stuck a mango wedge in her mouth. "I need a nap and a shower," she answered.

"Well, don't get too comfortable. We're not staying here."

"That's not for you to decide, Joshua," Wylie snapped. "If you want to go home, you can go home. But that doesn't mean I'm coming with you."

It felt good to stop bowing down to him. Wylie was almost an adult. She didn't need anyone telling her what to do anymore. She grabbed a towel from the bed and let the bungalow door slam behind her.

the inner circle

gregory Dalton couldn't wait any longer. He got up from his seat and paced across the lobby of the police station. Pacing was something he'd become an expert at lately. Walking back and forth. Thinking. Putting his hands on his waist. Eyeing the receptionist at the precinct as if to say *I'm a very important person, and you need to deal with me right now.*

Maura was sitting three seats away from where he'd stood up. So this is what had become of them: two people who were once so madly in love, they spent endless hours together. Now they couldn't even sit next to each other.

What was taking these people so long? In what universe did three missing kids not constitute an emergency? The night before, when he and Maura discovered the kids had snuck out, they both felt an initial sense of relief. Neither of them had been looking forward to spending an entire dinner together. Gregory wanted to celebrate his daughter's birthday and have one last night with his son before Joshua was moved into a juvenile detention center, but since they'd broken the news of the divorce, his kids looked at him like he was the sole reason their family was no longer functioning. They were young; there was a lot they didn't understand.

After the kids gave them the silent brush-off, Gregory had decided to go back to his hotel room and throw himself into his work. He told Maura he would meet her at the courthouse in the morning. It wasn't the first time their children had left without their permission and returned in the middle of the night. *It's what happens when you raise kids in the city,* he always told himself. *They think they're more mature than their age suggests. They're too independent. Transportation comes too easily for them. They don't feel trapped like those kids in the suburbs, who only go where their parents are willing to drive them.*

Maura and Gregory were so accustomed to the kids coming and going as they pleased, they didn't even worry anymore when they snuck out of the brownstone. Maura had stopped waiting up for them a long time ago. That night, they figured, like most nights, the kids would climb back up the fire escape way past their curfew (which was midnight), but they'd be safe and present at the breakfast table by morning. And maybe it was understandable that they wanted to spend this particular night without their parents. Gregory took great pride in the fact that his children loved each other as much as they did, though he refused to take any of the credit for it. He hadn't grown up with siblings, but he still knew that the kind of bond his kids had was rare.

It wasn't until he was stepping out of the shower at seven the following morning that Maura called him in a state of panic.

"The kids did not come home. The kids did not come home!" she'd cried.

No matter how often they snuck out, they always returned. And today of all days, with Joshua's court date, they knew it was vital for them to look well rested and presentable.

"I've tried all their phones," Maura had said frantically. "They all went straight to voice mail. And they haven't responded to any of my texts."

Gregory could feel his blood pressure rise. Straight to voice mail? Texts unreturned? Something was terribly wrong. His kids were glued to their phones. Despite his own fears, Gregory was able to get Maura to calm down. He told her the kids had probably spent the night at a friend's and would meet them at the courthouse. He would be at the brownstone in twenty minutes in a town car to pick her up.

Once at the courthouse, they were met by Joshua's team of lawyers. The parents of the girl in the coma were sitting across the aisle from them, but Gregory couldn't bring himself to look at them. They waited for their kids to arrive for close to an hour before the judge declared Joshua a no-show. What was his son thinking? He had already ruined his life, and now he was going to make things even worse.

Gregory couldn't control himself. He insisted to the judge that it didn't make sense. His son was a very responsible kid (apart from the time he drove drunk and put a girl in a coma). Something must have happened to him. The judge told him to sit down, or else he'd be in contempt of court. Out of the corner of his eye, Gregory could see the girl's parents shaking their heads at him. *No wonder his son nearly killed our daughter,* they must have been thinking. *His own parents can't even keep track of him.* The lawyers followed Gregory and Maura to the local police precinct, and they'd been sitting there waiting in the lobby ever since.

The cops would put an APB out for Joshua, since he was technically on the lam, but that had no impact on the fact that their oldest and youngest were missing along with him. Finally, after Gregory had paced the room a hundred times, he and Maura were taken into the police chief's office. The chief was a gruff, middle-aged man. His gut was protruding and his hairline was receding. He was either nursing a sunburn or his complexion was always a leathery red. He took a sip of his coffee as he faced the Daltons.

"When did you last see your children, Mr. and Mrs. Dalton?" he asked them.

"Yesterday evening, around six-thirty." Gregory answered. "It was Wylie's birthday, and I went to her room to give her a birthday gift. We spoke for a few minutes, and then I went back downstairs so she could get ready for dinner."

"Did any of them leave a note?"

"When was the last time a kid left a note for her parents after sneaking out?" he responded. Maura shot him a look. "No," he said. "They did not leave a note."

"Is it unusual for them to sneak out?"

Maura and Gregory looked at each other. What was the

right way to answer that question without sounding like deadbeat parents? She spoke up first.

"No. They do it all the time, but it's very unusual for them to not come home or answer their phones. I keep calling, and it keeps going to voice mail every time. They could be hurt. Someone could have taken them."

"Let's not jump to conclusions," the police chief said. "Do they have credit cards or debit cards in their names they might use as a means to spend money?"

"They all have debit cards," Maura responded.

"Wylie, our daughter, has a credit card as well," Gregory interrupted. Maura looked at him, confused. "I gave her one in her name to use when she sees fit. The bills come to my office." Maura shook her head. He knew what she was thinking—that he was trying to buy their daughter's love.

"Look, we have an APB out on your son," said the police chief. "If he contacts you, you need to tell us. He's in a lot of trouble. The other two, well, technically we can't report them missing until it's been twenty-four hours. I don't mean to pry, but is it true that you're in the process of getting divorced?"

Gregory and Maura nodded, not sure what the state of their marriage had to do with their kids disappearing.

"We'll do everything to find your kids, but when we consider your son's criminal history and the fact that he was being sentenced today, and the current family situation, it's highly unlikely we're dealing with a kidnapping or a child-endangerment scenario."

"What are you implying, officer?" Gregory asked, his anger bubbling just below the surface.

"Our working theory right now is that your children ran away from home."

Gregory and Maura let this sink in.

"In the meantime, if there's no sign of them after twenty-four hours, we'll start investigating. I'll need their computers, passwords to their social networking accounts if you have them, anything else that could help us."

Maura shuddered.

"I understand why you think they left home of their own accord, but I can't shake the feeling that someone *took* them," she said.

"Well, we're going to investigate all possibilities. Do either of you have any enemies? If you know of anyone who might want to hurt you, now would be a good time to let us know."

Maura and Gregory shook their heads. The only enemies they had at this point were each other.

✦ ✦ ✦ ✦ ✦ ✦ ✦

THE GIRL AT THE BOUTIQUE WAS RIGHT: THE DRESS fit Wylie perfectly. It hung off her curves and lengthened her legs. She felt glamorous in it, but also light and natural. Aside from the lip gloss she had brought with her, she had no makeup on. It had felt good to take a shower even if the water pressure left much to be desired. For the first time today, she smelled good. Her stomach was starting to growl, but the vegetable platter helped tide her over until dinner. Micah rationed what alcohol was left in his flask, while Joshua seemed slightly less on edge now. He lay down on the bed and tapped his finger on the wooden headboard.

It was hard to believe that just this morning they'd woken up on Phinn's boat.

Her brothers had changed out of their clothes into the linen pants and cotton T-shirts that had been left in the room for them. With their styles suddenly indistinguishable, Wylie realized how much they looked alike and how hardened Micah had become from wearing black every day. It was nice to see him in lighter colors for a change, even if he was visibly uncomfortable.

"Guys."

Wylie turned to see Joshua now sitting up on the bed.

"I feel like an idiot even bringing this up, because it sort of pales in comparison to everything that's happening right now, but if I don't get it off my chest, I'll go nuts." He looked down at his hands, clearly not wanting his siblings to see that he was close to tears. Wylie immediately sat next to him and put her arm around him.

"What's wrong?" she asked.

"Abigail broke up with me last night," he answered, his voice breaking.

"I'm sure it was just a fight," Micah jumped in. "She had too much to drink. She's probably sent you a million apology texts by now."

"Well, then she's gonna be even more pissed that I'm not responding to any of them. And maybe she was drunk, but alcohol just makes everyone more honest. She told me last night she didn't want to wait for me. I never asked her to. I never thought I had to—she just always said she would."

Abigail and Wylie had grown to be good friends, but

Abigail had never mentioned wanting to end things with Joshua. Then again, Wylie was his sister. She wasn't exactly the ideal person to confide in about that topic.

"Abigail loves you," she told her brother. "She just needs time, that's all."

Tinka entered the room without knocking, bringing their conversation to a halt. She now sported a form-fitting camouflage-print dress and wore her short hair slicked back. Micah practically had to wipe the drool from his mouth.

"It's time for dinner. Follow me."

The dining room was only a short walk away from the bungalow, but Tinka took the scenic route: back down the stairs and past the lagoon. Kerosene lamps, paper lanterns, and tealight candles lit up the grounds. The stars were magnificent. They seemed to cover every inch of the black sky above them. The ones they'd flown below in Manhattan looked dull in comparison. The dining room was filled with kids cleaning their plates, but Tinka took them to a private room off to the side of the common area, which was currently quiet and empty.

The table was decorated with small centerpieces filled with burro's tail and dandelions. The fish Lola had been preparing was now grilled and laid out on a large platter. The seasoning and marinade gave it a lavender finish, a hue none of the Daltons had ever associated with seafood. The fish was surrounded by sautéed vegetables, some of which Wylie couldn't identify. On both ends of the table, oysters on the half shell rested on ice. Each place setting also had its very own shrimp cocktail with a thick green dipping sauce. Wylie thought about how she could hone her cooking skills by helping Lola out in the kitchen, but even if that never happened and they left for home tomorrow, she knew this meal alone would make their journey worth it.

Eight empty chairs surrounded the table. Tinka pointed out their seats. Wylie and Joshua sat across from each other, both next to the head of the table. Wylie assumed the seat at the head was reserved for Phinn. Micah took the seat next to Wylie, and Tinka sat across from him.

After a few minutes of uncomfortable silence, Maz and Bandit, the two boys who had left the lagoon with Phinn, walked in and sat down. Lola, showered and changed from when they'd first met her in the kitchen, followed closely behind. She had her wet hair tied into a tight bun at the top of her head. With all the cooking and gardening, she probably didn't have time to fuss over her appearance—not that she needed to anyway. She grabbed the seat next to Maz, and they exchanged a quick kiss with the casualness of a couple who'd been together for a long time.

Bandit was the first of the group to speak up. "I hope you guys realize you've been given the opportunity of a lifetime by being here. Phinn's very selective about who he brings to the island."

Wylie was sick of all the veiled statements and mystery. She wished someone would just tell them why they were here, but she didn't expect any answers until Phinn arrived. They waited for him in relative silence, the giant platters of food taunting them. At one point, Micah reached across the table for a carafe of white wine, but Maz stopped him.

"We don't eat or drink until Phinn arrives," he said sternly.

"My mistake." Micah was so embarrassed, he barely got the words out.

"It's okay. You didn't know. Don't sweat it," Tinka intervened.

The whole room seemed surprised by Tinka's gentle tone. Until now, Wylie didn't think she was capable of being kind.

"Look, why don't we each share a little bit about ourselves," Maz said, softening his tone. "I'll start."

He told the Daltons he was born in New Jersey to an Iranian mother and an American father, but remembered very little of the Farsi he'd learned as a kid.

When Wylie asked how long Maz and Lola had been dating, they shared a knowing look and said too long to keep track.

Bandit had grown up in Brooklyn, but came to the island two years before. He'd been living at a youth shelter when he met Phinn and took him up on his offer to move here.

"It was the best decision I've ever made in my life," Bandit told them.

Phinn smiled at the sentiment as he entered the room, looking freshly showered and shaved. He kept his eyes focused on Wylie as he walked across the room and sat next to her.

"I'm starving!" Phinn declared. "Why isn't anyone eating? I hope you didn't wait on my account."

Phinn slurped down an oyster, then grabbed a beer from a nearby cooler, popped the cap off using the side of the table, and poured it into a chilled pint glass. Everyone else eagerly stocked their plates with the smorgasbord of seafood and filled their wine glasses to the brim, except Wylie, who opted for a glass of coconut milk, straight from the shell. Phinn held his pint glass up for a toast, and everyone followed suit.

"Splash!" he declared.

"Splash!" everyone echoed loudly. The Daltons smiled politely and wordlessly clinked their glasses.

"You say 'cheers' on the mainland. Splash is the term we use around these parts," Phinn translated.

"Oh, got it. Splash, everyone!" Wylie replied, awkwardly lifting her glass again.

For a few minutes, no one spoke as they devoured their dinner. Wylie doused her shrimp with the green dip and took a bite. The sauce tasted like lime and avocado, and the shrimp was so fresh, she could barely stop herself from moaning in delight. She washed it down with a sip of coconut milk that tasted sweeter than the canned kind she cooked with back home. How could Phinn ever crave fast food when he had farm-to-table dining at his disposal every night?

"What did you season the fish with?" Wylie asked Lola, unable to isolate the ingredients as she normally could.

"A chef never reveals her secrets," Lola replied with a smile.

"Lola, just tell her," Phinn ordered.

"Fine. Woodmeg and pame with a dash of salt. When you grind them up together, they turn lavender."

"We don't have those herbs on the mainland," Wylie said.

"Speaking of the mainland," Phinn said, "why don't we get straight to the point. Wylie, how old are you?"

Wylie, mouth full, swallowed her food quickly and nearly choked on it. "I turned seventeen yesterday, actually," she answered.

"Happy birthday," Lola said.

"And Joshua, what about you?"

"Sixteen," Joshua answered. Phinn gestured to Micah to answer.

"Fifteen," he said, and then with a glance to Tinka, "but people think I'm a lot older."

Phinn replied, "The people in this room tonight are members of what I like to call my inner circle. They're the people I trust most in the world." Wylie felt her stomach flip. It shouldn't have mattered, but she hated the idea of Tinka being that important to Phinn.

"How old are you guys?" Phinn asked the rest of the party. They answered in unison:

"Seventeen."

"And when will each of you turn eighteen?"

Again, they responded at the same time:

"Never."

Wylie could feel Joshua kick her under the table. She couldn't look at him, because she was certain they were both thinking the same thing. What did they mean they were never going to turn eighteen? Were the Daltons witnessing some sort of strange suicide pact?

Phinn laughed. "You guys look confused."

"We're just not sure what you mean by *never* turning

eighteen. Do you all plan to off yourselves or something?" Joshua asked.

"Nope," Phinn said, refilling his beer glass. "You could say we're timeless."

"Are we the butt of some elaborate joke?" Wylie asked, defensively. "Is this some weird hidden-camera show?"

"It's not a joke," Phinn assured her. "The reason we'll never turn eighteen is because we live on an island that's frozen in time. Hence the name Minor Island. You grow up to be seventeen, and then you stop aging. Told you I had a good reason for bringing you here," he added, clearly pleased with himself.

"You're full of it," Joshua said, examining all the faces of the inner circle. None of them gave anything away.

"This is a place where we don't answer to any adults or parents or *police officers*." Phinn made a point of looking at Joshua. "It's magical and tropic and we'd love it if you decided to stay. I know it's all been shrouded in mystery and you've had a lot of questions. Now I can answer them."

Wylie almost didn't want to allow herself to believe what Phinn was telling them was the truth. An island where no one aged past seventeen, but with all of the perks of being an adult? She could take care of herself and never age a day in her life. No mortgage payments or divorce filings. No diseases brought on by old age. If this was a joke, it was a cruel one.

Joshua asked the first question. "Okay, if this is for real, how did you guys even find this place?"

"My parents met and fell in love in the sixties. They had me and then five years later, my dad got drafted to Vietnam.

He didn't want to go, and my mom didn't want him to leave. So they left the States with a group of friends in a similar predicament. Maz's parents and Tinka's parents were with them. My mom insisted that instead of crossing the border, they sail to Nova Scotia. But they got caught in a storm and were lost at sea for hours until they washed ashore here. Lola's family was indigenous to the island, so they were already here. They took our parents in and let them stay."

Wylie's hands shook as she refilled her glass. Bandit was right—Phinn had given them the opportunity of a lifetime. He wasn't a psychopath after all. What he'd done on the boat wasn't a kidnapping; it was a rescue mission.

"Does your family still live on the island?" Wylie asked Lola.

Phinn answered for her. "There weren't many of them left by the time we got here. After some years of living here together, they decided to leave."

"Were they pushed out?" Wylie continued to press, uneasy with the notion that they'd be forced to leave.

"No," Lola was quick to respond. "It was their decision. In fact, we begged them to stay, but they wanted to move on. After meeting Phinn's parents, they became obsessed with the idea of getting older. Me, not so much."

Micah asked the next question. "So, what happened to all of your parents?"

The room fell silent and the faces around the table went dark. Phinn took a long swallow of his beer. Wylie could tell this was a subject no one liked to discuss.

"They died when we were all very young."

"How? When?" Joshua blurted.

"If you don't mind, I think we'll plead the Fifth on that one for now. It's not exactly a happy story," Phinn replied. Wylie wondered if he'd ever open up about how he'd lost his mom and dad. From the way his smile faded, she could tell it was still an open wound.

"I'm sorry for your loss," Joshua said quietly.

"So . . . can you guys live forever?" Micah asked.

Phinn shook his head.

"We're not vampires. But when you don't have to worry about the health issues brought on by old age, you live a lot longer than the average person. We've had some deaths over time, though they've been few and far between. There was a case of alcohol poisoning and a couple drownings. Ration your alcohol intake," Phinn said with a subtle glance toward Micah, "and you shouldn't have any of those problems."

Wylie played with the food left on her plate. She wanted to keep eating, but she was hung up on the fact that she was currently on an island where no one aged past seventeen.

"Why us?" she finally said. "Why did you decide to bring us here?"

"I started making trips to the States to recruit other teenagers to help populate the island once I turned fourteen and learned to sail, but I don't want to bring just anyone to the island. It's not fair for a rich person to win the lottery, right? So we extend the opportunity to kids who've been struggling on the mainland. Maybe it's their dysfunctional family, maybe it's legal troubles, or maybe they're just misunderstood. Whatever the problem, their full potential can't be realized the way it should. So, Wylie, when you told me about Joshua and some of your family problems, I thought this might be the best place for all of you."

"We should have been the ones to decide that for ourselves," Joshua said.

"And now you get to," Phinn replied.

Bandit cleared his throat and spoke up. "I was homeless when I met Phinn. My mom was in rehab. My dad was never around. One of my cousins had just been shot and killed by a cop. I knew my days were numbered. I was depressed. Phinn saved my life by bringing me here. There's no racism on this island. No homophobia. None of the old, traditional ideals we're used to back home. If that's not paradise, I don't know what is."

"Don't you miss what family you had, though?" Wylie asked him.

"They hurt me enough times. I'd have been a glutton for punishment to stay with them."

Wylie gave him an understanding nod.

"What's the scientific reason no one ages here?" Joshua asked.

"That, we can't answer," Lola piped in. "My tribe thought it had to be an environmental side effect of the island. Whether it's the air we breathe, the water we drink, the atmosphere—we're not certain."

"What we do know is that there's no age reversal," Phinn added. "If you come to the island like our parents did, already as adults, you won't get younger. Which is why we generally don't allow people to return to the States once they choose to live here. We believe once you go back, you revert to the normal aging process."

"But then how come you were in New York?" Wylie inquired.

"A few of us make occasional trips to the mainland for supplies and various errands. Our working theory is that once you turn seventeen, you have three hundred and sixty-five days to spare on the mainland. So far, I've used up only seventy days since my seventeenth birthday."

Wylie didn't want to ask her next question. He had already made the implication, but she was hoping her brothers didn't catch it. If they chose to live on the island, they would not be allowed to go home again. She'd have fewer than three hundred and sixty-five days to spare in New York, but even then it sounded like she wouldn't be allowed to go. She tried not to think about what would become of her mom if they abandoned her forever. How would she ever go on without her kids? Her dad would be fine. He'd already chosen to go on without them anyway. But there was also Vanessa to think of. She and Wylie had made a pact a long time ago that after college, they'd move to Paris together. Staying here would mean missing out on her entire senior year of high school. No prom. No graduation. No "Pomp and Circumstance." She felt silly thinking about it, but basketball playoffs were in two weeks, and their team had a perfect record this season. They wouldn't be able to win without their star point guard.

But on the flip side, if she stayed here, she could stop studying for the SATs. That one definitely made it into the "pros" column. Best of all, she wouldn't have to choose which one of her parents to live with. It was almost like

Phinn had granted her wish from the night they met. Thanks to him, she could choose to live on her own.

"How do you make sure no one talks about the island once you send them back?" Joshua asked. "What's to say we won't go home and tell everyone about this tropical island off the Atlantic coast where no one ages?"

"We have our ways." It was Maz who answered, his warm smile suddenly gone. Wylie shuddered. She wondered how they would be treated by these people if she and her brothers chose to go home. Would they be monitored all their lives just to make sure they never squealed about the island? As if sensing her anxiety, Phinn grabbed her hand under the table. She contemplated letting go, but there was something comforting about his callused palm against her skin.

"Do . . . you ever get bored?" Wylie asked. "Sure, there are drawbacks to getting older, but most of my friends and I, we can't wait to move out of the house, go to college, start our lives, see the world. Isn't there any part of you that wants that?"

"No," Bandit answered. "Take it from someone who's lived on the mainland most of my life—the life of an adult is highly overrated. Here, we get to party all the time. We keep the place running. We don't have to worry about any of the other crap that comes with getting older. Working some dead-end job, paying bills, getting our cholesterol checked. Go back to New York. I guarantee if you walked up to any forty-year-old and asked them what they'd do in your position, they'd stay here. No question."

Wylie let this sink in. He was right. Living here meant having all the freedom of adulthood and all of the freedom of youth at the same time. What could be better?

"I know this is a lot to process," Phinn said. "But I think we've covered just about everything."

"Wait," Wylie jumped in. "What's on the Forbidden Side?"

"It's a lot less dramatic than it sounds. You've probably heard of quicksand, right? Well, that portion of the island is prone to it. So we decided the area should be off limits, just to be safe."

Wylie breathed a sigh of relief. The notion of quicksand was frightening, but she knew it wasn't as dangerous as the way it was portrayed in movies.

"Who's Hopper?" Wylie asked.

Everyone at the table exchanged an uncomfortable look. Phinn smiled wide to overcompensate.

"Not one of our favorite topics," Phinn admitted. "He came to the island a couple years ago, but he wasn't a good fit. So we sent him packing. He had a twisted sense of humor and tagged parts of the island. That's why you'll see his name here and there."

There was obviously more to the story than Phinn was letting on, but Wylie didn't press him. She didn't want to hear any details that might deter her brothers from wanting to stay. And anyway, it was inevitable that not all recruits would fit in with the rest of the island. Hopefully, she wouldn't have that problem.

"It's getting late and you guys have a lot to think about," Phinn said, "I'm sure you want some time to make a decision."

"How long do we have?" Joshua asked.

"We can give you till the morning. Just remember, there's no going back on what you choose. If you stay, you can't change your mind and go home."

And if we leave, Wylie thought, *we can never come back here again*. How could they be expected to go back to their normal lives with the knowledge that a place like this existed? Joshua wanted to get married and have kids and be a dad someday. Wylie wasn't sure he'd be willing to give all that up, even if doing so extended his life span by about a hundred years. There was a very good chance they'd be sailing home tomorrow morning, and before long, she'd wonder if Phinn and this entire place were just a figment of her imagination.

"Well, then we should probably get back to our bungalow," Wylie said. "Thank you for the lovely meal. It was really nice getting to know all of you."

"Let me walk you back," Phinn insisted.

On the walk to the bungalow, Joshua and Micah strode ahead, locked in whispered conversation, but Wylie hung back with Phinn and listened as he pointed out tiny landmarks Tinka hadn't shown them on the tour.

"Nighttime is my favorite time on the island. It's so quiet and peaceful," Phinn said, reaching into a basket of glass jars in the Clearing. "These are for catching fireflies."

He handed a jar to Wylie and she quickly opened and closed the lid. She grinned as she watched it glow from the fireflies buzzing around inside. Phinn directed their attention to the sky, where a few insomniacs flew above their heads.

"I call them the night owls. They sleep all day and play all night. Sometimes when I'm feeling restless and can't sleep, I come down to the Clearing and roast sugar roots with them."

"What are sugar roots?" Wylie asked.

"A plant we have here. When you heat it up, it expands and bursts into a ball of sticky deliciousness. You guys want to try one?"

Joshua turned around. "No, thanks. We should get back to our room."

"Hey, if we're leaving tomorrow, I'm trying a sugar root," Wylie countered. "When in Minor Island, right?"

As Phinn pulled a bunch of red weeds out of the ground, he explained how important it was to respect the island's natural resources.

"Lola's tribe taught us that the island is sacred. We treat it as such. I guess you could say we're die-hard environmentalists. We take care of every inch of this place, and we're rewarded in spades."

The sugar roots were bulbous and the color of blood-orange pulp. Phinn pushed a stick into them and handed one out to each of the siblings. They stood around a lit fire pit and held their sticks over the flames. The bulbs expanded like balloons and when they popped, a glob of what looked like saltwater taffy sizzled into the shape of a ball.

"Blow on it for a second."

Wylie did as she was directed, then took a small bite. The sugar root tasted like a combination of marzipan and salted caramel. It was delicious.

"It was worth it, right?" Phinn asked.

They all nodded as they walked toward the bunga-low, munching on the melted plant the whole way home. When they arrived at the front door, Phinn gently held onto Wylie's wrist.

"Can I have a minute alone with you?" he asked.

Wylie glanced at her brothers. She didn't need their approval, but she also didn't want them to think that alone time with Phinn would sway her or cloud her judgment.

"Go ahead," Joshua said. "We'll be inside."

The door closed, leaving them alone for the first time since Wylie had fallen asleep on his boat. She stared at Phinn's face, trying to make sense of what she felt for him. His methods for bringing them here were wrong, there was no way around that, but did it matter anymore if his intentions were good?

"Do you forgive me for bringing you here?" he asked.

"I don't know," was the most honest answer she could give.

"What if I begged and pleaded?"

"That might help."

"Please forgive me. I could tell how much you love your brothers. I knew how much it would hurt to see one of them go to jail. I wanted to protect you from that."

"I don't need protecting," Wylie replied.

"We all do sometimes." He sounded so earnest, it nearly made Wylie forget why she was mad at him in the first place.

"I don't date older guys," Wylie blurted.

"I'm only seventeen."

"But you've been that age a lot longer than I have."

"Wylie, what if for the next thirty years, you stayed your age? Lived in the same house with your parents and brothers. Went to the same school. Hung out with all the same people. If you were frozen in time just like all of us are here, believe me, you wouldn't be a day older than seventeen."

Phinn's argument reminded her of a conversation she'd had the month before with her grandma on her seventy-fifth birthday.

"In my head, I still feel as young as you," she'd said to Wylie with a sigh. "And then I look in the mirror and I'm shocked."

Phinn was right. Living here on this island, without letting the aging process take hold, meant *being* a seventeen-year-old forever.

"Do you think you'll stay?" Phinn asked.

"Why couldn't you have just told us you were bringing us here instead of doing it without asking?"

"If I told you about this place, would you have even believed me?"

"No."

"I couldn't take that risk. I couldn't risk never seeing you again."

Before she even knew what she was doing, Wylie flung her arms around Phinn and breathed in his scent. His arms hung flat by his sides for a moment, and then he wrapped them around her waist.

"I'm glad I saw this place," she said.

"I'm glad you did, too," Phinn said, holding her even tighter.

"Good night, Phinn."

"Good night, Wylie."

"No matter what happens, it was really nice to meet you."

"It was really nice to meet you, too."

And then she let him go and walked inside, prepared for battle.

mea culpas

family meetings were Maura Dalton's favorite pastime. Halfway through Wylie's freshman year in high school, she got caught cutting class, and her mom insisted they conduct the meetings on a monthly basis. It didn't take long for the Dalton kids to realize that "family meeting" was just code for a lengthy, grueling parental lecture. Wylie usually zoned out and nodded her head at the appropriate times, while discreetly pinching Joshua and Micah for her own amusement. They always sat on opposite sides of her, and she liked to predict which one of her brothers would surrender to laughter first. It was usually Micah.

But now, with just the three of them, this family meeting was unavoidable. And its outcome would determine the rest of their lives.

They'd been talking in circles for hours, and so far the only thing they agreed on was that their decision had to be unanimous. There would be no scenario where Wylie would stay on the island and her brothers would leave. If they were going to live here, they were going to live here *together*.

But the chances of that happening were growing slimmer by the minute. Joshua was as adamant about going home as Wylie was about staying. For every point she made, he swung back with the perfect counterpoint. Wylie wasn't giving up easily, though. He could bully and debate her all he wanted, but she was not turning her back on this place. It wasn't a surprise to either of them that Micah stayed neutral for most of their discussion, even though Wylie was sure if they forced him to pick a side, she would win.

The only thing currently working in Wylie's favor was that the pot of woodmeg tea they found waiting for them after dinner was tapped out. Without any caffeine to keep him awake, Joshua began to yawn between sentences, and his eyelids started to droop. Wylie knew if he let his head hit the pillow and closed his eyes, he'd fall right to sleep. Maybe Joshua would agree to stay purely so she would stop talking and he could give in to his fatigue. That was, after all, how police officers coerced suspects into confessing to crimes they'd never committed—by mentally and emotionally exhausting them. Wylie was prepared to do both.

"I don't want to stay young forever. I want to get older," Joshua finally admitted.

This was the argument Wylie had been dreading all night.

"Don't you guys?" he continued. "I want to go to college one day. I want to get a job. Abigail and I had plans to get married, have kids, and grow old together. That's the point of living, isn't it? Experiencing everything life has to offer. Not staying in some strange state of arrested development."

"He makes a good point," Micah chimed in. "Honestly, fifteen hasn't been all that great for me. I don't know if I want to be a teenager forever."

Wylie was nearly fuming now. Micah had been quiet all night, and he decided to break his silence by siding with their brother?

"Growing up won't guarantee you happiness, Micah," Wylie announced. "It sucks, but it's true. The people who make fun of you now are going to grow up right along with us. But starting over on an island with people who don't know the Micah Dalton from Harper Academy? That could solve all your problems. You are a wonderful person, and you deserve to be around people who will finally appreciate you."

Micah looked down at his hands.

"What makes you think they won't hate me here, too?" he asked.

"Because they've invited you to stay. They want you here. If this island is high school, then the people we were at dinner with tonight are the popular kids, and they already like you. Especially Tinka. She was staring at you all night."

The last part wasn't entirely true, but when Wylie saw Micah's mouth form a smile, she knew it was a justifiable lie. Joshua wasn't the only kid in the family who could take a page from the politician's handbook.

"What about prom?" Joshua said, looking right at Wylie.

"What about it?"

"You're really okay with missing it?"

"Missing out on one night so I can be seventeen forever? Yes, I'm more than okay with that."

"What about falling in love and getting married someday? Don't tell me you've never dreamed of your wedding day, Dad walking you down the aisle."

Wylie rolled her eyes. It was so typical of a guy to assume that all females associated the word "future" with a white gown and a diamond ring.

"I can honestly say I've never dreamed about my wedding day. Why would I, with Mom and Dad fighting all the time?"

"What about being a chef? You've always wanted to have your own restaurant. You can't do that here."

"Maybe I can help Lola in the kitchen. I don't care who I work for as long as I still get to cook."

"What about Mom and Dad?" Joshua asked, rubbing his eyes. "Are you actually prepared to never see them again?"

"Yes." Wylie responded as confidently as she could. Despite the anger she felt toward her parents, the thought of never seeing them again was difficult to fathom. In one swift move, the Daltons would be declaring themselves orphans, and their parents would be as good as dead. Just like Phinn and his inner circle, except most of them didn't choose to lose their moms and dads.

"And you're okay with them just going on for the rest of their lives, not knowing what happened to us?" Joshua added.

"They never wanted us in the first place," Wylie countered. "And besides, they've always said they wanted the best for us. Well, this is it."

Joshua got up from his bed and paced the room. It was something their father did every time he was stressed out or frustrated. Joshua mostly looked like their mom, but his facial expressions sometimes bore a striking resemblance to their dad. Wylie wondered if he was pacing on purpose to mess with her head.

"The divorce isn't final yet. It won't be for a long time. Maybe Mom and Dad just need a little time apart. You know what they say, you don't know what you have until it's gone. I mean, it's not like there was cheating or abuse—something totally unforgivable between them."

"That's not entirely true," Wylie blurted, no longer able to keep the secret from her brothers.

"What's that supposed to mean?" Micah asked.

Wylie couldn't look him in the eye. "Dad had an affair."

"Dad would never do that," Joshua said suspiciously. Wylie raised her head and made herself focus on her brother's face.

"He would and he did. I found out a few months ago. We hadn't had one of our father-daughter dinners in a long time, so I went to his office to surprise him with Chinese food. When I got there, mostly everyone had gone home, but his door was open a crack. I almost walked in, but there was someone else with him."

"Maybe it was just a coworker," Micah interjected.

"They were kissing. And he told her it was only a matter of time before he left Mom and they could be together."

"You swear you're not making this up?" Joshua asked.

"I swear on my life. They do work together. Her name's Shannon. I heard them making all these plans. Getting their own little house in the Hamptons. Someplace cozy, but big enough for *all* the kids."

"She has kids?" Micah asked.

"Yeah, I looked her up. She has two kids. A boy and a girl around our ages. Dad was my hero—you guys know that," Wylie continued, trying to keep her emotions under control. "But in one moment, that changed completely. He's not who I thought he was. He left us for another family."

"Mom is going to have a nervous breakdown when she finds out," Micah said.

"She already knows. I went straight home. I was upset, crying. Maybe I should have kept it to myself, but that didn't seem right. So I told her."

"What did she say?" Micah asked.

"She said, 'We are never to discuss this again.' She changed her whole life for him. Gave up all of her dreams and plans. And even when he cheated on her, she wanted to sweep it under the rug, just like everything else."

"I hate them," Micah muttered. "I really hate them both."

Joshua stopped pacing and collapsed on his bed. "Don't say that."

"I didn't want to tell you," Wylie admitted, "but if we go home, we're not going back to the same family we left."

"I think we've reached a stalemate," Joshua said, defeated. "Let's get some sleep and pick this back up in the morning."

Sleep was a terrible idea. Wylie was certain she wouldn't

get an ounce of rest, with her future hanging in the balance. She knew what she was about to say would hurt her brother even more, but a little short-term pain was well worth a lot of long-term happiness.

"What's there to pick back up? Joshua, this is your 'get out of jail free' card. Aren't you thinking about what's waiting for you in New York? Micah and I have to deal with a broken home, but you have to deal with a four-by-four cell. A blue jumpsuit. A minimum of three years, locked up. A permanent record. An *ex*-girlfriend."

It was the mention of "ex-girlfriend" that got his attention.

"You said Abigail was just confused and that she didn't mean it when she dumped me."

"And I want to believe that, too," Wylie confessed. "But think about it. If she's already panicking, what's she going to be like when you're actually locked up? Maybe the first few years will be easy when she's still in high school, but what about when she's off at Harvard? You really think she's still going to be writing you letters and paying you visits on the weekend? I'm sorry, Joshua, but most relationships don't even survive people going to different colleges. I don't know if yours can survive jail time."

Joshua's olive skin was now a deep shade of red, and the vein in his forehead made its second appearance of the day. He walked up to Wylie, looked her right in the eye, and said:

"And whose fault would that be, Wylie?"

All the air went out of the room. No one spoke. Wylie was finally speechless. All this time, she'd thought if Joshua ever admitted she was the one responsible for the accident, it would be a relief. But all she felt right now was sheer disgust. Not for her brother, but for herself.

"Mine," Wylie answered. "And that's why I can't go back." As soon as she said it, she knew it was exactly the reason she wanted to stay. "If you're locked up for three years, you're never going to forgive me. And I'll never be able to live with myself. I already can't most days."

For once, Joshua didn't comfort her or downplay her guilt. Wylie knew it was because he didn't disagree.

"You were a no-show at your sentencing," Wylie continued. "You're a fugitive. They could put you away for even longer now. This is a second chance for *all* of us."

"She's right," Micah said. "I don't want you to go to jail. We've all tried to stay positive, but this is going to ruin your life. That girl might never come out of her coma. She could die. And then what happens to you?"

Joshua shuddered.

"I can't think about that. I don't want you guys changing your entire lives because of me," he told them. "I'll go back and face the music. I'll be out eventually, and then we'll pick up the pieces."

"Didn't you hear what Phinn said?" Wylie asked. "He brings people to the island who can't realize their potential back home. If that doesn't make you the perfect candidate to be here, I don't know what does. We could be really happy here. I can feel it."

"Are you saying that because you mean it or because you're into Phinn?" Joshua asked, with more than a trace of condescension.

"I don't have feelings for him. Sure, he's interesting and he's given us an incredible opportunity, but it wasn't right, what he did."

"Then is the accident the only reason you want to stay here?"

"No, it's not the only reason. There's nothing good waiting for us back home. Yeah, I'll miss my friends. I'll miss some things about school. I've worked hard for my cooking channel. I love being on the basketball team. Vanessa, she'll probably never forgive me for abandoning her, but the pros outweigh the cons. Back home, we'll get old and we'll die. We have more than a lifetime ahead of us here. Please don't make us go back. Please don't make us send you to jail, when we can all be free here together."

"I'm with Wylie," Micah said, finally choosing a side.

Wylie watched as their words sank in and the vein in Joshua's forehead slowly retreated.

"Okay. Let's stay." And then he grinned. "Let's be young forever."

They hugged and cheered and rejoiced in their decision.

"You're sure about this?" Wylie asked, nervous that Joshua would change his mind in the light of day.

"Positive."

With the debate finally over, it was time to go to sleep. Wylie lay awake in bed until she heard her brothers breathing deeply in their slumber. She quietly stumbled out of bed, slipped on her boots, and tiptoed out the front door.

The island was now eerily quiet. She'd assumed everybody partied till the wee hours of the morning, but she didn't hear any chatter or laughter or music. Maybe aside from the insomniacs, everyone went to sleep at the same time.

Manhattan was an island with a population of well over a million. No matter how late she stayed out, there were always enough people around to make her feel protected. According to Phinn, Minor Island currently had a population of fifty-three, and right now there wasn't a sign of anyone. She had taken her compass with her from the bungalow, even though she knew she wouldn't get lost. It was more than just a gift now, or a tool; it felt like a good-luck charm.

A girl's voice drifted toward her in the dark. As Wylie listened carefully, she realized the girl was reciting the poem from the dining room like a prayer: "'*Never forget to live life to the fullest. Do it for the troubled; do it for the lost. The days may feel shorter; the nights may feel long. But when we remember, our memories grow strong.*'"

"Hello? Is someone out there?" Wylie called out.

She felt a breeze pick up as the girl flew above her, too quickly for Wylie to make out her face. She thought about her parents as she repeated the words of the poem in her head. It seemed that Phinn had written it in honor of the family members and friends who were left behind on the mainland. Wylie squeezed the compass and picked up her pace.

Phinn's bungalow was nearly twice the size of all the other bungalows and easy to spot. The lights were off, but Wylie wouldn't let that deter her. She took a deep breath and knocked on the door three times. The door swung open, and Phinn stood in front of her, wearing nothing but boxers and a pair of slippers.

"I told you it's not a good idea to spend the night here," he said groggily.

"I'm not here to spend the night with you."

Phinn suddenly perked up at the sound of her voice.

"I'm so sorry. I thought you were Tinka. It's a long story. Please, come in."

Wylie stepped inside the room and heard the crunch of broken glass under her shoes. The ground was covered with clothing, broken picture frames, and other belongings. The dresser drawers were hanging precariously from their hinges.

"I'm not a slob, I promise," Phinn said. "Tinka likes to throw things when she gets mad. Luckily, her aim is horrible. So, do you have good news for me?"

"Yes. We'd like to stay."

"Really?"

"Really."

Phinn's eyes twinkled in the dim light as he looked at her. "You made the right choice." He moved toward her to give her a hug, but Wylie stepped back.

"I didn't come here to celebrate. I came to thank you. You gave my brother the one thing I couldn't: his freedom. And that's why I forgive you for the way you brought us here."

Phinn breathed a sigh of relief. "That means a lot to me. I won't take it for granted, I promise."

"You did the wrong thing, but you did it for the right

reasons. I've done that, too. I would be a hypocrite if I couldn't move past it."

"I appreciate that."

"It's been a tough year for my family," Wylie went on, "so I hope living here gives us a clean slate."

"This is a great place to start over. I hope you and I can do the same."

Phinn tucked a strand of Wylie's hair behind her ear.

"We can, but only as friends. If nothing happens between us, that has to be okay. I know it might be presumptuous to think you have any other expectations, but I'm not exactly interested in having a boyfriend."

"I have no expectations, Wylie. I like you. I think that's obvious, but I'll settle for friendship if that's what you want. Deal?"

"Deal," Wylie answered.

Phinn held out his hand and Wylie reached out to shake it. She suddenly felt her palms sweat as their skin touched. *Friends*, Wylie reminded herself.

"Great, then we both agree," Wylie said. "We can both be *adults* about this."

Phinn smiled and let go of her hand. "Bite your tongue, Wylie Dalton."

home

they stood at the top of the steps in height order. First Joshua, then Wylie, then Micah, who was still a few inches shy of being taller than his sister. The Clearing was decked out with lanterns, handmade piñatas, and brightly colored *papel picados*. Most of the kids were already dipping their feet in the lagoon or flying right above it, but they were much more dolled-up than when the Daltons had arrived on the island the day before. The same band was playing onstage, but this time the lead singer was singing instead of rapping, her sultry voice echoing off the palm trees. When she finished the song, Phinn stood on the step in front of the Daltons and hollered:

"Ladies and gents, I present the newest residents of Minor Island: Wylie, Joshua, and Micah!"

Wylie had to remind herself not to take a bow or wave like a beauty queen as everyone cheered below them. She wanted to believe their enthusiasm was sincere and wasn't just some show for Phinn's sake. Most of the residents looked genuinely pleased to have new friends among them, but there were a handful of smiles that looked rehearsed and almost robotic. Except for Tinka. She didn't bother to smile at all.

"You really do this for everybody, right?" Wylie asked Phinn, blushing from all the attention.

"Yup. It's a rite of passage," he answered. "Every person who's moved here from the mainland has a residency party." On Phinn's signal, the cheers of the crowd slowly tapered off. He escorted the Daltons down the staircase, where all the residents eagerly waited to meet them.

The entire day felt like a whirlwind. Once morning broke, Wylie and her brothers began the arduous process of settling in. First, they were asked to relinquish their cell phones. They were considered relics of the mainland and didn't work here anyway. Next, they were required to get a blood test and a full physical, followed by a proper fitting by the seamstresses, and then they were assigned to their permanent bungalows.

Aldo and Patrick were the two medics on the island. Despite their young age, they were both whip smart and had a gentle bedside manner. Aldo had come to the island in the eighties, when he was sixteen years old. He seemed more mature and buttoned-up than anyone the Daltons had met so far. Patrick arrived in the nineties, when the island was hit with a flu epidemic and Aldo needed an extra hand.

"I got a guy back on the mainland that gives us a stash

of flu shots now," Patrick explained. "All I have to do in exchange is give him one *parvaz* flower. It's a pretty awesome trade."

Patrick had perfectly formed dreadlocks tied into a low ponytail and a tattoo on his arm with the date he'd arrived on the island. Between his style and the casual manner in which he spoke, he was clearly the less conventional of the two.

"Everyone here is young and healthy, so we don't get a lot of patients. Mostly just minor cuts and bruises, things like that," Aldo assured them.

Unlike most of the other residents, Aldo and Patrick had come from stable home lives. Ultimately, it was their love of medicine that had lured them away from their families. They were both obsessed with cracking the scientific reasons for an island where no one grows up.

"It's still a mystery," Patrick admitted. "But we'll figure it out someday."

All three siblings passed their physicals and were next met by Nadia, the head seamstress, who walked them to the boutique to take their measurements.

"We get clothes from the mainland as often as we can, but most of our garments are handmade. We try to keep the designs simple and practical, but everyone still loves to add their own flair," Nadia explained. "It might take a couple weeks to get your new wardrobes, but we'll give you a rack of loaner clothes you can borrow in the meantime."

Once all their measurements were properly recorded, Nadia showed them to their new bungalows. The room they'd shared the night before was just a temporary space reserved for recent recruits or residents whose homes were under construction. Their new dwellings would be more centrally located.

Wylie had to withhold her opinion when they learned Joshua and Micah would be living in one bungalow together. Growing up, the Daltons had always had their own rooms, and sharing a space would be a big adjustment for her brothers. Perhaps down the road they could convince Phinn to bring Abigail to the island, and Joshua would never have to second-guess their decision to move here. Wylie was told she'd be moving into Lola's bungalow, a stone's throw from Phinn's place.

"Are you sure you're cool with me staying here?" Wylie asked Lola when she arrived on her doorstep. "I can always ask to be reassigned if you don't want a roommate."

"It's fine, really," Lola replied, pushing her clothes aside to make room in the closet. "I could use the company."

Wylie wasn't entirely convinced. She felt a sudden tightness in her chest as she thought about all the sleepovers, late-night phone calls, and strolls through Central Park she'd had with Vanessa. Sometimes they got so lost in conversation, they'd miss their stop on the subway and would laugh all the way up the stairs and across the platform to catch the next train headed in the other direction.

"I promise, you won't even know I'm here," Wylie said to Lola.

"It's nice to have a new girl around," Lola replied. "A lot of the time I'm stuck with Tinka, because of the whole inner circle thing, but we've never really been close. She calls me bridal all the time behind my back."

"What does bridal mean?"

"You know, stupid or dumb. Just like the entire custom of getting married. They don't say it on the mainland?"

"Not in the same way you guys use it."

"Hm. I tried to keep count every time Tinka rolled her eyes at dinner last night, but I lost track. Have you ever seen anyone look so miserable? She *hates* new recruits. I feel bad for her, though," Lola admitted. "Even though Phinn couldn't be less interested, she's been in love with him for decades. She's never coped well when it comes to other girls."

"But there's nothing going on between me and Phinn," Wylie was quick to point out.

Lola put her hand on Wylie's shoulder and looked her straight in the eye.

"That's what the last girl said before Tinka drowned her in the lagoon."

Wylie's eyes went wide, causing Lola to laugh.

"I'm just kidding. Tinka's harmless. Don't let her get to you."

"I won't. Thanks for the tip."

Lola moved the last of her clothes to the other side of the closet. She gestured to the desk next to Wylie's bed. "Those drawers are already empty if you want to throw anything in them."

Wylie thought of her desk at home, filled to the brim with books and school supplies. She didn't have anything here to put in drawers. None of her jewelry or makeup or the recipes she'd scribbled on note cards would ever find their way to the island. They were gone forever. Wylie opened the top drawer and discovered heaps of colorful string tangled with friendship bracelets. One had the name "Charlotte" spelled out on it.

"Who's Charlotte?" Wylie asked.

"I forgot those were in there." Lola hurried to the drawer and tossed the bracelets into a small trash bin.

"Was she someone you knew?" Wylie asked.

"She was my old roommate. She doesn't live here anymore."

"I thought nobody could go home once they decide to stay."

"Um, there are some exceptions to the rule," Lola mumbled. "If everyone hates you, you get voted off."

"Oh . . ." Wylie said, more than a little nervous about her fate on Minor Island. Tinka could have already turned half the population against her. And what if one of her brothers rubbed people the wrong way? Even back home, Micah was an acquired taste.

"Don't worry. That won't happen to you guys. Charlotte was an odd duck. She's better off on the mainland. What's it like over there?" Lola asked. "I'm the only true native here. I've never been anywhere else."

"You mean New York?"

"Yeah," Lola answered wistfully. "The big peach."

Wylie couldn't help but laugh. "They actually call it the Big Apple."

"See? I'm such an idiot when it comes to the rest of the world. What else can you tell me?"

"Well, it's really crowded. There's tons of restaurants, parks, museums. There's constant stimulation. It's amazing and overwhelming all at the same time."

"What's it like to ride in a car?"

Wylie smiled. It was almost like meeting an extra-terrestrial.

"It's not that exciting. And plus, they can be dangerous. You guys are lucky you don't have to worry about car accidents here."

Lola fluffed the pillow on Wylie's bed. "What if you tell me stories about what it's like to grow up on the mainland, and in exchange, I'll let you use the kitchen whenever you want?" she asked, her voice brimming with excitement.

If indulging her new roommate meant making a friend *and* getting access to a woodburning stove, it was more than a fair trade.

"All right. What else do you want to know?"

Lola dug under her mattress and pulled out a tattered journal. "Subways. Are they real? Have you ever been on one?"

"Every single day."

Wylie described in great detail what it felt like to ride a train, while Lola furiously jotted down notes in her journal. She grinned the entire time, as though her tiny world had finally burst open.

Later that night, the same look of unrestrained joy on Lola's face eased Wylie's nerves as Phinn announced their arrival at the residency party. Amid the sea of unfamiliar faces, Lola gave her a smile that said "You're going to be fine." Wylie slowly followed Phinn down the stairs and continued to wave to her new social circle. *Please don't vote me off the island,* she thought with every step toward the Clearing.

"I'll help you make the rounds," Phinn whispered in her ear. Her neck tingled the moment his breath touched her skin.

"That's okay. I can do it alone."

Once they reached the bottom of the steps, Micah drifted toward the outskirts of the crowd, barely acknowledging anyone on his way. Wylie watched as he casually approached Tinka. He said something that made her laugh and roll her eyes at the same time, and then she reluctantly handed him a *parvaz* flower and a beer. Joshua was already off and running, shaking hands and committing names to memory. If there were babies here, he'd have kissed all of them.

"You look like a deer in the headlights," a voice said. Wylie turned to find the lead singer of the band standing next to her. "It reminds me of the way I felt when I first came to the island."

"It's a little overwhelming," Wylie admitted. She was much more confident when she was among her own friends.

"Once you get to know everyone, it'll be easier. We're all very protective of Phinn, so we just want to make sure you're worthy of him."

Wylie considered telling the girl she was still trying to decide if Phinn was worthy of her, but sensed the comment wouldn't go over so well.

"I'm Bailey, by the way."

"Nice to meet you. You've got an amazing voice. I love your music," Wylie said.

"Thanks. We call ourselves the Youth Brigade. Phinn came up with the name. He's pretty brilliant, isn't he?"

Bailey explained to Wylie that she had been born in China, but was brought to the States by her adoptive parents. She grew up in a small town in Georgia, where she started singing in her church.

"They were strict and really religious. I couldn't leave the house. I could barely have friends. I met Phinn on a church trip to New York. He was so tropic. He brought me to the island, and I never looked back," she told Wylie. "That was twenty years ago. He changed my life. I'm grateful every day that I met him."

She gave Wylie a quick hug, then hopped back onstage to start a new set. The conversation with Bailey was a much-needed warm-up round. Wylie, more relaxed now, moved through the crowd and introduced herself to the residents, one by one. Every now and again, she'd catch Phinn giving her an encouraging smile. Normally, she would have felt smothered by the attention, but right now she was thankful for the support. And she was also glad to see him spending most of the party engaged in deep conversation with Joshua. From what she could gather, it looked like they were finally getting along.

During a rare reprieve from meeting people, Wylie snuck off to the buffet table to try out Lola's cuisine. So far, the purple yam pudding and the spicy crab sausages were her favorite dishes of the night. Most of the kids were enjoying beer brewed right on the island, but Wylie stuck to the nonalcoholic options. There were mocktails made out of fresh-squeezed sugar root and pineapple that perfectly complemented the food. If it had been up to her, she would have spent the entire party holed up next to the hors d'oeuvres. Instead, she only managed to steal a few bites before getting bombarded with more new faces and introductions.

Helen, Helen, Helen, Wylie repeated in her head, making sure not to forget the name of the resident she'd just been cornered by. Helen was a seamstress who worked with Nadia. She had four other siblings on the mainland, where she'd been raised by an exhausted single mom.

"Sometimes my mom would look at us, and I could tell she was thinking life would be so much easier if she had one fewer mouth to feed. There wasn't enough food to go around, but there wasn't enough love to go around either," Helen confessed sadly. The island had been her home for nearly three years. "When Phinn told me about this place, I knew it was my only hope for a happy life. I count my lucky stars all the time that I met him. He's just . . . incredible."

Helen introduced Wylie to Elliot. He and Helen spent most of the evening arm in arm, and Wylie had assumed they were a couple, but it turned out he was gay.

"I was homeless when Phinn found me. It was the dead of winter in New York, and I would have frozen to death," Elliot confessed. "I came out to my parents, and they kicked me out of the house. They disowned me. Phinn saved my life. I'm forever in his debt."

"Wow, that's incredible," Wylie said, glancing at Phinn. He gave her a smile and she smiled back.

"Isn't it nice not having to deal with crappy parents anymore?" Elliot asked.

Wylie hadn't mentioned her parents, but the general assumption seemed to be that anyone who chose to stay on the island was probably running away from something bad back home.

"More than you know," Wylie replied, without mentioning that her parents would have never kicked her out of the house if she'd been born gay.

Elliot was approaching his tenth year of living on the island and had helped build most of the ships. He worked closely with Douglas, the genius architect behind the bungalows and the guy they'd seen recovering from appendicitis the day before. A few years back, Elliot and Douglas's working relationship had blossomed into a romance, and Elliot had never been happier.

All the people she spoke with had different tragic stories, but there was one common thread among them: Phinn was the person who had rescued them. He was their hero, and from what Wylie had heard, he had rightfully earned the title.

"Phinn likes you. I can tell," Lola said, approaching from the dance floor. She and Maz had been inseparable all night, practically dancing cheek to cheek. For two people who'd been together too many years to count, they seemed like they were still in the honeymoon phase of their relationship. "I can tell by the way he keeps checking up on you."

"Well, I'm still trying to figure out if I like him back," Wylie admitted.

"Friendly warning: He doesn't handle rejection well," Lola said under her breath.

"Somehow that doesn't surprise me. Everyone adores him. He's like a god to all of you."

"I consider Phinn my brother," Maz replied, making his way toward them with water. "I'll never be able to repay him for everything he's done for all of us." Of all the people Wylie had met so far, she was certain Maz would be the first to take a bullet for Phinn.

"Speaking of brothers, it looks like yours is having a good time," Maz said, gesturing above them. Wylie followed his gaze and spotted Tinka and Micah whizzing through the sky, wearing nothing but their underwear. Wylie could tell from the way they were hooting and hollering at the crowd below that they were both drunk.

"At what point did they lose their clothes?" Wylie asked.

"Not sure, but if I had to guess, I'd say it was Tinka's idea. At least she's not following Phinn around like a puppy dog," Lola added.

"She is my shadow sometimes, isn't she?" Phinn, now standing behind them, chimed in.

"Sometimes is putting it kindly," Maz joked. "If I were you, I'd enjoy the space while you can." He took Lola's arm. "We'll see you two later. Welcome to the island, Wylie."

"Thanks," Wylie replied, giving the couple a wave good-bye.

"You've been avoiding me all night," Phinn teased her.

"I have not. I've just been busy meeting everyone."

"Can I at least have one dance?" Phinn gave a nod to the Youth Brigade, and they started to play a ballad.

"Wow. What power," Wylie teased back.

"What can I say? Running the island comes with its advantages."

The dance floor was moist and sticky from the combi-

nation of sweat and spilled drinks, but Wylie managed to
move her feet to the music. Phinn gently pulled her close.
He smelled like English soap and saltwater.

"Is everyone being nice to you?"

"Yes. They've all been sussing me out. They're trying to
figure out if I'm good enough for you."

Phinn laughed. "They've got it backward, don't they?"

"You took the words right out of my mouth," Wylie
joked.

"So, if you were back home today instead of here, what
would you be doing right now?"

Wylie tried to remember her schedule. They had basketball practice this weekend, to prepare for the playoffs, and
afterward all the girls from the team would probably go out
to eat together.

"Basketball practice."

"You play basketball?" Phinn asked.

"I made varsity my freshman year. I love being on the
court. It's the only time I can focus and stop thinking about
everything I was dealing with at home."

"Something tells me I wouldn't want to go up against
you in a game."

"Yeah, most of the girls from other high schools were
afraid of me. I can be a little competitive."

Wylie glanced over Phinn's shoulder to see if they were
being watched, but no one was paying them any mind. As
she scanned the Clearing, her eyes landed on a nearby palm
tree with something carved into its trunk. It was easy to
miss if you weren't looking for it, but if she squinted, she
could make out the words HOPPER WAS HERE. She made a

mental note to ask Phinn for more details on Hopper's exile once their slow dance ended. In the meantime, she placed her head on his chest and swayed to the music.

"*Get away from him!*" a voice suddenly howled maniacally.

Wylie, startled, looked up to the sky to see Tinka, eyes crazed, charging toward her. She had her mouth open, and Wylie could see the handful of *parvaz* flowers that sat on her tongue.

Tinka tackled Wylie to the ground in the middle of the dance floor, pulling at her long hair the whole time. Wylie, frantic, kicked and scratched back. Phinn tried to pull them apart, but Tinka, with Wylie still in her grip, floated up to the air just beyond his reach. Suddenly, they were assaulting each other in midair.

"Get off me, you psycho!" Wylie screamed.

It took four guys to grab on to their feet and pull them down. Tinka probably had enough *parvaz* in her system to keep her flying for a week straight. Phinn and Maz tackled her to the ground, giving Wylie an opportunity to catch her breath. She touched a throbbing pain in her chin, and her fingertips were dripping with blood. Tinka's long nails must have scratched her during the scuffle. Despite all the manpower against her, Tinka floated up into the air a few times before she was finally restrained.

"You're hurting her! Let her go!" Micah yelled at them, slurring his words.

Aldo pulled a syringe out of his pocket. Tinka thrashed violently when she saw the needle and screamed that they were all a bunch of "elders." Phinn and Maz held her arms down till Aldo was able to prick her skin with the syringe and inject her with something that instantly put her to sleep. For a terrifying second, Wylie thought that whatever they'd stuck her with had killed her, but then she saw Tinka's belly slowly moving up and down as she breathed.

Micah and Joshua were standing next to Wylie, all three of them frozen in shock together. She looked around to see if everyone else was equally petrified, but though a few people had been watching with mild interest, no one seemed fazed by the turn of events. It was like being on an airplane during bad turbulence. The air pockets always had her convinced the plane was about to go down, but when she looked at the flight attendants, they were casually making small talk and laughing among themselves. The band started back up again and the party resumed, while Aldo and Patrick dragged Tinka away. How was it possible that what had just happened was considered normal?

"Where are you taking her?" Micah flew after them without so much as a glance toward Wylie.

"He's drunk," Joshua said to Wylie.

"I know," Wylie replied. Surely if he'd been sober, he would have remembered to make sure his sister was okay, too.

◆ ◆ ◆ ◆ ◆ ◆

"SQUEEZE MY HAND IF IT HURTS," PHINN SAID.

"Ouch. It stings!" Wylie screamed, squeezing his hand.

They were sitting in the clinic now, the music and chatter from the party muffled in the distance. Once Patrick and Aldo had declared that the cut on her chin didn't need stitches, Phinn insisted on bringing her there to clean the wound himself. He tore what looked like a banana leaf in half and a gooey yellow liquid dripped out. Phinn used his finger to spread the liquid over the cut. As soon as it touched Wylie's skin, the pain subsided.

"What is that stuff?" Wylie asked.

"*Dava* plants. It's an old trick Lola's tribe showed us. The plants have healing powers. And luckily, I don't think this cut is deep enough to scar."

"I wouldn't mind if it did," Wylie said, half kidding. "It'd make me look tough."

"Tinka doesn't normally act that way. It was a bad side effect of mixing *parvaz* with alcohol. She has a tendency to go a little overboard at parties."

"She looked like she wanted to kill me."

"She'll spend the next few days detoxing and then she'll be fine. I won't let her hurt you again."

"Should I be worried about my brother?" Wylie asked. "I think he's falling for her. He spent the entire party hanging out with her. I didn't even see him talking to anyone else."

"You worry too much," Phinn responded.

"That doesn't answer my question."

"What I meant to say is, I know what it's like being the oldest. You're like the leader of your brothers. Just like you, I feel responsible for everyone. I want everyone to have a good time, I never want anyone to get hurt, I lose sleep worrying that people are unhappy or that newer recruits are missing their lives on the mainland. But do you know what I remind myself?"

"What?" Wylie asked.

"That you can't protect everyone all the time and you have to be okay with that."

"So you're saying she's going to hurt him?"

"No. I'm saying you have to let him figure it out on his own. And anyway, I think they make a cute couple."

"I'm so glad you approve of my brother falling in love with the girl who tried to dropkick me in front of the entire island."

"I wasn't worried for a second," Phinn said. "You could take her, no problem."

Although she didn't admit it, a small part of Wylie was relieved by what had happened with Tinka. It was strangely comforting to know that not everything on the island was perfect. She squeezed Phinn's hand tighter, even though the stinging had stopped.

"You're as good as new," Phinn declared as he gently dressed the wound and placed a bandage on her chin. It was nice to have someone take care of her for a change.

"My hero," Wylie said, with only a hint of sarcasm.

pills and potions

the room was cozy and inviting, but it didn't matter. No one had come by to inform Wylie what was going on since she'd been told to wait inside. She had woken up early, tired and groggy from the drama of the night before, to the sound of a knock on her bungalow door. She opened it to find Patrick and Aldo waiting on the other side.

"You have twenty minutes to shower and get dressed, and then you have to come with us," they told her, more friendly than firm.

As soon as she was ready, they took her to a private room adjacent to the clinic, that she didn't remember seeing on the tour. Warm corn tortillas with scrambled eggs and hot tea were waiting in the center of a long table. Despite the cozy surroundings, Wylie felt her anxiety bubble up as soon as she walked in. It was the same feeling of dread she'd had after waking up on Phinn's boat.

"Can you guys tell me what's going on?" Wylie asked

as Patrick and Aldo held the door open for her. "Or at least just give me a hint?"

"Don't worry, it's a good thing," Patrick said with a wink. The door closed behind them and Wylie sat alone.

Wylie's talent for conjuring up nightmare scenarios was working overtime, especially since she'd been ushered to this room by two doctors. Perhaps someone on the island needed a kidney transplant and they'd brought Wylie to a private room to put her on ice and harvest her organs. After she'd considered a few more morbid possibilities, the door opened and Micah and Joshua entered, freshly showered but visibly exhausted. Micah had dark circles under his eyes and Wylie could tell he was nursing a hangover.

"Do you know what we're doing in here?" Joshua asked.

"No idea. I just got here a few minutes ago. Aldo and Patrick woke me up and brought me here."

"Same thing happened to us," Micah said. "I'd barely even gotten back to our room."

"Where did you sleep last night?" Wylie asked.

"In the detox room, with Tinka. I wanted to make sure she was okay."

Joshua and Wylie exchanged a worried look. "And was she?" Wylie asked.

"No. She woke up in the middle of the night, throwing up everywhere."

"Then it's good she had you with her" was all Wylie decided to say for now. Wylie's mom used to call Vanessa a bad influence, and every time she bitched and moaned about her, it just made Wylie more inclined to be her friend.

"I've got good news," Joshua announced. "Phinn and

I talked for a while last night, and he says he wants me to help run the island. He's going to call me his chief of staff. He knows about my interest in politics and wanted to make sure I had an outlet for that here."

"That's amazing!" Wylie exclaimed, genuinely thrilled for her brother. Thanks to Phinn, now Joshua could live out some version of his dream on the island.

Finally, the door to the room opened, and Maz entered with a stack of handmade notebooks with stitched bindings that reminded Wylie of the fabric swatches in the boutique. He presented one to each of the siblings. A picture of the island was drawn on the cover, and the title read *The Minor Island Handbook*. Tinka's name was signed in the corner.

"Congratulations on garnering an invitation to join us on Minor Island," Maz said with all the excitement of a DMV employee. "Sorry for dragging you here so early, but it's important to get this under way. It shouldn't be too painful. Just a few guidelines to go over. Please open your handbooks."

Wylie and her brothers did as they were told. "This is your swearing-in ceremony," Maz continued. "By the time we're done here, you'll no longer be citizens of the United States. You'll be citizens of Minor Island."

Micah flipped through the handbook.

"Will we be quizzed on this stuff?" he asked, his voice groggy.

"No. It's only for reference. We'll go through it together, and then we'll have you sign some waivers, a nondisclosure agreement, and your certificate of citizenship. Think of this as an orientation."

"Does Phinn need to be here for this?" Joshua asked.

"We'd never bother Phinn with this kind of stuff. He's way too busy. I've always been in charge of our immigration practices, but Phinn wrote the handbook, and those who've been recruited to live here have all gone through the same procedure."

Maz walked them through the handbook page by page. It was mostly a review of things they were already familiar with, including a hand-drawn map and a directory of all the residents along with their jobs and responsibilities. But Maz insisted on going through each point in detail, and the meeting dragged on longer and longer.

He also passed around to all of them a Polaroid photograph of a young boy. He had fair skin covered in freckles, dark brown eyes, and curly chestnut hair to match. Wylie was certain she hadn't seen him at the party the night before. She was struck by the glimmer in his eyes and knew his face was one she'd remember.

"This is Hopper," Maz announced. "Take a good look. Commit his face to memory. He didn't leave on the best terms. If you ever see him anywhere, tell someone immediately."

"Is he dangerous?" Wylie asked.

"Possibly," Maz replied, but Wylie got the feeling he didn't want to alarm them. "We just don't want him back on the island, that's all."

Joshua waved the photo around. "What if we forget what he looks like? We've met a lot of people in the last day. It's not easy to keep track of everyone."

"His right hand is a dead giveaway," Maz replied. "It's

missing a few fingers. Let's just say he had a need to inflict pain on himself, and that's part of the reason he's not here anymore." Their raised eyebrows prompted Maz to elaborate despite his obvious reluctance.

"Sometimes," Maz continued, choosing his words carefully, "new recruits don't exactly work out as planned. In those rare cases, Phinn decides it's better to send those people back home. Hopper was a bully. He made people feel uncomfortable, so we got rid of him. It's only in the most extreme cases that we ship people off the island."

Maz passed around another faded Polaroid, this one of a girl named Olivia. According to him, she had left the island on a one-year sabbatical to travel the States and returned after her eighteenth birthday. Years after she came back, the residents slowly started to notice she was aging. From the picture, Wylie could see the slightest trace of crow's feet forming at her eyes, and a few smile lines.

"Olivia was another rare case of someone we had to banish from the island. We have her to thank for the discovery that staying on the mainland past our eighteenth birthdays has disastrous results. It took a lot of gray hairs to realize she was aging once she got back from her sabbatical, but when we did, we had to ask her to leave. If I've got the math right, Olivia would be in her late forties today," Maz told them. "Last I heard, she'd gone to medical school and was looking to start her own pharmaceutical company. It makes sense. She was a big science geek when we knew her."

The remaining pages were devoted to a set of laws that were grounds for exile if broken—all the things you would expect to be illegal: murder, attempted murder, treason, rape, and so on. There was a specific clause citing that any environmental crimes against the island would come with a swift punishment. Again, Maz went through each point meticulously, and Wylie began to wonder if they were actually going to spend the entire day in this room.

The last page contained a nondisclosure agreement the Daltons were required to sign. There was still no explanation of what would happen to them if they got kicked off the island and blabbed about its existence once they returned to the States. Wylie wondered if the punishment was death or a stint in a mental institution. It would be hard to convince the authorities that a girl ranting about a magical land where the weather was always warm, where teenagers could fly, and where no one ever grew up wasn't a raving lunatic.

"We know the mainland is all you've ever known," Maz said after they'd all signed, "but we ask that all new recruits adapt to the culture of the island. None of us here needs lessons on popular culture in the States. We don't need to know about your favorite albums or movies or websites. We certainly don't need to know what all the cool kids are saying. We have our own slang words and phrases. You'll adopt them along the way. We want to make the cultural shift as seamless as possible."

The back cover of the handbook included a vow the Daltons had to recite in order to gain their citizenship. Wylie expected confetti or trumpets when it was finally over, but all they got was a handshake from Maz and permission to go back to their rooms.

It had been a long and draining day. Wylie was looking

forward to taking a hot shower and getting in a nap before heading to the dining room for dinner.

"Wylie," Maz said, "I'm going to need you to stick around for a few more minutes."

Joshua and Micah lingered at the door, not wanting to leave her behind.

"I'll be okay, guys," Wylie assured them. "You can go."

Once they left, Maz nervously looked at his hands as he addressed her. *Great*, Wylie thought. *Here's where he tells me it's time to harvest my organs.*

"There's something else Phinn won't allow on the island."

The suspense was killing her. What could it be? Show tunes? Orgies? Crack cocaine?

"Procreation," he continued. "We don't have any parents here, and Phinn would like to keep it that way. So, although it's fine to have as much sex as you want, we can't have any of the girls getting pregnant."

Wylie laughed. This was the exact opposite principle from the one her grandmother had tried to instill in her. According to her, there was no point in having sex unless you planned to create life.

"Trust me," she reassured him, "we're on the exact same page. But this sounds like the kind of thing my brothers should be lectured on, too. Why am I the only one being told?" The sound of a bell chimed loudly through the island, saving Maz from answering her question.

"Perfect timing," Maz said. "Come with me."

Wylie followed him to the clinic. At least a dozen other girls were already waiting inside, and more had flowed in behind them. Maz stood back as the girls formed two lines, facing each other. Lola gestured to Wylie to stand next to her. She scanned the faces across from her, and aside from Tinka, who was probably still in detox, Wylie was almost certain every single female on the island was present.

Aldo and Patrick entered the room with charts and made their way down each of the lines. Wylie could see that Patrick was passing out a pill to each girl, while Aldo made notations on a clipboard.

"What is this?" Wylie asked Lola.

"Our daily dose of birth control," Lola whispered.

Wylie wasn't on the Pill. She'd lost her virginity a couple years before, but her escapades were few and far between and didn't warrant a very awkward conversation with her mom and a regular birth-control regimen. It creeped Wylie out to be standing in this room with all the other girls from the island, waiting to take an extra dose of estrogen, although all of them were in this together, at least. And that was why she didn't protest when Patrick handed her a tiny pill. Wylie simply placed it on her tongue and swallowed it down with water.

After all the pills were administered one by one, the girls were released, and Lola and Wylie headed back to their bungalow.

"The bell rings every day at five p.m. to alert us to head to the clinic and get our appropriate dose. Even if we're menstruating, we're still required to show up for placebo pills," Lola explained.

"Don't they trust you guys to just take them on your own? Do we really have to line up like cattle every day?"

Wylie asked, with more than a trace of judgment in her voice. She couldn't help feeling bothered that the onus of birth control was placed solely on the female population.

"Phinn thinks it's just easier this way. Some of us are very responsible, but others might forget, and then we'd have babies crawling all over the place."

Wylie wondered if accidental pregnancy was grounds for exile. It was nowhere in the handbook, but neither was the "no procreation" rule.

"It just doesn't seem right to have anyone else give us orders on what to do with our bodies."

"That doesn't happen on the mainland?" Lola asked.

"It depends on which state you live in, but shouldn't we be doing things better here?"

"I don't exactly disagree, but a friendly tip? I wouldn't go around talking about it to anyone," Lola said, lowering her voice. "Phinn doesn't like to be challenged."

"Well, then he shouldn't have invited me to stay on the island," Wylie said, stopping right in front of Phinn's bungalow.

Lola gave Wylie a quizzical look. She put her arm around Wylie's shoulder.

"I know I haven't said this yet, but I'm really glad you're here."

"It took you long enough," Wylie joked.

"But I'm going to let you fight this battle on your own. I'll be in our bungalow if you need me." Lola gave Wylie a peck on the cheek and skipped off toward their room. Before she could lose her nerve, Wylie knocked on Phinn's door.

"It's open," he called. "Come in."

Phinn hummed to himself while he hammered a shelf into the wall. He wore a pair of linen pants, but didn't have a shirt on. Wylie tried not to look at his bare chest and the scars scattered across his skin.

"Hey, Wylie," Phinn said, cocking his head.

Now that she was in his room and he was half naked, Wylie had no idea how to communicate like a normal person.

"I just had my swearing-in ceremony," she managed to say.

"That's great. Congratulations."

"I don't like the birth-control ritual," she blurted.

Phinn was expressionless. "Do you have religious issues with it?"

"No," Wylie said, nearly laughing. The Daltons didn't even go to church on Christmas. "I don't like being told what to do. The girls should have a choice whether they want to be on the Pill and if they do, you should trust us to take it ourselves."

Phinn shrugged. "We'll just have to agree to disagree on that one."

"That's it?" Wylie asked. "That's all you have to say?"

Phinn pulled a T-shirt on over his head. "Let's go for a walk. I want to show you something."

"I'm not done discussing this," Wylie said.

"Good. Neither am I."

They made their way through a trail behind the bungalows.

"Did Maz give you more information on Hopper?" Phinn asked.

Wylie nodded. "He told us to be on the lookout for him."

"Don't let it scare you. I just like to be cautious. The kid was mentally ill. We couldn't give him the proper help. Hopefully he's getting the treatment he needs back home."

As they continued down the trail, a popping sound in the distance grew louder. Wylie had heard it a few times around the island and didn't know where it was coming from. It sounded just like microwave popcorn.

"What's that sound?"

"You'll see," Phinn answered. "Now I want you to close your eyes."

Wylie didn't like where this was going.

"Are they closed?" he asked.

"Yes, they're closed. You know, this is a whole lot of buildup. It better be worth it."

"Oh, it will."

The popping sound moved at a steady rhythm as Phinn slowed to a stop.

"Okay, open them."

Wylie opened her eyes and let out a small gasp. They were standing in a field of *parvaz* flowers that seemed to go on for miles. The flowers were growing at a rapid pace, each new one making a *pop-pop* sound as it sprouted. In the background, the ocean glistened as the waves gently moved back and forth. Behind them stood a massive weeping willow. Phinn plucked a flower and another one instantly grew in its place.

"When you care for the island the way we do, its resources stay abundant," Phinn explained.

He offered the flower to Wylie, but instead of placing it

in her mouth, she slipped it behind her ear. The sun was setting and the sky was a neon pink.

"It's so peaceful here when the sun goes down," Phinn told her. "It's not just watching the stars come out or the light of the fireflies coming into view. It's that it gets quiet enough to hear all the natural sounds the island makes. The rhythm of the waterfall, the hum of branches moving in the wind, the *pop-pop* of the *parvaz* flowers—it's like an orchestra. Can you hear it?"

Wylie nodded.

"And you know what you can't hear?"

"What?"

"The sound of crying babies." Phinn looked at her straight-faced, then laughed. Wylie couldn't help but laugh along.

"Bad joke," he said. "For the record, I don't hate babies. But the whole point of living here is having all of the fun and none of the responsibility of adulthood. Raising a child is the ultimate act of being a grown-up. It's like the antithesis of what makes Minor Island paradise."

"I don't have a problem with that. I just have a problem with putting the burden on the girls. And I'm not the only one who feels that way."

"Who else has an issue with it?"

Wylie didn't want to sell anyone out, but maybe there'd be strength in numbers. Plus, Lola was a member of the inner circle. Phinn trusted her.

"Lola," she answered reluctantly.

"She should have explained to you that the burden is for everyone to carry. We require other forms of protection.

Especially with new recruits who could bring diseases to the island."

"I don't have any diseases," Wylie was quick to say.

"I know. My point is, we have to be careful. We have to take every precaution. And that includes monitoring all the girls and making sure they're on the Pill. Can I tell you a story?"

Wylie nodded.

"I was a kid the first time I saw the *parvaz* field. My mom and I stumbled across it together on a walk through the island, just a couple weeks after we got here. I was about five. Old enough to remember a few things about our old life on the mainland. We stood by this willow tree, blown away by the whole thing. I don't have too many memories of her, but I remember she had this unquenchable sense of adventure. Anyway, she let me run around the field by myself. I was so little, I got lost in the flowers. It's like a maze out here. I could hear her yelling my name and I would yell back, 'Mommy,' but she couldn't find me in the dark. And then after a while, she stopped yelling. Finally, I made it back to the willow tree, but she wasn't there anymore. I was by myself, in the dark, for hours. My mom and dad didn't come back to find me until the sun came up the next morning. I'd never been more afraid in my life.

"They failed me that night. They left me. And then they left me for good when they died. No one on this island is capable of being a parent, and I won't let another little kid go through what I did."

Wylie nodded. She thought back to being at her dad's

office and seeing him with a woman who wasn't her mom. She remembered feeling like he'd failed their entire family as she made her way down the office hallway and back to the elevator.

"I'm really sorry they put you through that," Wylie said.

"Wylie," Phinn said. "I'd like to renege on our deal. I don't want to be friends. I really like you." Wylie could feel her skin tingling just from being near him.

Phinn carefully lifted her chin up and moved his face toward hers. *Let him kiss you*, Wylie thought to herself. *Don't say another word. Let him do it.* But just as their lips were about to meet, Wylie pulled away.

"I don't want to kiss you under false pretenses," she blurted. "There's some things you need to know about me."

Phinn nodded, slightly unnerved. "I'm listening."

He sat down and leaned against the trunk of the weeping willow. He patted the ground and Wylie sat as close to him as possible. She took a deep breath.

"It happened a year ago. . . ."

CHAPTER 9

truth and consequences

every time Wylie relived the night of the accident in her head, it felt like she was back there again. It didn't matter that Phinn held her hand for moral support or that she had a view of the ocean and a field of *parvaz* flowers; she still felt like she'd time traveled to that harsh winter night in the Hamptons. More than a year had passed, but it was a memory she would never escape. And so, as she recounted the details to Phinn, she was transported to an entirely different island.

✦ ✦ ✦ ✦ ✦ ✦

CHRISTMAS IN MONTAUK ALWAYS FELT WRONG TO Wylie, but her parents insisted every year that they get out of Manhattan to spend a week in their Long Island beach house. Most families left town for fancy ski resorts or warmer climates and saved visits to the Hamptons for the summer. *That's exactly why we're going there now,* Wylie's dad would tell them. *To enjoy the peace and quiet.*

The beach house was a time-share split among several families from their Upper East Side neighborhood. None of the objects inside held any special significance to the Daltons. It didn't matter that Wylie and her brothers wanted to wake up on Christmas morning in their own bedrooms and open presents in their own living room. Maura wouldn't hear of it. Wylie had noticed her parents were a little gentler with each other when they weren't cooped up in the brownstone. The ceilings were higher, and the house got more light. Wylie always hoped the holiday would bring them closer together.

That particular Christmas, Joshua was the most adamant about wanting to stay in the city over the holidays. He told his parents that in a couple of years, Wylie would leave for college, which made it all the more important to spend the holidays together in the home they'd grown up in, but that was just an excuse. Wylie knew the real reason Joshua wanted to stay in Manhattan was because he couldn't stand to be away from Abigail for more than a few days. For Wylie, the only bonus to going to Montauk was that she could spend some quality time with her brother without his girlfriend clinging to him. She liked Abigail a lot, but whenever the three of them hung out, she felt like a third wheel. Kids at school even referred to them as "Jabigail" behind their backs.

Wylie knew for a fact that if Abigail were around, there would have been no persuading her brother to go to some random party in the Hamptons. It was pure luck that she'd been invited to the party in the first place. The morning after Christmas, Wylie decided to brave the cold to go for a walk. The beach was frigid and uninviting, and she considered turning around when she noticed two guys about her age roasting marshmallows over a small bonfire. Their names were Matt and Tyler and they were cousins. Tyler's family had a vacation home just a few miles away. Both sets of parents had gone to Europe for the holidays, and the boys had talked them into letting them stay in the beach house on their own.

"We're having a house party tonight for all the kids who are stuck out here," they told her. "Bring anyone you want."

"I don't want to go hang out with a bunch of people we don't know," Joshua said when she mentioned the invite. "Let's just stay in and watch a movie. Dad brought *Raiders of the Lost Ark*."

"Please," Wylie begged. "Think of it as practice for all those campaign fund-raisers you'll have to attend when you run for president. You have to get used to dazzling people you don't know. Even Micah wants to go, and he hates strangers. Right, Micah?"

"I don't hate strangers. I hate people," Micah responded, barely looking up from his phone.

"Going to some high school party in the Hamptons isn't going to help me become a politician. Try again."

Wylie debated whether going to the party was worth offering to be the designated driver. Would she even have fun with a bunch of randoms if she had to suffer through it sober? Yes, she told herself. She refused to be one of those people who always needed alcohol to have a good time.

"Fine. I'll be the designated driver."

Joshua smiled. "What time do we leave?"

They waited for their parents to retire to their bedroom and swiped the keys to Gregory's brand-new Mercedes. Wylie had gotten her learner's permit months before, but she generally preferred Joshua to drive them around. He didn't even have his permit, but he was a much more capable driver than his sister.

As they zipped their down jackets, Wylie suddenly got an inexplicable urge to nix the party and stay in watching movies. Maybe it was all the layers she was wearing or the recent snowfall outside, but the idea of driving in that weather didn't sound very appealing. But then she heard her parents fighting and decided staying home was no longer an option. Plus, the most epic evenings always seemed to happen when going out felt like a chore. The pull to stay in was probably a sign that they were about to have one of those nights they'd spend the next week reminiscing about. *Remember when you said this? Remember when we did that? That. Night. Was. So. Crazy.*

The drive to the party went smoothly. Wylie didn't even get annoyed when she noticed Joshua squeezing the door handle and slamming an imaginary brake with his foot every time he told her to slow down. They made it to the house without incident and only traded places behind the wheel so Joshua could parallel park the car for her. Wylie and Micah shivered in the snow as they helped him maneuver the car into a tiny space between two giant SUVs.

Wylie linked arms with both brothers as they walked up

the path to the house. The front lawn was already littered with red plastic cups, and a few drunken partygoers were filtering out to return to their vacation homes.

"Can we stick together tonight?" Micah asked. "I don't want to be abandoned with a bunch of people I don't know."

"Of course," Wylie reassured him. "I won't leave your side."

It was just one in the string of promises she would unintentionally break throughout the evening. The moment they entered the front door, Wylie was swept away by Matt and Tyler. They looked a lot cuter without their winter layers and snow hats, and she could tell from the minute they dragged her into the kitchen and offered to include her in a round of shots that they were competing for her affection. It was cute and flattering, and maybe, just maybe, she'd let one of them kiss her at some point.

Joshua and Micah made a beeline for the alcohol. Wylie introduced herself to Matt and Tyler's friends and kept the small talk going until her brothers were out of the kitchen. As soon as they ventured into the living room, she toasted her new friends with a tequila shot. If she had a shot or two now and stuck to water for the rest of the night, then she'd be fine to drive home. And worst-case scenario, they could always Uber. When Matt and Tyler launched into a drunken debate about their favorite NFL quarterbacks (Tom Brady versus someone she couldn't remember), any interest Wylie had in a potential hook-up vanished, but at least their argument gave her a chance to mingle.

Wylie walked into the living room to discover that an impromptu dance party had formed, and Joshua was hamming it up in the center of it. Micah stood on the outskirts of the circle and bopped his head awkwardly to the beat. Wylie hurried over and pulled him into the middle of the dance circle with her. At first Micah stood completely still, but then he seemed to realize it didn't matter what anyone at the party thought of them, and started jumping up and down like he was in a mosh pit.

Wylie couldn't remember at what point she abandoned the dance floor to stand in line to do a keg stand in the kitchen, but her legs were suddenly in the air as everyone yelled, "Chug, chug, chug!" *This is fine*, she told herself. They would take an Uber home and drive the Honda back in the morning before their parents were awake to pick up her dad's car. After she couldn't keep down any more beer, Wylie just barely managed to keep her balance as she lowered her feet to the ground. Even if these people were virtual strangers, she still didn't want to fall on her ass in front of them.

The rest of the party was a blur. Someone handed her a Jell-O shot and she swallowed it without using her hands. Anytime a good song burst through the speakers, she squealed excitedly and returned to the dance floor. She and Joshua played on opposing flip cup teams, and she brought her team to victory when she finished her beer before he did.

"It's cool," she told her brother after she high-fived her teammates. "We'll take an Uber home."

"It's Montauk. It'll take forever to get anyone here," Joshua responded, annoyed.

"Then I'll request one now. By the time it gets here, we'll be ready to take off."

Wylie took her phone out of her purse and fumbled with the passcode. Before she could manage to punch it in correctly, someone screamed the word everyone dreaded hearing at a party:

"*Cops!*"

It was a widely known fact that the police were brutal when it came to underage drinking on Long Island. Wylie and her brothers had heard enough stories about kids spending the night in the drunk tank to know they needed to get out of Dodge—immediately. Wylie grabbed her coat and didn't even bother to say good-bye to Matt and Tyler as they ran through the backyard. She and her brothers circled to the front of the house and ran to their car as fast as they could with alcohol in their systems and an inch of snow now on the ground.

Apparently at some point during the party, Wylie had told three other girls they could share a ride home with them, and somehow in the pandemonium, the girls had followed them to their car. The Daltons couldn't abandon them, but there was no time to wait for a car service. Micah was the most sober of the bunch, but he had never driven before in his life. The sirens of another cop car approached in the distance and Wylie quickly tried to get behind the wheel, but stumbled and fell as she opened the door.

"Joshua," Wylie said, slurring his name as it came out, "can you drive us?"

Joshua was incredulous. "I just drank a beer in that flip cup game."

"Okay, but how many drinks did you have total?"

"I don't know. Three?"

"We're not that far from home. You can handle it. You're a way better driver than I am."

The siren got closer. Joshua grabbed the keys from Wylie's hand and got behind the wheel. Micah sat shotgun, while the party stragglers and Wylie climbed into the backseat. It was a tight squeeze, and to complicate matters, the strays they'd picked up admitted they were visiting friends in the area and weren't entirely sure how to get back to their house. One of the girls searched for the address on her phone, while Joshua drove off, to at least get them away from the cops. With any luck, they'd still be home by midnight to rummage through the leftovers in the fridge and take turns curating their favorite YouTube videos. Finally, after about twenty minutes of aimless driving, one of the stragglers recognized the street they'd turned onto.

"This it is!" the girl screamed. "Just another mile down this road and we'll be there."

Everyone cheered. Wylie turned up the radio to celebrate. The heat was on high in the car, and she started to feel trapped in the backseat with three other girls. She leaned into the front seat and pushed the button to open the sunroof.

"Wylie, sit down," Joshua screamed at her.

The brisk air seeped into the car as the sunroof opened. Wylie leaned half her body out of the car and raised her arms in the air. Wylie's brothers grasped at her legs, yelling at her to get back in the car, but she wanted to enjoy the freedom for just a few more seconds. It was then that the headlights of a car in the neighboring lane washed over her.

The Mercedes hit a patch of ice. Under normal circumstances, without his sister halfway outside of the car, and no beer in his system, Joshua would have been able to remain in control. He was always a cautious driver, but the car veered into the other lane and collided with the oncoming vehicle. The three strangers in the backseat pulled Wylie in right before the collision and saved her life. The girl in the other car wasn't so lucky.

Katie Anderson. That was her name. She was sixteen at the time of the accident, just a little older than Wylie. She wasn't driving to a party or back to her parents' fancy Hamptons abode. There was no alcohol in her system, and no crazy sibling in the backseat of the car distracting her. Katie spent her school vacations waitressing at a seafood restaurant in Fort Pond Bay. The tips were good and it was a short drive away from a family friend's home in Montauk. They had a bedroom in the basement, and that was where Katie spent her time between shifts. She had stayed late at the restaurant that night to cover for another waitress who'd wanted to leave early to celebrate her one-year anniversary with her boyfriend. On any normal night at this time, Katie would have been back in the basement, under the covers, falling asleep.

After their car hit Katie's, it skidded across the road, then screeched to a stop. Joshua asked them if they were all right and though they were all shaken up, everyone in the car was conscious and had only suffered minor cuts and bruises. Before Wylie could ask Joshua if he was okay, he got out of the car and ran to the other vehicle.

Wylie and the others stood on the side of the road and watched as he pulled Katie from the front seat and dragged her a safe distance from the car. She wasn't conscious, but was still breathing. Wylie kept her eyes on Joshua as he pulled out his phone and dialed 911. From there, everything moved in slow motion. It felt like an eternity before the paramedics and police arrived, though in reality only a few minutes had passed.

"I'll say I was driving," Wylie told her brother while they waited.

"No way," he said.

"Please. This is my fault."

"It's not your fault," he told her, "I was driving. I'll take full responsibility."

And he did. When the cops arrived, Joshua admitted he had been the one driving. There was no mention of Wylie's reckless behavior in the backseat, or that she was supposed to be the designated driver. They asked for his driver's license, but Joshua simply shrugged and said he didn't have one. It was then that they smelled a trace of beer on his breath and administered the breathalyzer, then placed him in handcuffs. Wylie and Micah and the three stray girls sat helplessly on the side of the road as Joshua was driven away in a cop car and Katie was driven away in an ambulance.

If only they hadn't gone to the party. If only she'd kept her word and stayed sober. If only she hadn't told the other girls they'd give them a ride home. The girls walked from the accident back to their friend's house. Wylie would never see or hear from them again. Another police officer drove her and Micah to their house.

It didn't matter what Joshua had said on the side of the road; they all knew what happened would always be her fault.

+ + + + + +

PHINN PLACED HIS HAND ON WYLIE'S CHEEK TO WIPE away the tears that were now flowing in a steady stream, but she couldn't look at him.

"What happened to the girl? When I first read about the accident, there wasn't much information on her," Phinn said.

Wylie closed her eyes.

"She's been in a coma. A year of her life, asleep. The doctors say there's a chance she'll wake up, but there's no telling when that will be. And they're pretty sure that even if it happens, she'll never be able to walk again."

The tears had evolved into hiccups, and Wylie tried to hold her breath to make them stop.

"If I had kept my word, he wouldn't have been behind the wheel. And I was so careless on the ride home—I could have gotten us all killed. That's why I don't drink anymore."

Phinn pulled her close to him so that her head rested on his chest.

"It could have happened to anyone, Wylie."

"No. It happened to me, because I'm selfish and reckless. I want you to know the worst parts of me. I'd understand if you want us to go home. I have this rare talent for screwing up the lives of everyone around me."

"What happened doesn't change my mind about you. And you know what? If your parents hadn't been fighting that night, I bet you and your brothers would have stayed home and none of this would have happened."

Wylie had never thought about it that way, but as she examined every domino from that night, she realized hearing the argument upstairs was the first one to fall.

"The way my dad looked at us when he opened the door and saw the cops . . . I'll never forget it. He was so ashamed of us. But my mom was even worse. She didn't want to talk about it at all. Ever. 'Sweep it under the rug' is her motto in life."

"Looks like we both pulled the short straw in the mom and dad department."

"I guess that's something else we have in common. I don't want to be anything like my parents," Wylie admitted. "Old and miserable and full of regret."

"You won't end up feeling any of those things," Phinn assured her.

As they sat in the field together, Phinn picked a *parvaz* flower and one more rapidly popped up to replace it. Wylie wordlessly opened her mouth and Phinn placed the flower on her tongue. She took the flower from behind her ear and tossed it in the back of his throat. They didn't shoot up in the air like they had in Brooklyn. This time, they floated up slowly to the sky, embracing each other the whole time. Wylie suddenly felt dizzy and lightheaded from all the crying.

"Everything about you is unexpected," Phinn said. "The

way you nearly walked away from me at the bus stop when I gave you a hard time for not eating a *parvaz*. The way you demand answers to questions most people are afraid to ask. The way you tell the truth when it would be so much easier to lie."

"Is that a compliment?" Wylie asked.

"Yes. Has anyone ever called you a mermaid?" Phinn asked.

"As in the mythical sea creature? Can't say I've ever gotten that one before."

"They don't use it on the mainland the way we do here. We say it to describe someone who's smart, intelligent, not entirely of this world."

"Well, in that case, right back at you," Wylie said, her lips parting into a grin. "I mean, you brought me here. Clearly, you'd have to be smart to make such a wise decision."

"Some might even call me a genius."

"Teach me more words. I don't want to use any slang from the mainland. I want to talk the way everyone here talks. What do you guys mean when you say 'tropic'? I hear it all the time."

"Cool or awesome. I find you very tropic. Here's another adjective to describe you. Porcelain."

"Porcelain. That one I've heard before. Like the china? Does it mean fragile?"

"It means beautiful," Phinn replied.

"Then I think you're porcelain, too."

Phinn laughed, then placed his mouth next to her ear and said, "Wylie Dalton, you are beyond compare."

He pulled her toward him and kissed her as they drifted through the sky. His lips were dry but soft at the same time. It took Wylie a minute to get her bearings, floating there weightless, but once she did, she kissed him back harder. The wind picked up, but Wylie barely noticed. She was too busy falling madly in love.

CHAPTER TEN

ancient history

"san Fran-cisco. Am I pronouncing it right?" Lola asked.

"Yes, that's perfect," Wylie whispered, afraid that if she spoke too loudly, someone passing by would hear them.

"And it's in Cali-for-nee-a."

"More like Cali-*forn*-ya," Wylie corrected.

Lola made a quick note in her journal, then repeated after Wylie.

"Cali-forn-ya."

"You got it!"

"I like the way it rolls off the tongue . . . California. It sounds so tropic."

Lola had a secret obsession with the mainland. She swore Wylie to secrecy—even Maz didn't know she harbored a clandestine fascination with how the rest of the world lived. She claimed she had no desire to visit, but she kept Wylie up most nights asking questions about different cities and states, and writing down all the information in her journal by the light of a jar full of fireflies. Wylie noticed she'd retrieved the "Charlotte" friendship bracelet from the trash and was now using it as a bookmark. It seemed odd to keep a souvenir from a girl everyone hated enough to exile, but Wylie decided against asking her about it. She didn't want to be involved in any more of Lola's secrets. Especially when, one night when they both couldn't sleep, she confessed to Wylie that she was bored with the island.

"I've lived here my whole life. Sometimes I feel a little trapped," Lola whispered. "I would never leave, but I like to imagine what it's like in other places. You won't tell anyone, right?"

"Of course not," Wylie said.

"I mean it. Phinn can never find out. Promise."

"I promise." If Wylie didn't know both of them so well, she would have thought Lola was afraid of Phinn.

"Thanks. And don't worry, you've got at least another fifty years till you start to feel restless."

Wylie felt guilty. She'd taken an oath to abstain from discussing the mainland, and yet whenever Lola asked questions, she dutifully gave answers. Wylie even promised that once they got through talking about the mainland, she would tell Lola about other countries and continents. Part of her secretly liked reminiscing about home. If she never mentioned her old life, then pretty soon she would feel like it didn't exist.

"Do you ever think about your tribe?" Wylie asked. Up until now, she'd been too scared to broach the topic with Lola.

"Sure, all the time," Lola answered.

"Did they have a name?" Wylie asked.

"We called ourselves the Batcheha. I wish you could have met them." For a moment, Lola looked like she'd disappeared into a memory. She shook it off, then continued. "Sometimes I wonder what they look like now. They'd be so disappointed in me. I can barely remember how to speak Batchenise."

"Do you ever regret that you didn't go with them?" Wylie asked.

"No," Lola admitted. "It wasn't an easy decision, but in the end, I never could have asked Maz to leave and grow old with me."

"What if things hadn't worked out with Maz? Would you have regretted it then?"

Lola shrugged. "It never occurred to me that things wouldn't work out, but that's probably because everyone in my tribe kept their partners for life."

I wish that was true of my tribe, Wylie thought.

"Okay, stop changing the subject. What are some other cities in California?" Lola asked.

"I'll tell you tomorrow . . . *after* you take me to the kitchen with you," Wylie replied.

For the past two weeks, living here had felt like being on an extended vacation. Wylie had spent her days flying above the palm trees, getting to know the locals, and sunbathing near the *parvaz* field. Micah was usually holed up in Tinka's room, and Joshua was busy with his duties as chief of staff. Phinn had warned Wylie that most of his time was consumed with running the island, and he hadn't been exaggerating. The two of them usually didn't hang out till the evening, when they'd meet in the Clearing to roast sugar roots and share stories about their days. But most of her stories were beginning to sound redundant. Wylie wanted to find her niche. Lola had promised she would give her access to the kitchen, and it was time she kept up her half of the bargain.

"This, I can't live without," Lola said the next morning, holding up a long, wide knife with a rough wooden handle. The sunlight streamed through the kitchen window and shimmered against the blade. She sharpened it against a rock and handed it to Wylie with a basket full of onions.

"Onions, really?" Wylie asked. "Do you hate me?"

Wylie was actually quite skilled at dicing onions. Whenever things got really bad with her parents, she'd make French onion soup, and everyone would assume her tears were just a side effect of prepping the dish.

"If you run the knife, the cutting board, and the onion under really cold water, it won't make you cry," Lola advised.

"What are we making?" Wylie asked.

"Phinn's favorite: Fried chipney-onion cakes. It's an old Batchenise recipe."

"I have no idea what those taste like, but they sound amazing."

"Do you want to add anything? Maybe a dipping sauce for the cakes?"

Wylie had assumed she'd only be allowed to prep and slice ingredients. She never thought Lola would actually let her pitch in with a recipe.

"I make a mean pesto dip," Wylie said, trying to contain her excitement.

"What's pesto?" Lola asked.

"I'll show you," Wylie said, happy she had recipes she could teach Lola, too.

They spent the rest of the afternoon mixing the ingredients for the chipney-onion cakes, flattening them into the size of silver dollars, and setting them aside to fry right before serving. For a side dish, Lola whipped up a tomato salad with *parvaz*-infused dressing. Wylie watched and took dutiful notes, then walked Lola through the steps of making pesto. Lola only interjected once, when she suggested adding apple flower seeds as a substitute for pine nuts. After searching for them in the garden, Wylie discovered that apple flowers were a vegetable that resembled a giant red Brussels sprout. Lola directed Wylie to peel away the leaves and extract a cluster of edible seeds from the core for the side dish. Lola tasted the dip and nodded her approval.

"This is delightful," she declared. "We make a great team."

"If we lived in New York, we could open a restaurant together. No one's ever tasted food like this on the mainland. People would have to wait months to get a reservation."

Lola smiled wistfully. "There's no rule against dreaming, right? But for now, how would you like to help me plan the menu for prom? If we combine our favorite recipes, we could do something completely original."

"Prom?" Wylie asked, confused.

According to Lola, prom was an annual tradition Phinn

had established years before when he started bringing new recruits to the island. For residents who'd spent most of their lives here, prom was a fun novelty event. And for newer recruits, it helped soften the blow of milestones they'd be missing back home.

"Phinn never mentioned it to me," Wylie admitted.

"With everything he has to deal with, he probably forgot. I doubt he'd ask anyone else to be his date."

Lola walked Wylie out to the dining room and showed her a bulletin board decked out with a handful of Polaroids from the previous year's festivities.

"Phinn only busts out the camera for very special occasions," Lola explained.

Among the Polaroids, Wylie spotted a picture of Lola and Maz sporting wooden crowns on their heads.

"It's an embarrassing tradition," she explained to Wylie. "I don't know whether it's supposed to be sweet or funny, but they crown us king and queen every year. No one even votes on it. I guess it's our reward for being together the longest."

Wylie saw a picture of Bailey and Bandit, who, according to Lola, had been each other's date the previous year and were still casually seeing each other. Nadia and Patrick had gone to prom merely as friends, but they'd been dating ever since. Some of the pictures seemed to be missing from their allotted slots, but Wylie assumed those couples had kept them as souvenirs. And then her eyes landed on a candid photo of Tinka and Phinn. He had his arms wrapped tightly around her waist, and his mouth was perched right next to her ear. It looked like he'd just whispered something that made her laugh out loud.

"Phinn and Tinka went together last year?" Wylie asked.

"Only because no other guy had asked her, and Phinn felt bad. No one wants to waste their time dating her when she's just going to be infatuated with Phinn her whole life."

What had Phinn whispered in Tinka's ear just as the photo had been taken? The question ran through Wylie's mind as she walked through the garden, picking strawberries for dessert. She tossed one in her mouth. In New York, when her girlfriends had vented about their complicated dating lives, Wylie had tried to be supportive, but she sometimes felt like they were talking in circles. She'd always told herself that was why she didn't bother with relationships. They were too confusing and could turn the most confident girl into an insecure mess. Now she was finally seeing what it felt like from the inside.

"Stop thinking about it," she said to herself. The chickens squawked loudly, seeming to agree, but they'd just been startled by the creak of the kitchen door. Wylie looked up to find Phinn headed toward her, smiling ear to ear. He pulled her into a hug and gave her a tentative kiss on the lips. They were still in the early stages of their relationship and hadn't quite mastered the casual greeting.

"Is Lola working you to the bone?" he asked.

"Not at all—I love getting to hang out in the kitchen. I learned to make chipney-onion cakes today."

"Now you know the way to my heart. They're even better than Chicken McNuggets."

"Whoa. Coming from you, that's a huge endorsement."

"Do you have time for a break? I've got a surprise for you." Phinn smiled and bounced around on both feet. His energy was contagious and anxiety-inducing all at the same time.

"Uh-oh. Am I gonna wake up on your boat in the middle of the ocean if I follow you?"

"Definitely not. You'll like this, I promise."

She dropped off the tray of strawberries in the kitchen and followed Phinn outside. They rounded the corner to an outdoor dining area where all the benches and tables had been cleared away. Wooden beams created a rectangular boundary around the sandy dirt, which had been smoothed and leveled. It looked like Phinn had taken a couple of benches apart to construct the border.

"Check it out," Phinn said. He pointed to where a basket, woven together with bamboo sticks, hung from a tree.

Wylie had never considered herself sentimental, but this was quite possibly the nicest thing anyone had done for her. He had built her a basketball court.

"I love it," Wylie said. "The only thing missing is a ball."

Phinn handed her a box. Inside she found a rubber ball. It was the type kids used to play dodgeball or four square in grade school.

"Next time I go to the mainland, I'll bring you back the real thing."

Wylie turned the ball over in her hands and noticed PROM? written in large black letters. Her mind was suddenly bombarded by the visual of Phinn whispering in Tinka's ear.

"What's wrong?" Phinn asked, placing an arm around her. "I thought you'd be happy."

She took a deep breath, then told him about the photos Lola had shown her.

"I wish Lola hadn't done that," Phinn said.

"She didn't mean anything by it."

"It's not easy to explain my relationship with Tinka, and yes, she has feelings for me," Phinn replied, "but to me she's always felt more like a little sister. It would be like if I got jealous over how close you are with your brothers."

"It's not even remotely the same," Wylie pushed. "You guys have . . . slept together, right?"

Phinn sighed and looked up at the basket.

"Yes, but that's over now. It's been over for years."

Wylie nodded. There was no point in pressing him further. She believed him.

"Wylie, here's the thing," Phinn said. "I knew the moment we met on the rooftop that if I never got to see you again, I'd spend the rest of my life thinking about you. The memory of you would never be good enough. I wanted the real thing. So I didn't just bring you here to help your brother. I brought you here to make myself happy. Maybe that's selfish, but it's been a while since I've felt this happy."

It wasn't until she heard the sentiment that she realized it was exactly what she'd needed him to say.

"So, you want me to go to prom with you?" she asked.

"More than anything."

"Okay. I will go to prom with you, on one condition." Wylie handed him the ball. "You make this shot."

Phinn focused all his attention on the basket, holding the ball firmly in his hands.

"I've never even played before."

"Tough. Now, don't mess up," Wylie teased.

"This is a lot of pressure." Phinn took a deep breath. "But here goes." He popped a *parvaz* into his mouth, then flew straight up to the basket and tossed the ball in effortlessly.

"I made it! I'm taking Wylie Dalton to prom!" he shouted from the sky, flaunting his victory.

"That's not fair. You used performance-enhancing drugs!"

Wylie tossed a *parvaz* into her mouth. She grabbed the ball as it rolled down the court, then flew up in the air and dunked it like an NBA player. She gripped the rim of the basket and hung from it.

"This is amazing!" She whooped.

Phinn flew toward her and grabbed the other side of the rim, sticking his head through the basket.

"I did good?" he asked.

"You did good," Wylie confirmed. She pulled him into a kiss, then proceeded to crush him in a game of *parvaz*-enhanced one-on-one.

By the end of the game, all she could think about was how lucky she was to be here. It was the happiest she'd ever been in her whole life, and no one could ruin it.

CHAPTER ELEVEN

kings and queens

after all this was over, Gregory told himself, he would buy a new couch for the living room. The one he'd been sleeping on was hell on his back. There had been a glorious period in his life when every joint in his body didn't hurt so much when he woke up in the mornings. How naive he'd been to think that would never change.

It didn't feel right leaving Maura alone in a house that used to be filled with teenagers. She'd told him he could sleep in their bed if the sofa was too uncomfortable, but he was afraid he would reach for her in the middle of the night and she would pull away from him. And there was no way he could sleep in any of his kids' beds. All the artifacts they'd left behind, still in disarray from the police search, seemed to taunt him. Besides, as long as he stayed in the living room, he would be able to see them as soon as they walked through the front door.

One month had passed since his kids had gone missing. The police had sifted through their drawers and snooped through their computers, but found no evidence of plans to run away or clues that anyone might have taken them. Gregory had discovered that Wylie used her spare time to teach other teenagers how to poach an egg or make fresh pasta from scratch, and had quite an Internet following. The birthday gift he had given her was still sitting by her bed, unopened. Joshua's computer was filled with instant-messaging chats between himself and Abigail that he'd saved. Maura had insisted they read through them for clues, but all they found were a string of sweet nothings and plans for the future. Abigail's parents said she was inconsolable since Joshua had disappeared, and that he hadn't responded to any of her texts or phone calls.

And then there were the items they'd found in Micah's room. Gregory was well aware that his youngest struggled with social anxiety and that the medication hadn't helped as much as they'd hoped. He knew Micah was a talented artist; his desk drawers were filled with sketches and storyboards for graphic novels he wanted to write. But Gregory didn't know about the drinking. The police had found several bottles of alcohol under Micah's bed. Gregory requested they dispose of them before Maura had a chance to see them.

The NYPD hadn't officially closed its investigation, but all signs pointed to three teenage runaways. Joshua was a fugitive, so the manhunt for him would be ongoing, but the search lacked the effort that would go into a kidnapping case. Maura and Gregory already had a website, a hotline, a volunteer center, and friends posting flyers all over the city. They were also bombarding their Facebook feeds with photos, but no one had come forward with any tips on where their children might be, despite the handsome reward they'd offered. One month, and none of the kids had used their cards or cell phones. They had vanished without a trace.

Shannon had been relatively understanding about the distance Gregory had put between them. He had made her promises for the future, but ever since the kids had gone missing, Gregory couldn't bear to look at her or hear the sound of her voice. What if the affair was the reason they'd left? He didn't know for certain that Maura knew about his transgressions, but who else could have told Wylie? Though Maura had never mentioned it, he suspected she knew, from the way she looked at him like all of this was somehow his fault. Deep down, Gregory worried that she was right.

That was why he left the volunteer center early that day and waited outside Harper Academy until school got out. The other parents nodded at him politely; some even stopped to tell him they were praying that his kids would turn up soon. He didn't blame them for not knowing how to treat him. He was living out all of their worst nightmares, and nothing they could say would make him feel better.

Vanessa stumbled out of the building with a few friends Gregory recognized but didn't know by name. He felt his blood pressure rise when one of the girls said something and the rest of them, including Vanessa, collapsed with laughter. Wylie had been missing for barely thirty days, and Vanessa was her best friend. How could she be laughing like nothing in her world had changed? He crossed the street toward them. When they saw him approaching, they immediately went silent.

"Hello, girls." Gregory addressed them with all the parental warmth he could muster.

"Hi, Mr. Dalton," they mumbled back.

"Vanessa, can I speak with you for a few minutes?"

Vanessa nodded at her friends and they walked off toward the subway station without her.

"Is there any news about Wylie?" Her voice trembled as she asked, and Gregory felt slightly vindicated. Gregory shook his head.

"The police are still searching for clues, but they seem convinced the kids ran away. Vanessa, is there anything you remember from that night?"

"I already told the police everything I know."

Gregory couldn't get past the feeling that she was lying.

"You're absolutely certain?" he asked. "There was no one you saw them talking to? Nothing out of the ordinary?"

"I wish I knew more. We were all hanging out at our apartment in Williamsburg, and then the three of them left to go home. And that was the last I saw of any of them."

He wanted to grab her by the shoulders and shake her. He wanted to scream that her lies weren't protecting Wylie, they were only hurting her. The lengths kids would go to avoid getting their friends in trouble with their parents was infuriating.

"Nothing you tell me will get anyone in trouble. You understand that, right?"

Vanessa nodded.

"Did Wylie or either of her brothers ever mention running away? When they said good-bye to you that night, was there anything different about it? Did you get the sense that Wylie thought it was the last time she'd be seeing you for a while?"

"No. She seemed perfectly normal. I mean, we were all sad that Joshua was going to juvie the next day, but none of us really talked about it. We didn't want to ruin her birthday."

Gregory felt ridiculous now, standing outside of the school like he thought he was some sort of private investigator. He had only hoped he could return to the brownstone with some piece of news for Maura that would give her an ounce of hope to hold on to.

"Thank you, Vanessa. If there's anything else you remember, or if they try to get in touch with you, will you give us a call?"

"I will. Mr. Dalton, don't take this the wrong way, but if Wylie wanted to come home, she would have found her way back by now."

"It's not always easy to get home, Vanessa. You take care of yourself."

As Gregory walked off, he pulled a stack of flyers out of his briefcase and headed for the nearest bus stop. The glass wall was already covered with missing posters for a young boy named Bandit. Gregory did his best to tape up the flyers of his own kids without covering up the boy's picture. He looked at the date Bandit had gone missing—more than two years before. He thought about the kid's family. Clearly, they hadn't given up hope, if they were still posting flyers around the city, but after two years without their son, had they figured out a way to sleep at night? Did they still jump a mile like he did every time the phone rang or someone knocked on the door? He tore down one of the posters of Bandit, folded it, and placed it in his suit pocket. He would keep an eye out for him.

+ + + + + +

PHINN TUGGED AT HIS BOW TIE AND INTERLACED HIS fingers with Wylie's as they entered the dining room for prom night.

"Are you okay?" she asked.

"Great," he said, still fumbling with his tie. "I just feel like I'm being strangled by this thing, that's all."

Prom themes had been bandied about before Wylie and her brothers had even arrived on the island, but Phinn couldn't settle on one. Most had close ties to life on the mainland and didn't resonate with kids who'd spent their formative years here. So Phinn announced there was only one condition for their dress code: everyone had to look their most formal and elegant. That meant tuxedos for the guys and cocktail dresses for the girls. Nadia, Helen, and the other seamstresses spent months designing and sewing outfits that met Phinn's requirements. Tinka was normally in charge of the décor, but her stint in detox had slowed her down, and Bailey had taken over the responsibility this year.

Wylie's dress was originally intended for Charlotte, Lola's old roommate, but since she'd been exiled back to the States, the gown was available. After a few small alterations, it fit perfectly. The fabric itself was simple black cotton, but the beaded detailing added a wow factor. Shiny pieces of abalone shell were draped across it, causing the entire dress to sparkle with any small movement. To finish off the look, Wylie tied her hair into a low bun and used beets to stain her lips a deep burgundy.

All eyes were on Wylie and Phinn when they made their entrance. Over the past month, she'd forged friendships with a lot of the locals, but from the way they were staring, it felt like the jury was still out on whether she was good enough for their precious Phinn. Perhaps the food tonight would help win them over. She and Lola had labored over the menu for days, and pulled an all-nighter in the kitchen getting all the dishes ready for the dance. They were taking a huge risk: all the recipes were their own invention, and none were anything Lola had ever served in the past. It was Wylie who'd suggested they go with small bites, so they wouldn't have to spend all evening tending to the food.

"This place looks amazing. Maybe Bailey should handle the decorations every year," Phinn said.

"It's tropic," Wylie added. She still felt silly using slang words from the island, but she hoped that with a little time and practice, it wouldn't feel like she was trying too hard every time she spoke. Lola was always happy to give her a vocabulary lesson. Wylie knew now that "arthritic" meant weak, "elder" meant asshole, "silver" meant arrogant, and "midlife" meant tragic. But she found "tropic" was the most overused adjective among the residents.

But the place did look tropic. Every inch of the ceiling

and walls were strung with streamers made out of leaves and wildflowers. Tealight candles in mason jars lit up the room. All the chairs and tables had been moved aside to make space for the dance floor. Wylie had helped style the buffet table with herbs and dandelions, but she was most proud of the platters of appetizers: deviled eggs with a yolk and woodmeg filling, tiny mugs of French apple flower soup, lettuce cups brimming with sweet peppers, avocado, and baby three-legs (an edible bug on the island that was considered a delicacy), and individual *parvaz* crème brûlées for dessert. Wylie held her breath as Nadia and Patrick each took a bite from a deviled egg. She exhaled as their faces lit up and they filled their plates with more food.

A self-serve champagne bar was stocked with various juices and berries to mix with sparkling wine, but Wylie planned to stick to her favorite sugar-root mocktails. It wasn't a shocker to find Micah and Tinka already standing at the bar, topping off their glasses. Apparently Tinka's detox stint was meant to wean her off *parvaz* and not alcohol. Wylie felt a pang of anxiety as she watched them clink a toast. Micah needed someone to discourage his drinking habit, not enable it, but she would try her best not to worry about that tonight.

"You want to dance?" Phinn asked.

Wylie shook her head. She felt like they were being watched by everyone at the party, and she didn't want people staring at them as they danced together.

"No. I want you to try the food first."

"You know that's one of the things I like most about you."

"My big appetite?"

"No," Phinn said, laughing. "You're decisive. I can ask you what you want to do, and I know you're going to tell me."

It was true. She'd never been one to shrug her shoulders and respond with "I don't know. What do *you* want to do?" But the qualities Phinn appreciated about her continued to take Wylie by surprise. Most guys just complimented her looks.

"What's this?" Phinn asked, holding a mug.

"French apple flower soup. We boiled the apple flower, added a bunch of spices, and puréed it. There's a layer of fried dough and cheese on top."

Phinn sniffed it suspiciously, then downed the soup.

"Holy crap!" he blurted, crinkling his forehead.

Oh God, Wylie thought. *He hates it. He's going to puke it up right here in front of everyone, and they'll burn me at the stake for offending his taste buds.*

"It's . . . phenomenal."

Wylie grinned. "It's a party in your mouth, right?"

Phinn laughed at the expression. "Yes, it's a party in my mouth."

He tasted the other dishes, and they all solicited a similar reaction. Lola walked over with Maz, and he was just as complimentary as he stuffed his face with lettuce cups.

"We pulled it off," Lola whispered. "The food is a hit, lady."

Wylie put an arm around her. "We're basically culinary rock stars."

Within minutes, adoring residents surrounded Phinn,

and Wylie found herself pushed to the outskirts of the group. She gave Phinn a nod to indicate she didn't mind spending a few minutes without him, stocked a plate with food, and brought it over to Joshua, who was sitting alone at a table.

With all the time she'd spent in the kitchen the past few days, she hadn't even had the chance to ask him if he had a date to prom. Now she looked around the room at all the guests. Everyone was paired off. He was the only one who didn't have a date.

"I come bearing gifts," Wylie said as she grabbed a seat next to him and placed the plate between them.

"Don't feel bad for me," Joshua told Wylie, expertly reading the expression on her face. "It wouldn't feel right to be here with someone other than Abigail anyway."

"No wonder you don't have a date, if you didn't bother to ask anyone."

"I asked three girls. Everyone here already has a boy-friend—or isn't into guys."

"Maybe before Abigail turns eighteen, we can convince Phinn to bring her to the island."

"No!" Joshua was quick and adamant in his response. "She doesn't belong here."

"Okay, never mind. Sorry I brought it up."

"No, I'm sorry. I didn't mean to snap at you."

Wylie wanted to ask why he was so opposed to the idea of Abigail moving here. But unlike the Joshua from back home, her brother now kept most things close to the vest. The chief of staff title had gone straight to his head.

"Don't look now, but your favorite person's on her way

over here," Joshua said. Wylie glanced over her shoulder and saw Micah dragging Tinka over to their table.

"Do you think she's gonna to try to beat me up again?"

"I've got your back if she does."

Since Tinka's release from detox, Wylie had gone out of her way to avoid her. It wasn't that hard. Tinka spent most of her time with Micah behind closed doors, and when they did cross paths at the daily birth control ritual, or some evenings in the Clearing, they simply didn't acknowledge each other.

"Hi, Wylie," Tinka mumbled once they arrived at the table.

"Hi."

"Can we talk someplace private?"

"I'd rather not go anywhere alone with you," Wylie half joked, but she followed her to a corner of the dining room, close enough to the festivities, where anyone could restrain Tinka in case of an assault.

"I've been really unfair to you," Tinka spilled out. "My memories from the residency party are pretty fuzzy, but I've been told I attacked you. There's no excuse for what I did, and I'm really sorry. It won't happen again."

"Thanks for the apology," Wylie said. "But honestly, I just want you to promise you won't hurt my brother."

Wylie glanced at Micah, who was anxiously trying to gauge how their conversation was going.

"Micah? I won't hurt him."

"I mean it, Tinka. He really likes you. A lot. He didn't have many friends back home. He doesn't open up to many people. But he's different with you, and if you do anything to screw that up, it could destroy him. He's very . . . fragile. I don't want to worry about him drinking himself to death because the girl he's in love with is actually in love with someone else. Do you understand?"

"Completely," Tinka said, nodding. "Micah knows where we stand with each other. I've been honest with him from the beginning, and I won't hurt him."

"Good. Because if you do, I swear to God, I will make you regret it."

"I can respect that," Tinka said. "So, are you and Phinn official now?"

"Yes, I guess we are."

"Congratulations. I'm happy for you." Tinka smiled warmly. Perhaps the few days in detox had done her some good.

"Thanks," Wylie said. She had no desire to flaunt her romance in Tinka's face. Tinka and Phinn had a history Wylie could never compete with, and the best she could do was respect their friendship.

"I'm glad we had this conversation," Tinka said. "Maybe at some point we can even become friends." Tinka gave her a hug and whispered in her ear, "Be careful. He has the power to destroy you."

The moment she let go of the embrace, Tinka gave Wylie a sweet, unassuming smile. There was no acknowledgment of the cryptic warning she had just left her with. Wylie couldn't smile back as she let the words sink in. *Be careful. He has the power to destroy you.*

"Have a good prom! Phinn makes a great date," Tinka said brightly as she walked away.

She's just messing with your head, Wylie told herself. The warning was absurd, and Tinka must've said it to get a rise out of her. Wylie wouldn't give her the satisfaction; she'd focus on enjoying every moment of the night with Phinn. Across the room, he was still surrounded by a small crowd of residents. It was almost embarrassing to watch as they scrambled to get a word in or say something that would make Phinn laugh or nod in agreement. *This must be what it feels like to date a celebrity,* she realized. *You have to share him with all his adoring fans.*

Wylie gently pushed her way through the pack. Phinn was in the middle of a conversation, but she cut him off.

"Do you want to dance?" she asked.

"Sure," Phinn replied.

Wylie clutched his hand tightly and led him to the dance floor. She decided not to mention the conversation with Tinka. It would only piss Phinn off and ruin their night, which was exactly what Tinka wanted. So instead, she pressed her body against Phinn's, and they moved to the music together. They stayed like that for a long time, on the dance floor, laughing and talking and holding on to each other, so no one else would bother them.

After a couple of hours, the music tapered off and Patrick took the stage with an envelope in hand. It was time to announce the prom king and queen. Everyone stopped dancing and pretended to wait in suspense for Maz and Lola to reclaim their title.

"Ladies and gentlemen of Minor Island," Patrick announced. "I present to you this year's king and queen."

Patrick fumbled with the envelope, then frowned and

bit his lower lip. He cleared his throat and spoke into the microphone.

"Phinn and Wylie."

The dining room went quiet for a moment, until Maz and Lola made a point of applauding, and then everyone else followed their lead. Wylie was mortified. This was the last thing she wanted. She gave Lola an apologetic look, and Lola just smiled back as Phinn dragged Wylie to the stage.

"Why would you do this?" she hissed.

"'Cause I knew it would drive you crazy," Phinn whispered, smirking. "Come on. We'll laugh about it in the morning."

"Everyone is going to hate me now."

Phinn shook his head. "No, they're going to love you because they can tell you're hating every minute of this."

They stepped onto the stage. Wylie spotted Tinka in the distance, kissing Micah and pretending like she wasn't paying any attention to what was happening onstage. Patrick carefully placed the crowns on their heads.

Phinn was poised to address the crowd, but before he could speak, a loud boom echoed through the dining room, and the ground shook beneath their feet.

"What was that?" Wylie asked Phinn.

"Stay right here. Don't move."

Suddenly, it was pandemonium. Wylie heard Patrick scream to Maz that they needed access to the weapons. Maz fumbled for a key in his pocket and unlocked a cabinet filled with spears and bow and arrows. The guys lined up as Maz and Patrick swiftly handed out weapons. Tinka shouted that she wanted to go with them, but Lola held her back. Before Wylie could force someone to tell her what was happening, she found herself being dragged beneath the floorboards and engulfed in total darkness.

"Where are my brothers?" Wylie kept asking over and over, but no one would give her an answer. She wasn't sure how many people were even there with her.

"Can someone put a muzzle on her?" It was Tinka's voice, but it sounded far away.

"Micah? Joshua? Are you in here?" Wylie didn't care if Tinka wanted her to be quiet. She wouldn't stop asking for her brothers until she knew they were safe. She felt someone place a hand on her knee.

"They're not in here. It's just us girls in the basement," Lola said. "But Phinn won't let anything happen to them."

"We shouldn't be stuck down here," Tinka whined. "It's ridiculous to make all the women wait. We should be helping them."

No one else responded. It wasn't exactly the time to engage in a debate about gender politics.

"Can you tell me what's going on?" Wylie pleaded with Lola.

Lola's voice trembled when she answered.

"There's someone on the island who shouldn't be here."

CHAPTER TWELVE

hopper was here

"i knew he'd come back. They could all be dead out there. . . . Please don't let anyone else vanish. Please don't let anyone else vanish," a voice whispered.

In the pitch black, Wylie couldn't figure out who was speaking. Bailey's voice was raspier, Helen's was more high-pitched, and Nadia wasn't the hysterical type. Wylie wanted to reach out to the girl and find a way to comfort her, but she couldn't stop her own heart from pounding, and her limbs from trembling as the minutes ticked by. A few of the girls softly wept or quietly prayed, but most of them were too afraid to speak or make any sudden movements. The only thing Wylie was sure of right now was that if she got out of this basement alive, she would never hide down here again.

"It's Hopper. Phinn should have killed him when he had the chance," the girl continued. A small cry escaped from her throat, and then she started praying: *"Never forget to live life to the fullest. Do it for the troubled; do it for the lost. The days may feel shorter; the nights may feel long. But when we re-member, our memories grow strong."*

"Shhh. Did you hear that?" Lola whispered.

The prayers and cries came to a halt as everyone lis-tened: Footsteps, loud and thunderous. The boards above them shook, and all the girls clung to each other.

"Everything's okay!" It was Maz's voice calling to them. "We're all safe. I'm going to let you out now." The drum of multiple footsteps could now be heard as the door to the panic room opened. Light flooded the basement and Wylie closed her eyes, blinded by the brightness. When she opened them, everyone around her was clamoring to get out.

"Take my hand, Wylie," Maz ordered.

Wylie grabbed his hand and he pulled her aboveground. One by one each girl emerged, while the guys trickled in from the outside, still gripping their weapons. Reunions abounded as relieved and happy couples embraced and held each other tightly. Wylie spotted Phinn heading toward her, but she breezed past him and ran to the back of the dining room as Joshua and Micah entered, both clumsily holding spears. The last time they looked this scared and vulnerable, they were on the side of the road in Montauk.

"Are you guys okay?" Wylie asked, frantic with worry.

"We're fine," Micah said, fighting back tears. He was only fifteen. He wasn't old enough to go running toward an explosion without any explanation or warning.

"What the hell is going on?" Wylie asked loudly, more angry now than scared.

"You're asking the wrong brother." Micah gave a nod to

Joshua. "No one will tell me anything. Not even my own flesh and blood."

Tinka made her way over to them and punched Micah in the arm.

"Glad you're not dead," Tinka said, half joking.

"Right back at you," Micah answered.

The energy shifted in the room as the tears quickly evolved into a mix of laughter and elation.

"Are you going to tell me what's going on?" Wylie asked Joshua.

"I think it's better if you hear it from Phinn," he answered.

Wylie searched the room for Phinn and as usual, he was surrounded by a group of kids. From a distance, it looked like he was offering them hugs and words of comfort. Bandit followed closely behind, making notes on a clipboard as they moved from group to group. Wylie was Phinn's girlfriend. He should have checked on her by now, but she sensed she was being punished for hurtling past him and going straight to her brothers. She took a moment to gather herself, and then calmly walked toward him.

"Phinn." She said his name gently and he held up a finger, signaling for her to wait. After a few minutes of watching him console other residents, Wylie's patience ran thin.

"We deserve to know what happened," Wylie said, more forcefully now.

"Wylie, let it go," Lola whispered desperately.

"But we were locked in a basement," Wylie replied. "I think that warrants an explanation. Or does this happen all the time around here? 'Cause it didn't make it into the Minor Island handbook."

No one took Wylie's side or rallied behind her. They simply hung back and stared at her blankly. Even Phinn didn't bother to respond. Instead, he turned to Bandit and asked, "Is everyone accounted for?"

Bandit checked his clipboard and nodded. "Yes, no one's gone missing."

The room breathed a communal sigh of relief.

"Oh, thank God. I really thought it was happening all over again." The panicked voice from the basement belonged to a girl named Stacy. She was friendly with Lola, and the three of them had spent some afternoons together lounging around the *parvaz* field.

"*What* was happening all over again?" Wylie asked, but again no one answered. She was starting to feel like she was trapped in a zombie horror movie and she was the only one who hadn't been infected with a flesh-eating virus. "Can anyone hear me? Am I invisible?"

"Wylie, that's enough," Joshua said from the back of the room. He stormed over, grabbed her by the arm, and dragged her toward the exit.

"Let go of me!" Wylie said, doing her best to squirm out of his grip.

"Do what she says," Phinn spoke up, and Joshua instantly let go.

"Wylie has every right to be upset right now," Phinn said. "Stacy is referring to the lost kids."

"The lost kids? What do you mean?"

"Six months ago, some of our residents went missing. We call them the lost kids."

Never forget to live life to the fullest. Do it for the troubled; do it for the lost. The days may feel shorter; the nights may feel long. But when we remember, our memories grow strong.

The poem wasn't about those left behind on the mainland, Wylie realized; it was about kids who'd gone missing from the island.

"How did they go missing?"

"They wanted to camp out one night, but the next morning, they didn't come back. We searched the entire island for them, but they were gone."

"How many people?" Wylie asked.

"Twelve."

"Where did they set up camp?"

"On the Forbidden Side . . . before we knew it was dangerous."

"Did they go back to the mainland?"

Phinn shook his head. "None of our boats were missing."

Wylie turned to Joshua. "Did you know about this?"

"Don't be mad at your brother," Phinn urged. "He wanted to tell you and Micah, but I asked him not to."

Wylie glanced at Joshua, but he looked away guiltily. The only secret of consequence she'd ever kept from him was the one about their dad's affair, and even then, she'd finally come clean. No job title was worth betraying your siblings for. The entire room shifted uncomfortably as they continued to gape at her.

It reminded Wylie of one sunny afternoon in a downtown Manhattan park. "Keep your voices down," she'd begged her parents that day. "People are starting to stare." They were at her dad's company picnic, and her parents were dangerously close to coming to blows in front of all his colleagues. They were normally skilled at keeping their domestic disputes confined to the privacy of their home, but some comment her dad had made set her mom off and they ended up arguing loudly enough that other people could hear them. Wylie had never felt more embarrassed in her life. *Don't turn into them,* Wylie told herself now. She took a deep breath and turned to Phinn.

"Maybe we should talk in private," she suggested.

The two of them walked to Phinn's room in relative silence. But once they arrived at his bungalow and the door was closed behind them, Wylie allowed her rage to surface.

"Why didn't you tell us there were kids missing from the island?" she asked.

"No one's gone missing for months. The whole episode is behind us."

"But there was an explosion on the island tonight!"

"I hate that you had to go through all this on prom night," Phinn said. "But I won't let anything bad happen to you. I'm just trying to protect you."

"*From what?*" Wylie screamed, finally at the end of her rope.

"*From everything!*" he yelled back.

Wylie sat on the bed and let her face fall into her hands.

"Can you be more specific?" she asked, her tone quieter now, but no less angry.

"I'm trying to protect you from Hopper. If that means

arming all the guys with weapons and hiding the girls in a basement, then so be it."

"If he's so dangerous, why did you tell me I didn't need to worry about him?" Wylie asked.

Phinn explained to Wylie that this was a plan they'd always had in place. A drill they had practiced over and over again. If anything went wrong, the girls would hide in the basement and the boys would gather their weapons and fly or run to shore to ward off any possible intruders. So tonight, as the girls huddled beneath the floorboards, the boys had floated into the sky with their weapons aimed at the water's edge. Wylie pictured them still in their tuxedos, an army of James Bonds.

"The explosion was a couple of sticks of dynamite. Just a scare tactic. We didn't notice it till we were halfway up in the air, but there it was, in the sand . . . 'Hopper Was Here,'" Phinn explained.

Wylie felt a chill go down her spine.

"He was on the island?"

"We think so," Phinn nodded. "But there was no sign of a boat."

"Do you think he's responsible for the lost kids?"

Phinn shook his head. "We *know* he was involved. The only thing we found on the Forbidden Side when our friends went missing was the message 'Hopper Was Here,' written in blood. That's why we never go over there. It could be filled with traps and land mines."

"Do you think he . . . killed them?" Wylie asked.

"I hope not. He could be holding them hostage. He could

have taken them back to the mainland. We've looked for him everywhere, but we've found nothing. For a few weeks after they disappeared, his calling card would pop up on different parts of the island. Maybe someone has a twisted sense of humor and is just messing with us by writing his name everywhere."

"Who is this guy?" Wylie demanded. "What kind of person would do this?"

"I met him almost two years ago at a high school in Queens. It was career day, which is always a good resource when you're seeking out new recruits with talents that might be good for the island."

Hopper and Phinn had struck up a conversation outside the ROTC tent. Hopper admitted to Phinn that the only reason he considered joining the army was that eventually he wanted to be in the CIA. He was a spy junkie. He'd secretly bugged all the classrooms in his high school so he could eavesdrop on his teachers between periods.

"Also," Hopper told him, "I can skip class and still catch up on what I missed."

Hopper's talents went beyond surveillance. He lived with a foster family in a rough neighborhood in Queens, so he'd single-handedly created an alarm system for their apartment building. The irony was that when Hopper went missing in the middle of the night, his foster parents assumed his invention had failed them all, but in fact Phinn had convinced him to give up his dreams of being an agent and use his talents of security and surveillance elsewhere.

"The signs were always there. I just ignored them. It

was like having that one person at the party who makes everything a little uncomfortable or weird. He didn't make friends easily; he was aggressive, self-righteous at times. He didn't even make good on his promise to build us any sort of security system. I could tell people were afraid of him. They didn't like to be alone with him. I put up with it for an entire year. I kept thinking something might change, but it never did.

"And then the cutting started. First on his arms, then his legs. When he mutilated his own fingers, I knew there was something very wrong, and that I was only hurting him by keeping him here. Everyone else agreed, so we exiled him. A few months went by without incident, until we think he came back, out for revenge."

Wylie suddenly remembered Lola's roommate and the bracelet she'd found tucked away into her journal.

"Charlotte? Was she one of the people who went missing?" Wylie asked.

Phinn nodded. "She was . . . is . . . um . . . a really great person."

The beads of shell carefully strewn across Wylie's dress now felt heavy and confining. They had been meant for a girl who'd disappeared into thin air. No one knew if Charlotte was dead or alive, if she was safe or in danger. And here Wylie had been, prancing around in her outfit, worried that people wouldn't like her cooking.

"Lola told me she'd been exiled," Wylie managed to say.

"I told her to tell you that. Sometimes it's easier to pretend like nothing's changed, so most of the time, that's what we do. We thought about cancelling prom this year. It didn't feel right to carry on with traditions when so many of our friends were still missing. But if we lived in fear forever, then Hopper would get exactly what he wanted."

"I'm never going down to that basement again," Wylie said in response.

"I'm afraid you don't have a choice," Phinn said, holding her hand.

"You can't treat the girls like we're a bunch of damsels in distress. If we were on the mainland, it would be totally archaic to hide us away like we're some sort of liability. We shouldn't be left down there wondering if the worst is happening. We shouldn't have to worry that you all could be . . ." Wylie's voice trailed off.

What she'd really wanted to scream at Phinn in the middle of the dining room was, "How dare you make me love you, then put your life at risk?" But the voice she imagined coming out of her mouth sounded a lot like her mother's, so she held it back.

"Everything is going to be okay," Phinn promised her. "Hopper can't keep hiding forever. We'll stop him from hurting us again."

Phinn cupped her face in his hands.

"Wylie." It felt so good every time he said her name.

"Yeah?"

"I love you."

He almost seemed surprised as the words came out of his mouth. Like he hadn't planned to say them, but the moment had forced the truth out of him.

"I love you, too."

She let the words hang there and bridge the divide between them.

"I need you to promise me something," she said.

"Anything."

"No more lies. No more covering up the truth. I don't care if you think it's for my own good. If you're ever dishonest with me again, we're over."

"I'll never lie about anything again."

"Can I sleep here tonight?" Wylie asked.

Phinn nodded. Wylie put both her hands on his bow tie and gently loosened it. She could see his shoulders start to relax now that he didn't feel like he was being strangled. He brought his lips toward her face, but she pulled away again. She didn't want to kiss him yet. She finally had the courage to look straight into his eyes. And she kept her eyes fixed on him as she started to unbutton his shirt. Phinn put his hands behind her neck and fumbled for the zipper on her dress. It would have been easier for him if she turned around, but she wasn't done looking at him yet.

She knew it was early in their relationship to take this step, but it didn't matter. There was no one here to judge her and no rumor mill she had to worry about, like she did back in high school. Even though they lived on an island where time didn't function the way it did in the rest of the world, life was still short. Everything could change at a moment's notice, just like it did that night in the Hamptons. She didn't want to waste another minute.

"Are you sure about this?" Phinn asked, unzipping her dress.

"Positive."

As they melted onto his bed, Wylie decided that the few guys she'd hooked up with before no longer held significance. This was the only time she was giving herself to someone who knew there was more to Wylie Dalton than bright green eyes and pronounced dimples. Phinn knew the worst sides of her. He knew her mistakes and had witnessed her anger, and he wanted to be with her anyway. And she felt the same way about him.

trouble in paradise

"What was that?" Phinn asked.

"Nothing," Wylie answered.

"Was that your . . . stomach?"

"No!" Wylie pulled the blankets over her face and hid underneath them. Phinn slid down on the mattress and met her under the covers.

"That was definitely your stomach!" he teased.

Wylie placed both hands on her belly. Her stomach had a tendency to growl at the most inopportune times: in the middle of a final, during her first gyno appointment, throughout the eulogy at her grandfather's funeral. And now it had betrayed her again, in bed with her boyfriend. Why had no one invented a way to prevent belly groans from embarrassing the hell out of you?

"I'm hungry," Wylie explained. "I barely got a chance to eat last night, with all the commotion."

Grrrrrrrrr. Another rumbling sound filled the room, but this time it didn't come from Wylie.

"That wasn't me!" Wylie announced proudly. "That was totally your stomach."

"I know. They're talking to each other. Listen."

They both lay quietly as their stomachs continued to creak and moan like an old house settling.

"What do you think they're saying?" Wylie asked.

"Mine says, 'I can't believe this amazing girl told me she loves me last night,'" Phinn translated.

"Mine says, 'How can we get some food delivered to this bungalow so we can stay in bed all day?'"

"Your stomach knows what it's talking about."

Now that the sun was up, they could hear the rest of the island rising. Bungalow doors opened and closed as locals made the walk to the dining room for their first meal of the day. Luckily, Wylie and Lola had planned for this. A continental breakfast was the only way to go the morning after prom if they wanted to enjoy themselves and not wake up at the crack of dawn to collect eggs and cook omelets for a bunch of starving, hungover teenagers.

But even though she didn't have to get up, Wylie wanted the noises from outside to go away. She could hear bits and pieces of people's conversations as they walked past Phinn's window, recounting the drama of last night. She didn't want to think about any of that right now. Not the explosion, or the fact that kids on the island had gone missing, and definitely not the impending threat. Right now all she wanted to do was stay in bed with Phinn and pretend none of that had ever happened. The only memories she wanted to keep from prom were exchanging "I love you"s and spending the night together.

"Are you feeling okay?" Phinn asked.

"I'm just thinking about last night."

"I'm gonna recruit a team. We're going to do another search for Hopper's boat. He can't hide forever. We'll track him down eventually."

"Just don't send my brothers to find him. Joshua will want to go, but you can't let him. It's not his battle to fight. We don't even know Hopper."

"I won't let Joshua do anything that puts him at risk. You have my word on that."

Wylie sighed. "We can't stay in bed all day, can we?"

"I'm afraid not. I need to make sure everyone's okay after what happened. Try not to wander around alone. Stick with your brothers if you have to. There's safety in numbers."

"There's safety in pepper spray. I never left home without it in New York. I tossed mine in a drawer when I got here because I didn't think I'd need it."

"Maybe for now, it's not such a bad idea."

Wylie was suddenly struck by a thought: what if Micah wanted to go home now? Back home, her brother had been diagnosed with anxiety disorder. Living here seemed to remedy his symptoms, but that was before they knew a major kidnapping had been committed. Without knowledge of the lost kids, the Daltons had agreed to live on the island under false pretenses. If they insisted on returning home now, surely Phinn would have to make an exception. And Micah wasn't always rational when he was afraid. If he thought his life was in danger, Wylie's youngest brother might try to sail away in the middle of the night.

"I should check on Joshua and Micah and see how they're holding up after last night."

"Good idea," Phinn answered.

Wylie slipped out of bed and put her prom dress back on. Once she got to her room and changed out of it, she would never wear it again. It didn't feel right to keep it, when it belonged to someone else. Her feet still ached from wearing high heels, so she decided to walk back to her bungalow barefoot.

"I wish we could hide out here a little longer," Phinn said.

"Me too," Wylie replied.

Phinn grabbed her by the hand and pulled her back into bed. *Kissing him will never get old*, Wylie thought. Fifty years was considered an eternity to be married in normal people time, but with the way time functioned on the island, Wylie and Phinn could be together for twice that long. But in ten decades, Phinn would be as beautiful and energetic and strong as he was right now.

"You're making it impossible to leave," Wylie whispered between kisses.

"I know. That's the point."

They kissed some more until Phinn pulled away. He hopped off the bed and took a painting from the wall. Behind it was a tiny cupboard.

"What are you doing?" Wylie asked.

"I want to give you something."

Phinn fished a key from inside his desk drawer and used it to unlock the cabinet. Inside Wylie glimpsed a stack of photographs, a worn-out teddy bear, and a rusted cigarette case. He took out the cigarette case, locked the cabinet, and sat down next to her.

"I keep my prized possessions in there," he explained. "They're artifacts from when we first came to the island. The teddy bear was the only toy I had with me and there are a few things that belonged to my parents."

Phinn handed her the cigarette case. "Open it."

A tiny antique hand mirror, strung on a silver chain, glittered inside. "It's an old family heirloom that belonged to my mom," Phinn explained. "It's one of the only things I have of hers. I want you to have it."

"I couldn't possibly—" Wylie started to say, but Phinn cut her off.

"Don't argue. It's been gathering dust in there for years. I'd rather have someone I love wear it."

"I don't know what to say."

Wylie swept up her hair as Phinn helped her clasp both sides of the chain together. The mirror hung right below the hollow of her neck.

"Thank you, Phinn. I will never take it off."

"Every time I look at it, I'll remember how I see things so much clearer with you in my life."

Wylie toyed with the charm with her thumb and index finger as she left Phinn's room and walked back to her bungalow.

Living in Manhattan, she'd borne witness to more than a few walks of shame. They usually happened on Sunday mornings. Messy hair, smudged eyeliner, a dress way too sexy for a brunch date. The men and women usually kept their heads down as they paid the cab driver and walked up their stoops. Wylie hadn't expected the stroll to her bungalow to feel like a walk of shame, but as residents passed her on their way to breakfast, they didn't even try to mask their judgment. She knew exactly what the whispers and stares meant: none of them thought she was good enough for Phinn, especially after she confronted him in public last night.

It doesn't matter what they think, Wylie kept repeating in her head, but the truth was, she hated that she couldn't separate her romance with Phinn from her friendships with the other kids. She was starting to feel like she could single-handedly bring down Hopper and they'd still think Phinn could do better.

Once she had a little time to hide in her bungalow and decompress from the walk home, Wylie braved the outdoors again to check on her brothers.

"You guys can't stay mad at me forever," Joshua said as he let Wylie in.

"You lied to us," Wylie argued.

"And so did Phinn, but from what I hear, you've forgiven him."

"Phinn was wrong to lie," Wylie admitted. "But you're our brother. You should have warned us that our lives could be in danger."

Joshua tried to explain his rationale for keeping the secret. He was following orders; he didn't want to scare them; if he was president of the United States, there'd be plenty of classified information he wouldn't be allowed to tell his family. Wylie realized she was making him grovel, because for once, it was nice that he had to be the one to apologize for something.

"It's okay," she finally said. "I get it."

"I do, too," Micah agreed. "Tinka also kept it from me all this time. If I'm not going to hold it against her, I'm not going to hold it against my own brother. Just don't let it happen again, or I will shave your head in your sleep."

Joshua agreed that the previous night's developments provided them with a loophole to return to New York, but none of the Daltons were in the mood for a drawn-out debate about whether they should stay on the island. Instead, they agreed to write "stay" or "go" on a piece of paper. This way, they could each answer honestly without feeling bullied into an opinion.

Wylie was the first to drop her piece of paper into a jar. Joshua dropped his response in next. Micah hesitated for a few minutes before jotting down a word and tossing his answer in.

"Who wants to do the honors?" Wylie asked.

Joshua stuck his hand into the jar and took out the first scrap of paper. He read it out loud: "Wylie votes to stay."

He grabbed another piece of paper and slowly unrolled it. "This one's mine," he said. "I vote we stay."

Joshua tilted the jar, and the last piece of paper fell into his palm.

"It's unanimous," he said. "We all want to stay."

Wylie left their bungalow feeling good about their decision. After all, New Yorkers didn't move out of the city for fear of terrorist attacks, and Californians thought the sunshine was a fair trade-off for the occasional earthquake. Every place had its drawbacks, and Minor Island's was Hopper. Eventually, they would capture him, ending his reign of terror, and everyone could go back to being a carefree teenager. In the meantime, Wylie would do her part to help.

Compared to most of her classmates in New York, Wylie didn't consider herself the activist type. She had plenty of opinions, but never felt compelled to march down the street holding a sign. She even rolled her eyes when her classmates filled her newsfeeds with trendy political hashtags. Vanessa could post about the environment till the cows came home, but she never even bothered to recycle. But if no one else was going to effect change, then Wylie had no choice but to do something.

"I don't know," Lola said when she heard Wylie's idea. "It's a big risk."

"Come on, Lola, please. I can't do it without you. Everyone is still figuring out if they like me. But if you're with me, they'll get on board."

"It's dangerous. You know that, right?"

"I do, but I think it's worth it."

"Fine. I'll do it. For Charlotte," Lola said. "If she were still here, she'd be all for it."

"I'm sorry about what happened to her," Wylie replied, not sure what the appropriate thing was to say. No wonder Lola had been hesitant to get to know her when she'd moved in.

"I should have told you the truth. Phinn didn't want to

scare you all off. It was stupid of me to lie, but if it helped keep you here, I'm kind of glad I did. I really can't imagine this place without you now."

"This is my home. I'm never going anywhere else."

"Good."

"So . . . on a scale of one to complete and total terror, how scared should I be of Hopper?"

"We should all be extra cautious. But we can't just hide in our rooms in fear. And anyway, the island knows how to protect us from predators."

"It does?" Wylie asked.

"That's what my tribe always said. My parents told me those who don't respect the island would meet an untimely demise. I'll admit, I've never seen it happen. Maybe they were making up stories, but I choose to believe them. After all, this place is magical."

"Yes, it is," Wylie replied. She took some comfort in Lola's words, even if it was just an old family legend.

Once Lola agreed to Wylie's plan, the two of them knocked on the door of every bungalow that belonged to a female resident.

"How do you feel about hiding out in the basement?" Wylie asked each girl who opened the door. The answer was always some variation of "I hate it" or "it's scary in there" or "that place gives me panic attacks."

Next, Wylie presented each girl with a hammer and a handful of nails and invited her to meet her and Lola in the dining room in exactly one hour.

Most of the girls showed up right on time. Even Tinka

didn't refuse the invitation. Curiosity was a great way to mobilize the masses. Wylie stood onstage, above the basement they'd all been crammed into together.

"I know I'm the new girl on the island," Wylie said. "And I realize I haven't had a chance to get to know all of you, but I do know something we all have in common. Even you, Tinka."

Some of the girls snickered at Tinka as she raised one eyebrow.

"What could we possibly have in common?" Tinka asked. It seemed that without Micah around, she forgot to be nice to Wylie.

"We all hate being treated like fragile creatures who need to hide away in the basement the second something goes wrong. The guys think we're arthritic, but we're not."

"Obviously." Tinka relented. "None of us likes being treated like we're weak and useless. What's your point?"

"My point is we don't have to agree to go along with it."

"I second that," Lola added. "We have every right to be on the front lines like the guys."

Some girls nodded their heads in agreement, while a few retreated to the back of the dining room.

"We're as strong as they are," Wylie continued. "And we don't need boys to protect us from everything. I'd like to play a part in changing the way we're treated, and I invite you to join me."

Wylie opened a small box filled with metal brackets. She placed a wooden slab over the entrance to the basement and hammered a nail into it. Some of the girls gasped in response, others cheered, and a small faction hustled out of the room.

"Is Phinn okay with this?" Bailey asked.

"Don't worry about Phinn," Wylie said. "Now, I could use a little help here."

The girls edged toward the stage with their hammers and nails. Wylie assumed there'd be some reluctance, but she didn't expect they'd be practically terrified to join in. Nadia nervously glanced toward the entrance of the dining room and then handed her tools back to Lola.

"Sorry, guys," she said as she walked out. "I can't do this."

"I can," Tinka announced. She was the first to join Wylie onstage and hammer a nail into the slab. Lola joined them next. After a few minutes, no one could hear each other talking over the sound of the pounding. They hammered away and cheered each other on until the floorboards that opened up to the basement were nearly sealed shut.

"What's going on in here?" Phinn's voice bellowed through the dining room, loud enough to cut through the hammering. The girls instantly dropped their tools.

"Busted . . ." Tinka said under her breath.

"What does it look like?" Wylie turned, answering Phinn with a smile as he approached. Maz, Bandit, and Joshua trailed behind him. "We're closing up the basement. The girls and I don't want to hide down there anymore."

"I never approved this," Phinn replied. His tone was so serious that Wylie stumbled over her response.

"It wasn't, um, it wasn't up for debate."

"This was your idea, Wylie?" Phinn asked.

"Don't be mad at her," Lola quickly jumped in. "It's my fault. I'm the one who told her it was a good idea. We should have talked to you about it."

"We're so sorry, Phinn," Bailey explained. "We'll take out all the nails right now."

"Like hell we will," Wylie said. "Last night was terrifying. We're not going to stand back and let you guys fight our battles."

"That's not up to you. I make those decisions." Phinn was addressing her like a child and yet Wylie could tell he was struggling not to completely blow up at her.

"My mistake," Wylie replied. "I didn't realize we were living under the rule of a dictator."

Joshua gave Wylie a look that said "Please shut up," but she just glared back at him. If there was one person in the room she expected to defend her, it was her own brother.

"Can you all give me and Wylie some alone time?" Phinn phrased the question less like a request and more like an order. The girls quickly made their way out of the room. Tinka brushed close to Wylie.

"Just because he gave you his mom's necklace doesn't mean he'll do what you want," she whispered as she followed the rest of the girls out of the room.

Phinn's expression was cold and aloof as he approached her. What happened to the guy who'd covered her with kisses that morning?

"Don't ever talk to me like that in front of anyone again,"

Phinn snapped. "You did it last night and I gave you a pass, but now you're making a habit out of it."

"This isn't about you, Phinn. This is about the girls on the island. I don't agree with the way we're being treated. We have every right to stand up for ourselves. You don't have to be such an elder about it."

"I can't give you special treatment because you're my girlfriend. Lola should have told you this was a bad idea. I don't know what she's trying to prove—"

"She's not trying to prove anything," Wylie said, cutting him off. "Let's just start over. The girls and I don't want to hide in the basement anymore. Can we have your approval on that?"

"No. I don't know how much more clearly I can spell this out for you, Wylie. Hopper's dangerous. It's safer to keep you girls hidden."

"It doesn't feel safe down there."

"Wylie, enough!" Phinn yelled. "I've lost a lot of people in my life. I won't lose you! End of story!"

Phinn left without so much as a hug or a handshake. Once he was gone, Wylie tried to take out the nails, but her hands were shaking. She didn't mean to upset Phinn, and she didn't want the other girls to think she believed she deserved special treatment from him. *This is what happens when you get political*, Wylie thought. *You just end up ruffling feathers and pissing people off.*

"Trouble in paradise?" Tinka walked back into the dining room and handed Wylie her hammer.

"Phinn was right. It was a bad idea," Wylie replied.

Tinka shook her head. "For a second there, I thought Phinn liked you because you were different, but you're not. You're just like every other girl he's dated . . . doing everything he wants."

"I made a mistake. I'm fixing it. That's all."

"Right. Just sweep all your problems under the rug."

"That's not what I'm doing!" Wylie retorted sharply.

"Careful. The more you tell yourself that, the more you'll start to believe it."

disappearing act

a rough patch. That's what Vanessa always said when her relationship of the moment was headed for disaster. Wylie, dubious, would nod in agreement, even though she knew a breakup was imminent and she'd have to drop everything to cheer up her best friend once again. And now here she was in the throes of her very own rough patch, and Vanessa wasn't at the ready to make her feel better.

It had been six agonizing days of kill-me-now awkwardness between her and Phinn. They continued to kiss and hold hands when they were together, but something felt *different*. The kisses were shorter and his hands didn't hold on to her quite as tightly anymore. Phinn had thanked her for pulling every last nail out of the floorboards, but Wylie couldn't shake the feeling that he still expected her to grovel for forgiveness.

"He's busy. Don't take it so personally," Lola said, trying to comfort her.

"He was busy before and he didn't act like this. Next time I come up with an idea so stupid, will you just slap me repeatedly until I get over it?"

"It wasn't a stupid idea."

Wylie and Lola had spent the better part of the morning planting seeds and watering the vegetables in the garden. Access was limited to only a few locals, so it was always quiet and peaceful. Even the chickens seemed to be shrieking less. Maybe Wylie's nonstop chatter about Phinn had put them straight to sleep.

To be fair, Phinn *was* busier than usual. He had called together a group of residents to form an unofficial army. They would use all five of the island's sailboats and spread out over the ocean in search of Hopper. Since they would all technically be aging as they sailed in the waters off the island, they would have to do it in brief shifts. Wylie noted that none of the girls had been asked to volunteer, but if anyone was opposed to Phinn's plan, they kept their concerns to themselves.

Wylie couldn't decide what was more upsetting—the events of prom, or Phinn's icing her out. Never in her life had she lost sleep over a guy, but for the past week, all her fears about Phinn kept her mind racing. It didn't help that the sudden awkwardness had started right after they'd slept together for the first time.

"Maybe I was just really bad in bed," Wylie blurted.

"I didn't want to tell you, but that's actually the word on the street," Lola said sarcastically. "I can't go anywhere without hearing everyone say 'Wylie Dalton has no idea what she's doing in the bedroom.' You're probably never going to have sex again."

Wylie splashed Lola with water playfully. "That's just evil."

"More evil than spending the entire day talking about Phinn when you promised you'd teach me more about Austin, Texas? Maybe I should revoke your kitchen privileges."

"You wouldn't dare!" Wylie said.

"Try me. Now, where did we leave off? You said Austin was a liberal city, even though Texas was a red state. I can't remember what any of that means. How many colors do states come in?"

But Wylie couldn't get into a lengthy political discussion. She had become a girl possessed.

"Are you sure Phinn's never exiled an ex-girlfriend?" Wylie asked as she walked into the coop to collect eggs.

"I'm positive."

"Ugh. I'm sorry. I can barely stand myself right now. Thanks for listening to me. I don't know what I would do without you," Wylie admitted. "Tonight we'll talk about nothing but Texas. And as a token of my love and affection, I'll take care of dinner. You go spend the day with Maz."

"Now *that's* the spirit!" Lola replied, never one to turn down time off from the kitchen. "What's on the menu, Chef Wylie?"

"One of my favorite family recipes. A hearty stew of pickled turnips, a handful of basil, fried eggplant, and a big spoonful of honey to balance the sour ingredients. It's called Sweet Honey Stew. My dad taught me how to make it."

Lola's smile faded. Wylie walked out of the coop with a basket full of eggs.

"I know it sounds gross, but I swear, everyone will be like, 'Please sir, I want some more.'" Wylie said it with a British accent, mimicking the famous line from *Oliver!*, but the reference was lost on Lola.

"I'm sure it's delicious," Lola replied, "but we're low on turnips, and a few people are allergic to eggplant. How about that seafood stew I taught you a few weeks ago?"

"Sure. No problem," Wylie said, trying not to sound disappointed. She had thought of Sweet Honey Stew because she was feeling a little homesick, but the familiar taste would have probably left her in a sadder state of affairs.

"I'm gonna go find Maz," Lola said. "Thanks for making dinner. And try not to obsess over Phinn. No guy is worth driving yourself crazy over."

It took nearly three hours to water the rest of the plants, pull all the weeds from the garden, and prep the seafood stew, but Wylie stayed focused and barely thought about Phinn. Once all her tasks were completed, she grabbed a basket from the kitchen and stocked it with plantain and pame butter sandwiches, along with a jug of lemon sugar root juice filled with sprigs of rosemary.

She passed through the Clearing and watched as residents took turns jumping off the waterfall. Tinka and Micah were also there, painting still lifes from the lagoon, but there was no sign of Phinn. She knocked on his bungalow door, but he wasn't there either. She finally found him in the clinic, where Aldo was bandaging his hand.

"Are you okay?" she asked as she walked in.

"I'll be fine. Just a little cut from a loose nail on one of the sailboats," Phinn replied.

"Have you had time to eat lunch? I brought food."

"You must have heard my stomach growling all the way from the dining room."

"It *is* freakishly loud," Wylie joked. "I thought maybe we could go to the beach."

They took the same trail they'd walked the first day Phinn had brought Wylie to the island. As they made the trek toward the dock and the ocean, past the yellow lady-bugs and the stalks of bamboo, Wylie thought of the girl who had entered the island not too long before, all suspicious and confrontational. Phinn must have found her attitude amusing, knowing in just a day she'd happily agree to stay forever. So much had changed in such a short time.

"Are you going to dump me?" Wylie asked point-blank as they laid a blanket out on the sand and opened the picnic basket.

"No, I've just been distracted."

"There's this word we have on the mainland: 'bullshit.' Maybe you've heard of it? It's what you say when someone's not telling you how they really feel."

Phinn silently contemplated his next move, then spoke up. "Fair enough. I'm still mad about our fight."

Wylie nodded. "I appreciate your honesty. But I've already apologized. I don't know what else I can do."

"And I forgive you. It's just hard to forget when your girlfriend calls you a dictator."

Wylie cringed. "I didn't mean it. All the girls were finally starting to warm up to me and I felt humiliated in front of them."

Phinn sighed.

"I hate fighting," Wylie continued. "It reminds me of my parents."

"Look, Wylie, relationships aren't perfect. Sometimes we're going to fight. It doesn't mean we're turning into your parents."

"Famous last words," Wylie mumbled.

Phinn took a long chug of the lemon sugar root juice, then wiped his mouth and raised the jug to Wylie. He pointed to the remaining liquid.

"Half full. That's the way I try to see the world," he said.

"Wow. You just blew my mind," Wylie deadpanned.

Phinn smiled sheepishly. "My point is, it's all about perspective."

"Right, except the stakes in this relationship are a lot higher for me than they are for you," Wylie said, turning serious. "Your life hasn't changed much since I came here. My life has changed completely. Yeah, I stayed here because I wanted to be seventeen forever, but I also stayed here for you. My mom did the same thing for my dad. She gave up all her dreams so she could be with him. She ended up miserable, and he ended up leaving her for another woman."

"I didn't know that."

"It's a topic I prefer to avoid. So, I *can't* end up like them. I *can't* look at you in ten years and see the losses. I have to see everything I've gained by being here."

"You will."

"Then don't pull away from me every time we don't see eye to eye. You can't punish me if this is going to work."

She wasn't sure how well Phinn would handle her honesty, but if she wasn't truthful with him, she'd be planting the first seed of resentment in the pit of her stomach.

"I screwed up. It won't happen again," Phinn confessed. "I love you."

Wylie felt the knot in her belly loosen as her appetite finally returned after its weeklong absence. Now they could simply enjoy each other's company.

"I love you, too."

Wylie took a big bite of the plantain and pame butter sandwich. If she could sell them on a food truck back home, she'd make a quick million.

"When does Operation Hopper get under way?" she asked.

"In a few days, hopefully. We're not ready quite yet."

The sun was hotter than normal today. Wylie felt her skin heat up and knew she'd get a nasty sunburn if she wasn't careful. The waves of the ocean crashed against the sand, and the cool, foamy water stopped short at her bare feet.

"It's hot," Wylie said as sweat began to drip down her forehead. "Let's go for a swim in the ocean."

"We can't," Phinn replied. "Being off the periphery of the island makes us age—that's why we save all our swimming for the lagoon."

"Come on!" Wylie said. "Just ten minutes."

"It's against the rules."

"But *you* make the rules. You can choose to break them.

No one's around. Everyone's been too scared to come out here since the explosion on prom night. We'll have complete privacy."

"I don't know."

"We'll have to strip to our underwear," Wylie said flirtatiously.

"I can't."

"Do I have to get down on my hands and knees to beg? Because I'll do it."

Phinn dug his fingers into the sand, then said under his breath, "I don't know how to . . . swim."

"Are you serious?"

"My parents died before they got a chance to show me how. The lagoon is shallow enough that it doesn't matter, but I'll drown in the ocean."

"Not if I teach you to swim. You'll be safe with me. There's just one rule to remember: never turn your back on the ocean."

Wylie pulled off her shirt and pants, keeping only her bra and underwear on. Phinn stripped down to his boxers, and they linked arms as they walked toward the water. In the time they'd known each other, Wylie had never witnessed Phinn's confidence wavering. He was always self-assured and cocky, even arrogant at times. But as they stepped knee-deep into the water, she could almost hear his heart beating out of his chest. A wave crashed against them, knocking them off-balance.

"I've got you. Don't worry," Wylie told him.

"I don't want to go out much further. My feet won't reach the ground."

"You're tall. You'll be fine. Don't you trust me?"

Until now, Wylie thought the question of trust was an issue only for her. She had to decide if Phinn could be trusted after the way he'd brought her to the island and his decision not to tell her about the lost kids. It had never occurred to her that he had to learn to trust her, too.

"Phinn, do you trust me?" she asked again.

"I don't know," he answered.

"Well, right now, you're going to have to," Wylie responded.

They waded into the ocean until the water reached their chests and the waves grew still.

"It's a lot like flying," Wylie explained. "Only you're in the water."

Wylie flipped onto her back and let her arms and legs splay out as she floated on the surface of the ocean. The clouds rolled in, shielding them from the relentless heat of the sun. They looked almost gray and ominous and Wylie wondered if it was going to rain for the first time since she'd come here.

"You try it now. Just float on your back the same way you would in the air."

"I'll sink."

"No, you won't." Wylie maneuvered back to her feet, placed her hand on Phinn's back, and held him as he floated faceup.

"Now put your hands out," Wylie instructed.

"Don't let go," Phinn begged.

"You're doing great. A few more lessons and we'll have you swimming in no time."

She knew if she let go, Phinn would float on his own, and he'd leave the water feeling proud and giddy. But he'd asked her not to, and she didn't want to betray his trust. If keeping her hands propped under him made him feel safe, then that's where she'd leave them. Phinn closed his eyes and Wylie let herself count the freckles scattered across his nose.

A bell rang out in the distance. It was almost five p.m. and time to gather in the clinic for a dose of birth control.

"I'd better go. I can't miss the Pill."

Wylie helped Phinn get back on his feet and they walked to shore. They quickly got dressed as a light mist showered them from above.

"Now that I'm ten minutes older, will you promise not to leave me for a younger woman?" Wylie teased.

Phinn answered the question by giving Wylie a long kiss. She kissed him back just as passionately. Once they came apart, they each tossed back a *parvaẓ*.

"Don't get weird on me again, Phinn," she told him as they hovered in the sky, poised to fly their separate ways.

"I won't. You have my word."

Wylie watched him fly off, then whizzed past the trail to the Clearing to make a quick stop in the kitchen. Lola had been late to the last few birth-control rituals, and Patrick and Aldo were beginning to lose their patience. When she got lost in a recipe, even the sound of the bell couldn't snap her out of it. Right about now, she was probably tasting the seafood stew to make sure the flavors of the broth met her standards, even though Wylie had told her to take the afternoon off.

"Loles!" she called as she landed in the garden, but there was no sign of her. She hurried into the kitchen, but it was empty.

"Lola, are you in here? The bell rang. I'll see you in the clinic!"

The girls were all in their places when Wylie arrived. She grabbed a spot at the end of the line and scanned the room for Lola, but she was nowhere to be found. Maybe she actually did take the day off with Maz and lost track of time? Patrick and Aldo gave her a look, but Wylie just shrugged.

"I checked the kitchen. She's not in there. I'm sure she'll be here any minute."

"This is the fourth day in a row she's late," Patrick said, making a note on his clipboard. "Phinn's got strict guidelines. We ring a bell for a reason."

Wylie placed a pill on her tongue and washed it down with a cup of water.

"She'll be here. No one has to tattle to Phinn." She said the last part loudly, signaling to the rest of the girls to keep their mouths shut.

"Maybe she's pregnant," Tinka chimed in.

"That's not funny, Tinka," Aldo said.

A half hour passed, and Lola still hadn't shown up. The latest she'd ever been was fifteen minutes, but today she'd set a new record.

"When was the last time you saw her?" Patrick asked.

"This morning. We were in the garden together and she left to find Maz. Phinn and I went to the beach, then I stopped by the kitchen to get her, but she wasn't there."

Tinka reached out and touched a strand of Wylie's hair.

"Your hair is wet. You didn't convince Phinn to let you swim in the ocean, did you? 'Cause that's against the rules. If word got out he was bending them for you, well then, it would be total anarchy," Tinka said. The other girls stared at Wylie, waiting for an answer.

"I showered after the beach and then came here. Hence the tardiness and the wet hair," Wylie lied. "Like I said, Lola will be here any minute."

＊ ＊ ＊ ＊ ＊ ＊

BUT LOLA NEVER SHOWED UP. THREE HOURS HAD passed and they'd all been ordered to gather in the Clearing. They had scoured the entire island, but everyone had come up empty. Wylie's brothers had paired up on the search, and they were the only two who had yet to return. *Please*, Wylie thought. *This can't be happening.* They would find Lola, and tonight she'd tell her everything she knew about Austin, Texas.

"When did you last see her?" Maz asked Wylie for the tenth time.

"This morning, in the garden. She said she was going to see you."

"I haven't seen her all day," Maz said, raising his voice.

"That's what she told me!" Wylie said.

"You shouldn't have let her go anywhere alone!" Maz snapped.

"This isn't Wylie's fault," Phinn intervened. "She didn't do anything wrong."

"Well, the love of my life is missing and I want an expla-

212 ～ Sara Saedi

nation." Maz's voice quivered as he tried not to break down in tears.

"We're going to find her." Phinn's voice was calm and even. It was the same tone Wylie had used as a kid when her parents erupted into an argument and her brothers tiptoed into her room. She knew it was difficult for him to keep a brave face, but he had to. Otherwise, the entire island would go into panic mode.

The leaves of the palm trees rustled as the rain started to pick up. It had been sprinkling all night, but right now the weather was the least of their worries. Joshua and Micah, both out of breath, landed in the middle of the Clearing.

"We found something," Micah confessed.

Phinn squeezed Wylie's hand as they followed her brothers through the dining room and into the kitchen, where Wylie and Lola spent their days laughing and arguing over cooking methods.

"There," Micah pointed.

Carved right into the wooden counter were the words HOPPER WAS HERE.

forbidden sides

fourteen days had gone by with no sign of Lola, and every inch of the island looked different to Wylie now. It didn't matter that the lagoon sparkled in the moonlight or that thanks to days of rain, the *parvaz* field was even more lush than usual. All that mattered was that Lola was gone, and no one knew if she was ever coming back. No more hushed late-night conversations about the mainland. No more strolls through the garden. No more recipes to taste-test and adjust accordingly.

The hours in the kitchen were the most agonizing part of Wylie's day. The island still needed to eat, and she was the obvious candidate to replace Lola as the resident chef. But feeding fifty people without any help proved exhausting. Wylie tried to honor her friend by making only the recipes Lola had taught her, but most were far too labor intensive and took double the time to cook by herself. So lately it was salads all day, every day. The vegetables in the garden were starting to wilt, and sometimes the chickens had to go without being fed, but it was inevitable that a few tasks would fall through the cracks. How had Lola ever done this alone?

"I can sand the wood down if you want," Bandit said, pointing to Hopper's carved inscription on the counter.

"No. Leave it. It's a good reminder," Wylie told him as she sliced open an avocado.

It was Phinn who had insisted on the bodyguards. He refused to leave Wylie alone in the same place Lola had been abducted from, so he recruited several of his strongest men to trade shifts in the kitchen. Bandit was her afternoon bodyguard and talked ad nauseam about how grateful he was to Phinn for bringing him to the island. Wylie tried to nod and smile and agree, but "grateful" was no longer a word she'd use to describe her state of mind. Her fingers grazed the letters.

Hopper was here. But how? Wylie kept thinking. How had he managed to enter the island and walk all the way to the kitchen without anyone seeing him? How was he able to kidnap Lola and drag her back to his boat without anyone hearing her scream or struggle?

"He's resourceful," Phinn said that night as they lay in his bed together. Wylie had practically moved into his bungalow. She couldn't bear to sleep at her own place next to Lola's unmade bed. It also made Wylie think about the three empty bedrooms in New York that would torment her parents for the rest of their lives.

"She told me she was going to see Maz. That was hours before the bell rang, and Maz said he hadn't seen her all day. Plus, I went to the kitchen right before the clinic. Lola wasn't there, and nothing was carved into that counter. The timeline just doesn't make sense to me."

"You didn't notice the carving, because you weren't looking for it. A lot of us searched the kitchen for Lola, remember? And your brothers were the first to see that Hopper had left his calling card."

The lack of emotion in Phinn's voice left Wylie troubled. He was either getting impatient with her, or he just didn't know how to comfort her anymore. Wylie knew that everyone grieved differently, but she couldn't help but wonder why he sounded so bored every time she mentioned Lola.

"You don't want to talk about this, do you?" she asked.

"No. I don't like to see you upset."

"But why aren't *you* more upset? Lola's one of your closest friends. A member of the inner circle. Maz's girlfriend. And yet you haven't had a single normal human reaction to what happened."

"That's not fair," Phinn said. Wylie could tell she'd offended him by the way he abruptly pulled away from her. "I don't have the luxury of losing it. I have to keep calm for the rest of the island. If anyone knew I was afraid or upset, it would be chaos."

"No one's here but us," Wylie pointed out.

"And you're upset and scared and I'm trying to be strong for you." Phinn moved back toward her. "Let's get some sleep." He gave her a kiss good night, but Wylie wasn't ready to go to sleep.

"What if she went to the Forbidden Side? She said there were herbs that grew over there that she missed cooking with. Maybe she crossed over and got trapped in some quicksand. Why can't we go look for her there?"

"Because Lola knew not to go near that place. Even Maz won't cross over, and no one loved Lola as much as he did."

Loved. Wylie had also overheard Maz use that word in the past tense a couple days before in the dining room: "I loved her so much." Like he knew she wasn't coming back.

"Generally when things like this happen on the mainland, the boyfriend or husband is responsible," Wylie said. "How do we know Maz didn't do something to her and he's trying to cover it up?"

"Wylie, don't take this the wrong way, but you sound like a crazy person. Last night, Bandit and Joshua had to wrestle Maz to the ground when he tried to sail away by himself to look for her. I have someone guarding the boats and his bungalow so he won't sneak off."

Wylie didn't blame Maz for taking matters into his own hands. Operation Hopper had only set sail a handful of times and so far, their search was fruitless.

Wylie had one other theory she couldn't mention to Phinn: that Lola had faked her disappearance and finally decided to find a way to the mainland. She could be on a plane right now to California or Texas. But Lola would never leave without Maz and couldn't make it off the island without a boat.

"Take the day off tomorrow," Phinn said. "I can find my way around a kitchen; I'll make food. Some of us put a memorial together down by the Clearing. It'll make you feel better to see it. For now, try to get some sleep."

Wylie closed her eyes and tried to slow down her thoughts. If only her parents were fighting in the next bungalow. Then she wouldn't have any trouble passing out. But all she heard were the quiet sounds of Phinn's breathing.

"Phinn?"

He didn't respond. He was already asleep.

+ + + + + + +

Charlotte, I miss your laugh and your weird sense of humor. The island hasn't been the same without you. Love, Elliot.

Danny, remember our morning flights through the parvaz field? I think about them often. I haven't been able to fly over there since you've been gone. I'll wait for you to get back and then we'll go again together. xoxo Helen.

Jersey, the band hates being short a bass player. We sound like crap without you. We will have a tropic jam session once you come home. Hopefully soon. Love you, goose. Yours, Bailey.

"I can't read all of these. It's too sad," Micah said. Dark circles had taken residence under his eyes, and Wylie could tell she wasn't the only one who wasn't sleeping much these days.

"I feel like we owe it to the missing kids to read them," Wylie replied. "But yeah, it's pretty heartbreaking."

During the hours Wylie had spent slaving away in the kitchen, the residents had erected a memorial for the lost kids. Phinn had discouraged it in the months right after the tragedy, worried it would feel too much like they were dead. But with Lola now gone, everyone agreed they needed an outlet for their pain. The memorial itself was constructed by stringing several yards of twine between two palm trees. Nadia had cut squares of cloth from leftover fabric, so that each of the residents could draw art or write messages on them, then hang them from the twine. It was strange to see all the names and personal jokes written to people Wylie had never met or known existed.

> *Lola, I miss your cooking. I miss how you were always kind to everyone. I even miss the way you were always late for everything. Maz is a wreck without you. You have to come back and put the poor guy out of his misery. Love, Aldo.*

Lola had only been missing a couple of weeks, and some of the tributes sounded like excerpts from a eulogy. The locals had known Lola for much longer than she had, but Wylie got the sense that they didn't know the real girl. She grabbed a piece of cloth and a Sharpie pen, but couldn't find the words to memorialize her best friend. Instead, she just wrote *Don't mess with Texas* and hung it up next to the other messages. Hopefully she wouldn't get in trouble for making a reference to the mainland, but ever since she and Lola had made their way through the cities in the Lone Star State, Lola liked to remind her not to mess with Texas right before they fell asleep.

"How are you doing?" Wylie asked Micah before he left.

Back in New York, the smallest mishap could raise his anxiety. "You look exhausted."

"Have you looked in a mirror lately? 'Cause you look like the walking dead."

"Geez. Thanks a lot."

"What I mean is, you don't have to worry about *me* so much," Micah replied.

"I'm your older sister—worrying about you is a job requirement."

"I know you, Wylie. A bunch of kids went missing. Lola's gone. Now you're worried the same thing could happen to one of us, and it would be all your fault for running off with Phinn and taking us to his boat."

"It *would* be my fault. I'll never forgive myself if anything happens to you guys."

Micah glanced up at the bungalows. "My life sucked before we came here. Back home, someone like Tinka wouldn't even try to get to know me." His face lit up when he mentioned her name. Wylie could tell that for him, this was not a fleeting romance.

"What's up with you two these days?" Wylie asked. "I haven't seen her around much."

Micah stuck his hands in his pockets. "She won't leave her bungalow. She won't even let me in. I leave her food and talk to her through the door to make sure she's okay. She said she's certain she's going to be Hopper's next victim and that he's 'going to come after her for what she did to him.'"

"What did she do to him?"

"She won't tell me. For a while, she slipped me notes under the door, because she was convinced someone was listening in on our conversations. Honestly, I'm worried she's losing her mind a little. She's got this weird theory. . . ." Micah looked around to make sure no one was eavesdropping.

"What theory?" Wylie asked.

Micah took a note out of his pocket and handed it to Wylie. On it were the words: *The Forbidden Side.*

"Flip it over," Micah directed.

The back of the note read: *That's where Hopper lives.*

"What does she mean Hopper lives on the Forbidden Side?" Wylie asked.

"I don't know. She won't say anything else about it. I showed it to Joshua, and he said she's being paranoid and that I shouldn't worry. He told me to only go to that part of the island if I had a death wish."

Wylie hadn't talked to Joshua much recently. When he'd learned Wylie had asked Phinn not to send him out on any of the search missions, he'd stormed into the kitchen and told his sister she had no business using her boyfriend against him. He could have shouted at her till every *parvaz* flower wilted and died, and she still wouldn't have backed down. Since the argument, Joshua had been keeping his distance. It didn't matter. She'd rather have him alive and angry than the alternative.

"If Tinka says anything else suspicious, let me know," she told Micah. "I can talk to Phinn and see if he can help her." She didn't want him to carry the burden of Tinka's questionable mental state on his own.

"That's the problem," Micah whispered. "She made me swear I wouldn't mention it to Phinn."

"She's lucky she has you to check on her," Wylie said with as much sympathy as she could muster.

"Someone has to," Micah replied as he walked away.

Wylie watched her brother make his way up the rickety stairs to the bungalows. She waited until he turned the corner and then she meandered past the small crowd that had gathered at the memorial. In two weeks, the only time she'd been alone was in the bathroom. She needed some air and to get away from all the heartbreaking sentiments hanging in the Clearing. Phinn would be furious if he found out she was wandering around alone, but she had her pepper spray and compass, and more than a few *parvaz* flowers in her pocket. She would probably need the entire supply for where she was going.

The weeds and brush had grown thick around the entrance to the Forbidden Side, making the caution tape and barbed wire almost unnecessary. Someone had covered up Hopper's calling card, but the layer of paint was starting to peel. No one had tended to the barricade, too afraid to get within inches of where a heinous crime might have been committed.

Wylie wasn't sure what exactly had brought her here, but her gut kept telling her that Lola was not snatched from the kitchen. The timeline didn't add up, and anyone could have carved "Hopper Was Here" into the counter. Even if she didn't find Lola, maybe there were some clues on the other side of the barbed wire that Phinn had overlooked.

I, Wylie Dalton, solemnly swear to abide by
all the rules presented to me in the Minor Island

Handbook. I understand I am not allowed to leave the island of my own accord. I will not cross over into the Forbidden Side. . . .

If the roles were reversed, Lola would cross over for me, Wylie thought. The fence was high, but with the help of a *parvaz* flower, anyone could easily hop it. Wylie slipped one into her mouth, chewed quickly, and took a deep breath as her feet floated above the ground.

From a bird's-eye view, palm trees and foliage obscured the Forbidden Side. If you were flying right above the island, you couldn't see into it at all. But as Wylie's body slowly rose above the fence she spied a patch of land not much bigger than the Clearing. She glimpsed what looked like a row of empty cages, but before she could maneuver past the barrier to get a closer look, a body crashed into her, knocking her straight to the ground.

"What are you doing?" Phinn asked frantically, pinning her down.

"Nothing!" Wylie responded, trying to catch her breath. "You scared the hell out of me."

"Don't lie to me, Wylie. Why were you over here?"

"I was looking for clues."

"It's off-limits."

"Why?"

"Because twelve people went missing on that side of the island!"

"Okay," Wylie said. "You didn't have to tackle me to the ground."

Phinn loosened his grip as they both stood up and dusted themselves off.

"I've told you over and over again it's dangerous, but you don't listen."

"I'm not going to give up on Lola!"

"Well, you're not going to find her here."

"Says the guy who's lied to me on more than one occasion," Wylie snapped.

"So that's what this is about." Phinn held her by the shoulders and looked straight into her eyes. "Listen to me. I am not lying to you right now. I love you. I would never do anything to hurt you."

Wylie let out a sigh and nodded.

"I'm sorry. I just feel so helpless. There's nothing I can do to bring Lola back."

"Well, you won't be able to find her if you get yourself killed in the process."

Together they walked back to the memorial. The Clearing was still filled with residents paying their respects to all the kids who had gone missing. The Youth Brigade was performing a new ballad they'd written as a tribute to their lost friends. Lola's disappearance had unearthed all the feelings they'd kept buried for the past few months. It was proof that what had happened to the lost kids wasn't an isolated incident. They were all still at risk, and at any point, one of them could be the next person to disappear.

Wylie didn't want to take part in the vigil at the moment. Aside from Lola, she didn't have personal experience with the friends they were mourning. She didn't want to pretend she understood the gravity of their pain. And part of her wanted to scream that throwing together a memorial and singing sad songs wasn't going to solve anything.

"I'm going to my room," Wylie told Phinn.

"I'll come with you."

"No. I'll be safe there. I want to be by myself."

The bungalow looked like a time capsule of happier times. Wylie had only been there once since Lola's disappearance, to gather some belongings. Maz, too fragile to comb through Lola's things, had also avoided it.

"Where are you, Loles?" Wylie asked the question out loud as she collapsed on her bed.

Wylie looked at Lola's messy ball of sheets. A few weeks before, they'd had a ridiculous argument over the fact that Lola never made her bed.

"What's the point if I'm just going to mess it up again tonight when I go to sleep? It's a waste of time."

"But it makes the room look nicer."

Wylie had taken to making both of their beds most mornings, because she couldn't live with the mess. Lola would usually fall asleep writing in her journal and the next day, Wylie would unearth it from the blankets and place it back under the mattress. She scanned the bed and spotted the leather binding peeking out from under the pillowcase. Wylie had never been tempted to snoop through it before. But as she grabbed the journal from under the pillow and held it in her hands, she contemplated whether or not to read it. Cracking it open would be a huge breach of privacy, but it seemed forgivable under the current circumstances.

A small laugh escaped her throat as she skimmed through

the notes Lola had taken during their late-night conversations. Sometimes when she could barely stay awake, she told Lola fake stories about the mainland to amuse herself. Thanks to Wylie, Lola now thought Beyoncé was the president of the United States and had won the election after a televised dance-off with her opponent, Taylor Swift. There were a few recipe ideas scribbled among the pages and a love note to Maz she'd never had a chance to give him. Wylie tore it out and stuck it in her pocket. Between the pages of notes and recipes were full-length diary entries. One of the earliest entries had Wylie's name in it:

> *I didn't think it was true, but I guess you can't put anything past Phinn these days. ~~He~~ brought new recruits. We all agreed we shouldn't bring any new people to the island until we found everyone who'd gone missing. Not like he's ever listened to what anyone's told him before. It's three siblings. The oldest is a girl named Wylie and it's so obvious he's interested in her. I can't figure it out, but something about the three of them feels different. Like he <u>really</u> wants to impress them and he's nervous they might not want to stay on the island. Phinn told me if they stick around, Wylie will be my roommate. Charlotte's only been gone for a few months. What's it going to look like when she comes back to Minor Island and all*

*of her stuff is gone and a new girl is living
with me? I am the worst friend in the
entire world.*

Wylie quickly placed a chair under the doorknob.
They didn't have any locks on their door and she didn't
want to run the risk of Phinn walking in on her while
she read the remaining entries. Some of them were just
passages about how much Lola loved Maz and what their
life together might look like if they ever lived on the
mainland. Wylie already felt conflicted about looking
through the journal, so she just scanned the entries for
one word: "Phinn."

*I never thought prom night would end
with us hiding in the panic room. Wylie
and I had slaved away in the kitchen for
hours. Everything was going great. I didn't
even really care when Phinn and Wylie
were crowned king and queen instead of
Maz and me. But then an explosion went
off and the girls all had to hide. No one
was hurt and no one went missing, but we
know it was a warning from ~~Hopper~~. ~~He's~~
going to come back again and we might
not be so lucky the next time. Everyone
trusts Phinn will keep us safe, but no one
ever talks about what he did to the lost
kids. ~~He's~~ to blame for what happened to
them. No one will say it, but it's the truth.*

He was awful to them. Charlotte didn't deserve to be treated that way. Neither did the others. Of course, I would never say anything like that out loud. He'd probably lock me up on the Forbidden Side and throw away the key.

The last entry was written just a week before Lola went missing:

I'm such an idiot. Wylie wanted to seal up the floorboards to the panic room and I said I would help her. Ugh. I know better. I just got swept up in the whole idea and I thought about how much Charlotte would have loved it, too. I should have talked her out of it and instead I helped her rally all the girls. Who knows? Maybe I secretly want to be exiled. Anyway, Phinn walked in on us hammering at the basement door and he completely lost it. He even yelled at Wylie, so I told him it was all my idea. I'm not going to lose another friend because of him. Maz was so mad at me afterward. I think he was just afraid for me. And I don't blame him. I guess I'm afraid for me too. Maybe if I cook Phinn some chipney-onion cakes for dinner, he'll forgive me. Yeah, right. He doesn't forgive anyone.

Wylie thought back to when Lola made her swear not to tell Phinn of their late-night discussions about the mainland. Even then, Lola sounded like she was afraid of Phinn, and now the journal confirmed it. She tore out a few blank pages and slipped the diary under the mattress. She placed a pen in her back pocket, moved the chair from under the knob, and walked out the door with purpose. Once she'd arrived at her destination, she pounded on the bungalow door with both fists.

"Tinka!" she called. "Let me in!"

"Go away!" Tinka shouted back.

"Not until you open the door!" Wylie was prepared to knock and yell until her knuckles bled and her voice gave out.

"I haven't let anyone in here for almost a week. Why would I make an exception for you, of all people?"

"Because it's important."

"Not to me."

Wylie used her pen and scribbled *I think Phinn is hiding something* on a piece of paper. She slipped it under Tinka's door and finally heard some movement. The door opened a crack and Tinka pressed her face against the small opening. She crumpled the paper into a ball, placed it inside her mouth, and spit it out at Wylie.

"This is me not giving a shit," she replied.

Just as she moved to close the door, Wylie placed her foot in the frame and pushed it all the way open. It slammed behind her as she barged into the room.

"Get out!" Tinka shrieked.

The stale air hit Wylie's nostrils and she nearly gagged. If this was payback for the time Wylie had breathed into Tinka's face, it was quite the revenge. The bedroom was messier than normal, with art supplies and plates of food strewn around the floor. From the look of Tinka's greasy hair, Wylie could tell it had been days since she'd showered.

"What?" Tinka asked nonchalantly.

"It's just a little stuffy in here, that's all."

"You don't say. I'll crack open a window."

Tinka pulled the curtains aside and a cool breeze helped fumigate the room as she opened the window.

"You haven't left your room in seven days?" Wylie asked.

"I've left to use the toilet. Micah's been bringing me food. I can tell Lola's still missing from the lackluster meals."

It was typical of Tinka to get in a dig, but Wylie wouldn't take the bait.

"What are you hiding from?"

"Oh, I don't know. A psychopath who's been kidnapping people from the island. I'd say that's a pretty solid reason to stay inside and sleep with a knife under my pillow. It doesn't sound like I've missed much, aside from a few vigils and some sappy Youth Brigade songs. Those guys are really losing their touch. Now, if you don't mind, I need to get back to lying in bed and being dead to the world."

"Do you really think I would be here unless it was absolutely necessary?"

"Right, it's absolutely necessary because Phinn is hiding something. Phinn is *always* hiding something. It's who he is. I've learned not to question it."

"Lola was afraid of him, did you know that?"

Tinka shrugged. "No, but what does that matter?"

"I don't know. Maybe Hopper didn't have anything to do with her disappearance."

"I know she was your friend, but you're living in a fantasy world. That's precisely what happened."

"Do you know why Phinn brought me and my brothers here?"

Tinka lit a stick of incense and held it between two fingers like a cigarette. "I'm bored with this conversation. If you're having doubts about your boyfriend, his ex isn't exactly the person you should be talking to."

"His *ex*?" Wylie said, letting out a snort. "Phinn says you're like a little sister to him. He said it's been years since anything happened between you guys."

"He said that?" Tinka replied, raising an eyebrow. "Wow. So then, he didn't tell you that I spent the night with him two days before he brought you to the island?"

"You're making that up," Wylie blurted defensively.

"I wish I was."

Tinka had every reason in the world to lie. And after a week of being cooped up in her room, she was probably in desperate need of a little entertainment. But there was no way Wylie would let herself get derailed by jealousy.

"Whatever happened between you and Phinn before I came here is your business," Wylie replied stoically. "The only thing I care about right now is whether Phinn's hiding something about the lost kids. Did he do something to Charlotte before she disappeared?"

"I'm not at liberty to speak about that."

"I'll take that as a yes. Lola wrote in her journal that it was his fault they all went missing."

"You read Lola's diary? That's an elder move."

"I was looking for clues."

"Aww, cute. You're like a detective now."

"I need to know what else he's hiding."

"Why? Why do you care?"

"Because . . ." Wylie wasn't sure how to answer the question.

"I'm waiting."

Wylie's silence whipped Tinka into action. She slammed the window shut and closed the curtains. She put out the stick of incense and crawled into the bed, pulling the covers over her. After letting out a dramatic yawn, she closed her eyes and pretended to snore.

"Because I want to know who I'm in love with," Wylie finally admitted. Tinka opened her eyes.

"No, you don't. Trust me. I don't know why Phinn brought you and your brothers here, but ignorance is bliss, Wylie. If I were you, I'd leave here right now and go back to your bungalow and forget about what you read in Lola's little diary. She was always too introspective for my taste anyway."

Wylie glanced around the bedroom. Some of the walls were now covered in Micah's artwork. He'd drawn a gorgeous portrait of Tinka wading in the lagoon, but his interpretation of her was much more delicate than the tough and abrasive girl Wylie had come to know. And then Wylie saw it again: the photograph of Tinka and Phinn from prom night. Tinka had taken it from the dining room and placed it right next to her bed. Except now, she spotted something she hadn't noticed the first time she looked at the picture. Tinka's chest was adorned with a small antique hand mirror hanging from a silver chain. The same necklace Wylie was wearing right now.

"What did he say to you right before that photo was taken?" Wylie asked.

Tinka shrugged. "I don't remember."

"Sure you do. What did he say to you?"

Tinka looked away. "He said that I was beyond—"

"—compare," Wylie finished her sentence. "I guess he says that to all the girls."

"Why did you come here? To break my heart all over again?"

"I came here because I didn't have anyone else to go to." Wylie paused for a moment, then pointed at Micah's drawing.

"It's really beautiful, the way he sees you," she said. "I know he doesn't see anyone else that same way."

Tinka didn't respond. She wiped the corners of her eyes, grabbed the knife from under her pillow, sat up, and put on a pair of beat-up sneakers.

"Fine. You asked for it. You want to know the truth? Come with me."

sketch artist

wylie nearly had to jog to keep up with Tinka as they trekked through the *parvaz* field, moved around the perimeter of the island, then made a sharp right turn that led them to another trail. The ground was muddy and slippery from the recent rain and Wylie wished she'd brought her galoshes to the island.

"Why can't we take a *parvaz*?" Wylie asked. "We'll get there so much faster if we fly."

"I can't touch that stuff anymore," Tinka reminded her.

"Right, sorry."

"And anyway, we can't risk anyone seeing us, so stop complaining. I'm armed and dangerous," Tinka replied.

Tinka may have brought along the knife as a weapon, but the deeper they moved into the trail, the more she needed it to clear sharp branches and leaves out of their way. Wylie, winded, tried to catch her breath. She'd been wrong to think flying actually counted as a form of exercise. After all this was over, she'd start a workout regimen that did not include mixing basketball with *parvaz*. She referred to her compass throughout the hike, but keeping track of every direction they moved in had quickly become out of the question.

"Are you just taking me to some quiet and secluded place so you can murder me?" Wylie asked, trying to lighten the mood.

"Nah. You're not worth getting exiled for."

Wylie's shoe caught on a rock, which flung her forward and onto the ground. She landed with a thud and let out a small cry. She half expected Tinka to keep walking, but she actually turned around to check on her.

"You okay?" Tinka asked, offering a hand.

Wylie grabbed Tinka's hand and she pulled her up. Mud was caked in Wylie's hair and all over her clothes.

"I'm fine."

They continued to hike to their mystery destination. As the minutes ticked by, Tinka started humming quietly to herself. Wylie had to listen closely to place the melody. It was the song "I Am a Rock" by Simon and Garfunkel. When she was growing up, her dad used to sing it to her and her brothers when they couldn't fall asleep.

"Did Micah teach you that song?" Wylie asked.

Tinka shook her head. "No."

The trail finally came to a dead end, blocked off by trees and thick ivy. Wylie had lost all sense of direction and wasn't sure what part of the island they were even on. If Tinka abandoned her, Wylie would have no idea how to find her way home.

"Wait here for a minute," Tinka directed. "I want to make sure no one else is around."

She pushed her hands into the ivy and pulled it apart, peeking through the other side.

"We're good. Squeeze in."

It was easier for Tinka to fit her compact body through the plants. She stood on the other side of the blockade and helped Wylie through, but the vines and branches still scratched at her face and skin. On the other side of the shrubbery, they found a lone bungalow. It was made of logs and looked far more secure than the rooms they bunked in. There were no windows or doors.

"Where are we?" Wylie asked.

"Phinn's man cave or secret lair. I prefer 'secret lair.' It's way more badass," Tinka said. "Don't worry. Only a few people know about it."

"Has he brought you here before?"

Tinka let out a laugh. "Once. But you don't want to know what we did inside. He's never brought me back, though."

"How on earth did you remember how to get here?"

"Being a borderline obsessive stalker comes with its advantages."

Tinka walked up to the bungalow and felt around the logs. There was no discernible entrance. She leaned her body against a wall, but nothing budged.

"I've never tried to get in before," she admitted.

"Then how do you know for sure there's anything secret in here?"

"It's in the middle of nowhere on an island that's already in the middle of nowhere. It has no windows or doors. I can assure you, he doesn't store party supplies in here."

"Why haven't you ever gone in to snoop before?"

Tinka fumbled over a loose log. She pushed it forward and a small door opened into a pitch-black room.

"If Phinn ever found out I was in here, he'd probably never forgive me. Are you coming?" she asked as she tiptoed inside.

Go in there, Wylie told herself. *Do it for Lola. Do it for your brothers. Who cares if Phinn never forgives you?* She stepped inside and the door instantly shut behind them, leaving them in the dark. Tinka struck a match and used the flame to light a nearby kerosene lamp. The cavelike space was circular in shape with a small table at its center, surrounded by stools. A map of the island was on the wall, and curtains had been hung to block out any cracks between the logs. Wylie spied wooden file cabinets and a stack of newspapers from the mainland. The one on top was from February, the day she and Phinn had met.

Tinka pulled at a file cabinet, but it was locked.

"Typical Phinn. Always so paranoid."

She tried to pick the lock with her knife, but it wouldn't budge.

"Are you going to help me find a key or what?" she asked Wylie.

"Forget it. Let's go," Wylie said. "So he's got a place where he conducts business. I was stupid to think he was hiding anything. Sorry I made you drag me all the way out here."

"I think you're just afraid," Tinka said with a trace of kindness.

"Of what?"

"Of what you might find in here. And what it might mean."

"I'm not afraid," Wylie insisted. "We can snoop if you want, but it'll just be a waste of time."

It only took a few minutes for them to locate the set of keys that opened all the locks. Tinka found them stuck under the table. Figuring out which key belonged to which lock was a much more excruciating process. When they finally unlocked the first file cabinet, they gave each other a spontaneous high five.

"Finally!" Tinka cheered.

"Okay, before we look inside," Wylie said, "I think we should make a pact. If we don't find anything suspicious, then Phinn never has to know either one of us was in here. It stays between us. Agreed?"

"Agreed."

"You weren't crossing your fingers, were you?" Wylie asked.

Tinka placed her palms out in front of her.

"Nope."

Wylie opened the drawer and found it filled to the brim with cell phones. Her phone rested on top of the pile. Wylie wished the battery wasn't dead so she could turn it on. She wondered why Phinn didn't let them at least use the cameras on their phones. Maybe he would reconsider once they ran out of Polaroid film. Underneath the Daltons' phones, the cell phone technology quickly devolved into the past. Wylie spotted a few flip phones and one brick phone that looked larger than her head.

"This one's Micah's, isn't it?" Tinka asked, pulling out a more recent phone in a skull-and-crossbones case.

"Yup," Wylie answered, a shiver going down her spine. She couldn't help thinking how often her parents had tried to call or text since they'd gone missing.

"I wish I could take it to him. He misses it so much," Tinka said.

"We can't steal anything. It'll give us away."

Tinka reluctantly tossed the phone back in the drawer.

Some of the other drawers were filled with more out-dated gadgets from the mainland: a Game Boy, a Discman, even a bulky old laptop. Phinn had kept organized files on each of his recruits with the dates he'd brought them to the island, along with their medical records and other tidbits of information he'd kept track of. Wylie was surprised to see up-to-date notes on where all of their families currently lived. Phinn must have carved out time for research on his trips to the mainland.

"Wow," Tinka said. She slid Bailey's folder over to Wylie. It included a printout of an obituary. Her mother had died of cancer ten years prior.

"Do you think she knows?" Wylie asked.

Tinka shook her head. "I don't think she'd want to know."

They'd been poring over the files for at least an hour, and they still needed enough time to get back to the clinic for their daily birth control. Ever since Tinka had become a recluse, Patrick and Aldo had started making house calls to give her the Pill.

"It's not the first time I've refused to leave my bungalow for days at a time," Tinka confessed.

Wylie took great care in putting the files back exactly as they had found them. Phinn was meticulous enough that if one piece of paper was out of place or if one file wasn't in alphabetical order, he'd know someone had been going through his drawers. Though Wylie was disappointed not to find any clues concerning Lola's disappearance, she also felt a sense of relief as they stuck the keys back under the table. Nothing they had found was all that shocking or unforgivable. Phinn was simply running a very tight ship.

But just as they pressed against the logs to find their way out, Wylie glimpsed a tiny scrap of paper peeking out from behind one of the curtains. She pulled the curtain open and discovered a bulletin board covered in article clippings about the Daltons. Most of them were about the accident they'd had in the Hamptons. Tinka stood next to her and examined the collage.

"Oh my God," she blurted. "I know why Phinn brought you to the island."

＋ ＋ ＋ ＋ ＋ ＋ ＋

MAURA'S HAIR SMELLED DIFFERENT. SHE MUST HAVE changed her shampoo since Gregory had moved out. He tried not to inhale too deeply as they held on to each other. They hadn't touched one another in months, and he didn't want to do anything that would make her break the embrace. The closeness felt new and familiar all at the same time, and he didn't want to let go.

Gregory had fantasized about this moment, but he'd thought it would occur under happier circumstances. The police would call and tell them they'd found their children safe and sound. Gregory would hang up the phone, announce the good news to Maura, and she would throw her arms around him. Instead, the call Gregory had received that morning was to inform them that the police were officially putting an end to their search. He had waited all day to tell Maura, but he couldn't put it off any longer.

"How could they do this to us?" Maura cried in his arms.

"It's going to be okay. This doesn't mean we have to stop looking. We'll hold another press conference."

"We're never going to see them again, are we?" Maura asked him.

Neither of them had ever said it out loud, even though they'd both been tortured by the possibility.

"Don't think that way," he whispered. "We're going to get our kids back, safe and sound. That is one promise I will never go back on."

A knock on the door forced them out of the embrace. Maura reached for a box of tissues and wiped at her eyes as Gregory checked the peephole. He opened the door to a tearful Vanessa.

"Hi, Mr. Dalton," she said.

Gregory let her in and Maura poured her a glass of water.

"I just heard the news. I'm so sorry," Vanessa told them.

"We all are," Maura replied gently.

"No." Vanessa shook her head. "This is all my fault. I didn't tell the cops everything I knew. I thought I was protecting Wylie. . . . It's stupid, but I thought if she didn't want to be found, then I had to respect that. But I never expected her to be gone for so long. . . ."

Gregory froze. "What are you telling us?"

"I saw her leave the party with someone. A guy. Not anyone who went to our school. I'd never seen him before."

Gregory and Maura looked at each other. It was the only piece of new information they'd received in weeks. Vanessa was clearly in a fragile state, and if they didn't tread lightly, she might fall to pieces and refuse to help them.

"Do you remember what he looked like?" Gregory asked.

Vanessa nodded.

"Would you be willing to describe him to the police?"

"Yes."

Gregory praised Vanessa for her courage, but he wanted to scream at her for withholding information from them for so long. They took a taxi to the police station and this time, the wait to speak with an officer was much shorter than the day they'd reported the kids missing. Gregory and Maura held hands while Vanessa gave her description to the sketch artist. The sound of the pencil scratching the page made every hair on Gregory's arms stand upright as he listened to Vanessa describe the guy. Tan, sandy-colored skin. Auburn hair with hazel eyes. A scar above his eyebrow. An oval-shaped face. A strong chin with stubble on it. Slightly crooked teeth. A few freckles along his nose. *Gorgeous*, she emphasized. About five feet eleven inches. Lean but toned.

"How old would you say he looked?" one of the cops asked.

"He acted like a college kid, but he only looked about seventeen."

The police officers looked over the sketch and nodded.

242 ⌒ Sara Saedi

They told the Daltons they would run it through their database to see if it matched anyone with a criminal record.

"We might already have the guy in custody for something else," the police officer explained.

Vanessa was the next person to look at the sketch.

"That looks just like him," she proclaimed.

Maura looked at the picture and shuddered, then passed it to Gregory. He looked at the image staring back at him.

No.

That day in the police station, they'd asked him: *Do either of you have any enemies?*

"Do you recognize this man?" the police officer asked them.

Maura shook her head. Gregory couldn't move.

"Mr. Dalton? Do you recognize him?"

"I've never seen him before in my life."

It took another hour for Gregory to get Maura home and wait for her to take a sleeping pill so she could get some rest. As soon as she drifted off, he bolted out of the house and hailed a cab.

The workday was coming to an end, but there were still some employees lingering in their offices and cubicles. As he ran down the hallway, everyone pretended to shift their attention back to their computer screens. Shannon called out his name, but he kept running.

He shut the door behind him as he entered his office, then upended his penholder on the desk. A key fell out that he used to unlock the bottom drawer on his file cabinet. Gregory pushed the files all the way to the back of the drawer, revealing a small wooden box that lay underneath them.

He carefully took the box out of the drawer and opened it. Inside was a small pile of tattered Polaroids. All he had to do was look at the images and he was flooded with memories. The warm temperature of the water in the Clearing. The yellow ladybugs. The *pop-pop* sound of the *parvaz* flowers. The last time he'd looked at the photos was after Joshua's accident. For a brief period, Gregory had actually debated sending Joshua away to the island. It was always in his worst moments that he was gripped by nostalgia for his old life.

He sifted through the photos until he landed on one from his last few days on the island. Lola had taken the picture, and Maz and Tinka were in it. Gregory was in the middle, right next to Phinn, who still looked exactly like the person in the police sketch.

Attached to one of the photos, Gregory found a folded piece of paper. The ink was faded, but he could still make out a map of the island, along with its coordinates. Tinka had slipped it to him in case he ever changed his mind and wanted to return.

If you leave, I will find a way to make you regret it, Phinn had snarled at Gregory the day he'd announced his departure.

Tears began streaming down his face. Maura had been right to suspect all of this was his fault. Phinn had made good on his promise. He had gotten his revenge. He had taken Gregory's children from him.

hostages

"that's Gregory," Tinka said.

When Wylie swept the curtain aside and discovered a wall devoted to her family, she assumed Phinn had been keeping tabs on them after Joshua's accident. He'd admitted to her that night in Brooklyn that he knew about the accident, and maybe he never let on just how closely he'd followed it or how long he had planned to rescue them. But Tinka was pointing to the photo of Wylie's dad from his wedding day.

"Yeah," Wylie replied slowly. "Has Micah told you about our parents?"

"Gregory is your dad," Tinka responded.

"I know, it's weird. Why would Phinn do this much research on someone's parents before he brought them here?"

"You're not understanding. Your dad *lived* here."

Wylie laughed. "Nice try, Tinka, but I'm not falling for that."

"I'm not making this up." Her hand lingered on the photo. "Gregory. Sweet, lovely Gregory. Stubborn as hell and loyal to a fault."

"My dad's from upstate New York."

"No, Wylie. He was one of the kids brought over with the rest of us. Your dad grew up right here on the island. His last name wasn't Dalton then. I guess he made that name up, hoping Phinn would never find him."

Wylie had only witnessed her father cry once. It had been during a family trip upstate, to where he said he'd been raised. They'd parked the car in front of a small house on a street lined with maple trees, and her dad announced they were looking at his childhood home. Wylie remembered how his voice had quivered and his eyes had welled up when he'd looked at the small white Victorian with a wraparound porch and a bright red door. She'd thought the tears were for her grandparents, who had died in a car accident long before Wylie was born.

But none of that had been true.

A sharp pain flooded Wylie's skull. The room appeared to be spinning. Her legs suddenly felt like wet noodles as they wobbled beneath her. Tinka pulled out a stool.

"You should sit down."

Wylie eased herself onto it. "I think I'm going to be sick," she announced.

"Just put your head between your legs for a minute. You'll feel better." Tinka rubbed Wylie's back as she knelt down to stop herself from passing out.

The printouts dated all the way back to the mid-nineties. There were articles on Gregory from the *Fordham Observer*, the paper at his alma mater, reporting on his internship at a prestigious bank. There was a faded wedding announcement for Gregory and Maura in the *New York Times*. Wylie had been just a kid when her dad was featured in *Forbes Magazine,* but the interview was pinned to the wall. And then the focus of the articles shifted from Wylie's dad to his children. They were mostly fluff pieces from their high school paper: an article on Joshua's campaign for class president, another about Wylie's cooking channel on YouTube, and a few comic strips created by Micah, followed by a series of articles from real publications on Joshua's trial.

"Even if he was a hundred years old, I would still recognize him," Tinka said, pointing to a photo of her dad on the wall. "Your brothers don't look anything like him."

"They look more like my mom. He and Joshua share a lot of facial expressions and gestures, but you'd have to spend a lot of time with both of them to notice. People say I'm the perfect combination of both my parents."

The aching in Wylie's head only got worse as she watched Tinka skim through the clippings, but she didn't feel like she was going to faint anymore. She sat up straight and let out a shaky exhale.

"Go ahead," Wylie said to Tinka. "Tell me everything. Don't leave anything out."

"Your father is the only person who's ever broken Phinn's heart."

Wylie did her best to listen as Tinka recounted an entire history about her dad that was not the one she'd been told her whole life. Gregory's parents may have lived upstate at some point, but his dad (also known as Wylie's grandfather) was drafted to Vietnam and refused to go to war. Tinka explained that Phinn's parents and several other couples sailed away together to dodge the draft. It was the same story Phinn had told Wylie and her brothers their very first night on the island. But Phinn had left out one tiny detail: Wylie's grandparents and father were among the families on that boat. Gregory and Phinn were the two oldest kids making the journey, and according to Tinka, they were as close as brothers. Gregory looked up to Phinn, especially once their parents died and the kids were left to fend for themselves. Wylie's grandparents weren't killed in a car crash. They died on the island. Wylie was too afraid to ask how.

"Your dad never questioned Phinn. Gregory had complete faith in every decision Phinn made for the rest of us," Tinka explained. "It was actually kind of like the dynamic between Phinn and Joshua now."

"So what happened?" Wylie asked. She wondered what her dad had done to get himself exiled.

"What happened is what always happens. A girl got between them." Tinka seemed to shake off a memory as she drew the curtain closed.

"Who?"

Tinka covered her face with her hands. "Me."

Wylie gripped her stomach, then placed her head back between her legs. It would be a miracle if she got through this conversation without puking or fainting. She took a deep inhale through her nose and breathed out through her mouth.

"You dated *my dad*." A part of her wished she'd never set foot in this bungalow and could have remained in a state of blissful ignorance.

"Oh, God. Micah's never going to look at me the same way again, is he?" Tinka asked, her voice going up an octave.

"I don't know. This changes everything."

"I hate Phinn," Tinka mumbled, her tone cold. "How could he do this?"

"Finish the story," Wylie said. She didn't have it in her to cry or scream or throw things. All she felt now was numb.

Tinka collected herself, then continued. "Gregory was the smart choice and Phinn wasn't. Believe me, I've tried to turn off my feelings for Phinn for years. And for a while, it was working. I was happy with someone else. Phinn had made it clear he only wanted a friendship with me, so I moved on. But he didn't like that either. It was okay for him to not want me, but it wasn't okay for me to stop wanting him. So one night, I was supposed to camp out in the *parvaz* field with Gregory, but Phinn convinced me to go to the beach with him. He brought a bottle of wine he'd smuggled from the mainland. He seemed so interested in me. I kept thinking, I need to leave to meet Gregory, but one thing led to another and I stayed. And your—Gregory found us. I'll never forget the look on his face. He was devastated."

There were no baby pictures of her dad. The only photos she'd ever seen of him were from his college years. He'd told them a flood in the basement had destroyed all his childhood photographs.

Tinka continued. "Gregory knew the only way he could

hurt Phinn as badly as he had been hurt was by leaving.
So that's what he did. He's the only person who's ever left
the island without being forced to. Phinn was furious. He
promised that one day he'd get his revenge."

"And that's what I am? Revenge?"

Keg stands at the party in the Hamptons. Flying around
New York with some mysterious stranger. Convincing her
brothers they'd be far better off living on some twisted island. Wylie had to find a way to right her wrongs. She
would get her brothers, and they would go home.

"Look. It doesn't always matter *why* he brings people
here," Tinka said, trying to soften the blow. "For all its
problems, it's still the most amazing place you'll ever live. I
bet there hasn't been a day since he left that Gregory hasn't
missed it."

Wylie couldn't picture a younger version of her dad living here. What was he like when he was her age? Did he
spend his days whizzing above the island? Had they both
jumped off the same waterfall and swum in the same lagoon? Did he like to dig his heels into the same warm sands?

"Everything he told me was a lie." It wasn't until after
the words came out that she realized she wasn't sure if she
was referring to Phinn or her father.

"He loves you," Tinka conceded. "I don't think that was
part of the act."

"I don't care," Wylie answered.

The warning bell rang. The sound was faint from inside
the secret bungalow, but they both heard it.

"We have fifteen minutes to get to the clinic. We'd better
hurry," Tinka said, defeated.

"Screw that," Wylie replied, feeling around the walls for the hidden door. "I am done following Phinn's rules."

With the fear of Hopper looming over their heads, Wylie had made a habit of traveling with *parvaz* flowers in her pocket, in case she needed to take a quick flight. The ones she'd been carrying for the past couple of days had started to wilt.

Wylie didn't want Tinka to relapse on *parvaz*, but they couldn't lose time hiking back to the Clearing.

"Put your arms around my neck and I'll fly us both there," Wylie ordered.

Tinka bit her lip and rolled her eyes, but did as she was told.

The sight of Wylie landing in the Clearing with Tinka on her back was enough to grab everyone's attention. There were remnants of dried mud in Wylie's hair and in her clothes, making her look just as crazed on the outside as she was feeling on the inside. Some of the girls had already headed to the clinic, but most of the locals were scattered around the lagoon. *Good*, Wylie thought. She wanted everyone to witness what was about to happen. Micah was the most surprised to see Tinka out of her bungalow and with his sister. Joshua didn't bother to acknowledge them, still upset with Wylie for interfering in his work life.

"What's going on here?" Phinn asked, even more chipper than usual.

He looked so different to Wylie now. The mouth full of crooked teeth she'd once found endearing now seemed almost repulsive. His auburn locks seemed dirty and rusted.

And his chin with its little bits of red stubble looked like a sad version of a child trying to grow a beard. Tinka's warning echoed through her head on repeat. *Be careful*, she had said. *He has the power to destroy you.*

Only if I let him, Wylie thought.

She walked up to Phinn. "I know the truth," she said flatly.

"About what?" he asked, still smiling.

"About why you brought me here." She placed her hands on his chest and shoved him against a tree.

Phinn's fan club gasped and shrieked on his behalf. Joshua didn't drag her away this time or ask her what the hell she was doing. He just shook his head disapprovingly, as if to say, *Typical Wylie*. She expected Phinn to go into a rage or maybe even shove her back, but he just looked at her like a wounded bird.

"I was revenge," she said, her voice controlled. She wanted so badly to get through this without crying.

"What?" Phinn asked.

"I was revenge," she said, louder this time. "And so were my brothers. You tricked all three of us." She turned from him to address the crowd. "I know you were all wondering why Phinn brought us here. Why did he like me so much? Why did he make my brother, a guy he barely even knew, his chief of staff? I finally know the truth."

"Wylie," Phinn interrupted. "Please, it's not what you think. Whatever Tinka told you, she's making it up. She'll do anything to get between us."

"I had nothing to do with it," Tinka chimed in.

"How many of you knew Gregory?" Wylie addressed the crowd. "How many of you remember when he left the island?"

About half the crowd raised their hands.

"And how many of you have heard of him? The one guy who left of his own accord?"

All of the hands went up in the air. Joshua and Micah looked at their sister, not exactly sure what she was saying.

"Gregory is my dad. Our dad," Wylie said. She turned to her brothers. "This was Phinn's plan all along. My dad used to live here, but he abandoned the island, and Phinn brought us here to get his revenge."

"That's not true. She's lying," Phinn insisted.

"Phinn," Wylie said. "You kidnapped us. You brought us here under false pretenses. You lied to us the entire time. But it stops now. We want to go home."

They would go back to New York, and Wylie would break the ultimate rule. She would alert the authorities about the island and the sociopath who was stealing runaways and at-risk kids from the mainland and bringing them here. They'd send a real army to the island and find Lola and the other lost kids.

"You can't make that decision for all of us," Joshua intervened.

"What are you talking about?" Wylie asked. "There is no decision. We're leaving."

"I'm not going back," Joshua replied.

"Did you not hear anything I just said? Phinn only brought us here to mess with our parents. It's my fault we came here, but I'm getting us home. Nothing Phinn's ever done or said has meant anything."

"You don't believe that, Wylie," Phinn said calmly.

Wylie looked around the Clearing as the locals started closing in on her. No one cared about what they had just heard about Phinn. They glared at her without sympathy or remorse.

"I don't care why Phinn brought us here," Joshua said. "I'm not leaving."

"It doesn't have to be like this," Phinn said as he took a step closer to Wylie. "Listen to your brother."

"Let us go home," Wylie begged.

"Take them to the Forbidden Side," Phinn ordered. "*All* of them."

The residents leapt into action as they surrounded Wylie and her brothers. Nadia and Bailey grabbed Wylie's arms. She was strong, but Wylie couldn't fight off both of them. Maz and Bandit grabbed Joshua, while Elliot and Doug held Micah down. Tinka skipped to the palm tree, opened the cupboard, and pulled out a coil of rope. She used her knife to cut it into three equal pieces.

"Why are you doing this?" Micah asked Tinka as she restrained his hands with the rope.

"I'm just following orders," Tinka replied casually. She moved on to Wylie and tied the rope tightly around her wrists.

"Tough break, Wylie," Tinka said with a wink as she patted her down. She was so busy gloating, she managed to miss the pepper spray and the compass in Wylie's pockets.

"He's all yours now," Wylie snapped. "The two of you deserve each other."

The walk to the Forbidden Side felt like it took an eternity. Phinn led the way and Wylie stared at the back of his head. He kept looking over his shoulder to see if she was okay, just like he had on the day he brought them to the island, but she refused to make eye contact. Instead, she kept her head down and caught sight of the mirror dangling from her neck. She felt silly now, for having felt so honored to wear it.

"I don't want to go to the Forbidden Side," Micah kept saying over and over again. He wheezed between breaths, in the throes of an anxiety attack. But Joshua was the one who talked the most. He begged and pleaded with Phinn to show them some mercy.

"You don't have to do this," he said. "Give me five minutes with my sister. I'll calm her down. I'll convince her not to go home. Please. We'll die over there." Phinn ignored him.

Once they reached the Forbidden Side, Tinka used her knife to cut through the caution tape and the weeds that had grown around the barricade. Phinn grabbed a key out of his pocket and unlocked the fence.

It was darker on this side of the island, with most of the overgrown trees blocking out the blue sky. It was hard to tell what time of day it was. The stench of urine made Wylie wish her hands were free so she could plug her nose. Small patches of sand were cordoned off and the cages Wylie had spotted from above the gate looked much larger up close. Each was big enough for a human being to fit snugly inside. She glanced around and found Hopper's bloody and faded calling card on a giant wooden box. Because she'd stared at the inscription in the kitchen countertop for hours, she could swear this one was in a different handwriting. Phinn opened the doors to the box, revealing whips and handcuffs and more rope.

There was a reason the Forbidden Side was off-limits. It wasn't the quicksand or land mines or the threat of Hopper. It was the fact that this place was being used as a prison camp.

"Don't put them next to each other." As soon as Phinn made the order, Wylie and her brothers were flung into separate cages and the ropes were replaced with handcuffs. At least five cells separated Wylie from Micah, while Joshua was placed in a cell about a hundred feet across from them.

"I'm sorry," Nadia mumbled quietly in Wylie's ear. She unlocked one of the cuffs from Wylie's wrist and clasped it around the wire framing.

"Maz," Phinn said, "We'll need a guard schedule again for the fence. I want two people here at all times to make sure they don't get away. I'll take the first shift. You're all dismissed."

Tinka gave Wylie a little wave good-bye as she skipped off. She didn't acknowledge Micah at all. Once they were alone, Phinn crouched down next to Wylie's cage.

"I never wanted this to happen," he told her.

"How can I even believe that?" she spat. "*Everything* you've told me from day one was a lie!"

"Not everything. I love you, Wylie."

Wylie let out a laugh. "The only person you love is yourself."

Puddles formed in Phinn's eyes. "That's not true. No,

it wasn't an accident that we met. Yes, I was planning for a very long time to bring you here. But I never, ever planned to feel the way I feel about you."

The memory of locking eyes on the rooftop in Brooklyn would no longer fill her mind with silly words like "destiny" and "soul mates." It had all been premeditated and carefully planned out.

"I love you," he said again.

"You only brought me here to hurt my dad!" Wylie yelled.

"The second we spoke to each other, I knew I was going to fall for you, and it changed everything."

"You lied to me over and over again."

"People lie to each other all the time, Wylie. It's what human beings do. They lie until they think it's safe to be honest."

"That doesn't make it right." When her parents had started dating, Wylie's mom pretended to like oysters for months, because they were one of her dad's favorite foods. Those were the kinds of lies normal people told each other, but Phinn's indiscretion was in a category of its own.

"I'm sorry I brought you here to hurt your dad, but you stayed because you wanted to hurt him, too."

"What the hell is that supposed to mean?"

"You and I have something in common. Gregory Dalton left us both." Phinn was crying now. Seeing him in tears brought up emotions for him Wylie didn't want to have: sympathy, longing, compassion.

"What's your point, Phinn? We're both equally terrible people?"

"We're not terrible, but we lash out when people hurt us. I know I deserve it, but after everything we've gone through together, it hurts that you want to leave. It hurts to know you're okay with never seeing me again."

Wylie could lie to him like he'd lied to her all this time. She could pretend she really was okay with never seeing him again. But the fact was, she didn't know what it would feel like to go on without him.

"I don't know if I'm okay with never seeing you again." It was the most honest response she could give.

"Then I want you to know that I'm happy your dad left the island," Phinn confessed. "If he hadn't left, then you wouldn't exist. You're the best thing that's ever happened to me, Wylie."

Wylie clanked her handcuff against the cell. "You have a funny way of showing it."

Their time on the island kept rotating through Wylie's head on an endless loop. Their first kiss in the *parvaz* field. Roasting sugar roots together in the Clearing. Flying through the air and shooting baskets. The day at the beach when she gave him a swimming lesson. It wrecked Wylie to think she would never be that version of herself again. This was what it felt like to get older, she realized. Being an adult meant accepting that life hadn't turned out the way you planned. It meant having that constant, troubling feeling of regret and disappointment. A feeling that would probably take hold of her the second she found her way home.

"I never wanted to grow up this fast," Wylie said sadly.

Phinn reached into the cage and took her hand. "Maybe growing up isn't such a bad thing," he said.

258 の Sara Saedi

Wylie was suddenly consumed by a memory of the day her dad moved out of the house. Maura had knocked on Wylie's bedroom door. She'd said she needed some air and asked if she could sit on the fire escape. She crawled through Wylie's bedroom window and sat on the ladder wearing nothing but a robe, despite the chilly weather.

"Mom, you're going to freeze to death," Wylie had warned her, but she didn't budge.

Wylie placed a coat around her mom's shoulders and sat with her, half scared she might leap off the fire escape.

"Do you want to hear something sad?" Maura asked. Wylie didn't know how to respond.

"What?"

"After all the lying and the fighting and the cheating, I still love him."

That is *sad*, Wylie thought. *And maybe even a little pathetic.* But she didn't say that out loud.

The memory on the fire escape took on a different meaning now. Wylie's mom wasn't weak after all. She was just human. Maura was trying to explain that love didn't operate like a light switch. You couldn't just turn your feelings off, even when someone has hurt you over and over again. Wylie didn't understand it at the time, but it was exactly how she felt right now as she stared at Phinn. She nearly let out a laugh. Her worst fear had been realized: she could relate to her parents.

"We could leave the island together, Wylie," Phinn said. "We could start over. We could travel the world and grow old together."

Once he said it, Wylie knew exactly what she wanted. To

live in the real world and to see every part of it. To have the freedom to make her own decisions without consulting any handbooks or showing up for a daily dose of birth control. To forge her own path. She looked at Phinn and told herself that one day, she would be able to stop loving him. She would meet someone else who was good and honest and didn't use people. In time, she would look at that person and not see everything she had lost by leaving the island, but instead everything she had gained.

She held Phinn's gaze and did the one thing she knew would hurt him as much as he'd hurt her. She used her free hand to rip off the necklace that had belonged to his mother and dangled it in front of him, then said as coldly as she could:

"I would rather die young than grow old with you, Phinn."

It might have been a lie, but she could tell by the broken look on his face that he bought every word of it.

rescue mission

the water started out choppy, but Gregory managed to keep the boat afloat. He had to make this journey alone. The police department wouldn't be easily convinced that he suspected his children were being held captive on an island no one knew existed. The circumstances of their disappearance haunted him even more now that he'd seen the sketch of Phinn. Were they smuggled to Minor Island, or did they go willingly? Did they know Phinn's connection to their father? Were they living there freely, or were they being held prisoner? If his voyage continued to go smoothly, he would have all the answers by tomorrow.

Though he hoped for an easy passage, Gregory had given his lawyer a sealed envelope and asked him to release it to Maura if no one had heard from him in a month's time. For now, he had told her he was going on a quick trip to raise funds to help continue their search efforts. Maura might think he was insane after reading the contents of the envelope, but he directed her to get in contact with Dr. Olivia Weckler. Olivia was the only other person who could confirm to Maura that the island actually existed. She'd been exiled from Minor Island when, after returning from a one year sabbatical on the mainland, she started showing signs of aging.

Gregory wondered what Olivia would think if she came across the police drawing of Phinn. The sketch was already plastered everywhere in the city, but Gregory knew there was little point in looking for Phinn in New York. His visits were rare, and when he did come to the mainland, he never stayed very long.

And he couldn't wait any longer to find his kids—or to tell them the news he'd just received.

The call from Joshua's lawyer had come a couple days before, and Maura was the one who had answered the phone.

"Katie Anderson came out of her coma," he said. "It's too soon to tell if she'll be able to walk, but she's awake. She has a long road ahead of her."

The irony wasn't lost on Gregory. The Andersons had their daughter back, while their kids were still missing. But not for long. Gregory placed Wylie's birthday present at the top of the things in his suitcase. The gift was an old painting of *parvaz* flowers that Tinka had made him years before. He'd had it restored and framed for Wylie. He had wanted so badly to give his daughter a tiny piece of his past, even though he'd planned to lie and tell her he'd found the picture at an antique shop. The thought of giving it to her in person helped keep his nerves at bay once he boarded the sailboat and maneuvered it away from the docks.

262 ~ Sara Saedi

Decades had gone by since he'd sailed on his own, but he couldn't hire a captain for the ride. Bringing a stranger to the island was far too great a risk. Sailing a boat was like riding a bike, he tried to convince himself. As soon as he hit the open waters, it would all come back to him. And it did, for the most part. He remembered how to hoist the sails. It wasn't easy to accomplish by himself, but he managed to shackle the clew, release the mainsheet, pull the halyard tight, then cleat it. First the mainsail, then the jib, all with the objective of keeping the boat steady.

It was several hours into the ride when he noticed an anvil-shaped cloud up ahead: the sign of a white squall. Phinn had taught him that. The bow began dipping as the wind quickly picked up speed. Gregory thought of using the GPS to turn back to New York, but then an image of his kids came into his mind. Wylie, Joshua, and Micah. The three best things he'd ever done with his life. The reasons he never regretted leaving the island. No threat of bad weather would stop him from rescuing them. Phinn didn't know anything about being a parent. He had no clue the lengths a father would go to protect his children. But he was about to find out.

+ + + + + +

IT WAS COLD AT NIGHT ON THE FORBIDDEN SIDE. Instead of a lagoon, there was a thick swamp with mosquitoes buzzing around. Wylie's arms and legs were already covered in red welts where they'd bitten her as she tried to sleep. A small patch of flowers and herbs grew along the periphery of the cages. They were probably the plants Lola had mentioned she missed cooking with. After three days locked up behind the caution tape, she no longer found the smell on this side of the island as offensive as on the day they'd arrived. The stink of urine was not as strong, and Wylie knew it was only because her senses had gotten used to it.

So far, the routine had been the same every day. Wylie, Joshua, and Micah were let out of their cells for a few minutes to relieve themselves and stretch their legs. Tinka was assigned to Wylie. It was humiliating, squatting behind a tree to go to the bathroom with Tinka handcuffed to her, to ensure that she wouldn't try to run away. Once they were locked up again, Phinn would arrive to bring them leftover scraps from breakfast, along with water. He fed her brothers first, then made his way over to Wylie.

"Please tell me you've changed your mind about going home," he'd plead, and Wylie would always answer the same way.

"No."

"You don't know how much it hurts me to see you like this," he'd say, on the verge of tears.

"You're the one who's doing this to us," Wylie reminded him.

"Because you didn't give me any other choice."

"I don't want to go home!" Joshua would yell from across the way. "Please! Let me out!" But Phinn always ignored him.

"You're all staying here until your sister changes her mind."

Once the narrow streams of sunlight faded, Wylie would

sit awake in her cage, unable to sleep. It wasn't just the whine of the mosquitoes that caused her insomnia, but also the racing thoughts about her parents. She wondered if her dad suspected where they might be, or if her parents had stopped searching for them. Wylie liked to imagine that the tragedy had brought her mom and dad closer together. Perhaps the loss would remind them why they fell in love with each other in the first place. She knew it was wishful thinking, but maybe once she and her brothers found their way back home, they could all be a family again.

"Why are you doing this?" Joshua called to her the next morning, after Phinn had left and they'd finished their breakfast. "Why can't you just forgive him and put us all out of our misery?"

"What he did was unforgivable!" Wylie yelled back. "He's going to let us go home eventually. He can't keep us here forever." Maybe if she kept telling herself that, she'd eventually believe it.

"I don't care if Phinn brought us here because of Dad. I'm not going back to New York just so I can rot in jail."

"We're already rotting in jail," Wylie mumbled to herself.

Over the course of the past few days, Micah had been so quiet that Wylie had to call his name just to make sure he was still alive. She had contemplated not telling him about Tinka's past with their dad, but she worried someone else on the island might taunt him with it. He was better off learning about the secret from his sister, even if she wouldn't be able to hug and comfort him from the confines of her cage. He didn't say much when he heard the truth, and though it was probably disturbing, Wylie suspected what hurt him even more was the way Tinka ignored him now. She didn't ask if he was okay or try to sneak him art supplies. Cooperating with Phinn had put her back in his good graces, and that was exactly how she wanted it.

"Micah!" Wylie called out.

"I'm alive," he managed to say.

The nights were long and scary. Any sudden sound or noise kept them on edge. This was, after all, where Hopper had kidnapped the lost kids. Lola's journal had said Phinn was just as much to blame for their disappearance, and now Wylie knew what she'd meant. The lost kids were never camping out on the Forbidden Side. They must have been prisoners, too, when they went missing. Each of them had done something to offend their fearless leader, and they had been punished for it. She tried to imagine the look on Phinn's face as he entered the prison camp to feed the delinquents, only to find the entire place empty.

The crunch of leaves startled Wylie from her near slumber. It was probably a bird or a small, harmless animal, she told herself. There was nothing to be afraid of. If Hopper did show up, someone on the other side of the island was bound to hear them scream. And then she heard footsteps.

"Micah," she said as loudly as she could without yelling, "Do you hear something?"

No response. The sound got closer and closer, and then she heard the faintest whisper of a girl's voice.

"Wylie. It's me. Don't scream."

"Lola?" Wylie asked, her heart in her throat.

"No, you idiot. It's Tinka. Don't make a sound. I've come to help you."

This was obviously a trap, and Wylie was not going to step into it.

"Go away. You're just going to get us killed."

"We don't have much time. Most of the island's been hit with a bad case of dysentery, thanks to a little something I snuck into the food. Phinn's stomach is apparently made of steel, but a medical emergency was the only way I could get rid of Patrick and guard the gate by myself."

"And you came to set us free," Wylie said sarcastically. "How dumb do you think we are?"

"Who are you talking to?" Micah asked.

Tinka felt her way through the dark to his cage. "Micah, it's me. I want to help you guys go home."

"Why? So you can get rid of us and walk into the sunset with Phinn?" Micah snapped. It was the most her brother had said since they'd been taken captive.

"I expected more from you, Dalton. Did you learn nothing about me during those hours we spent in my bungalow? Phinn trusts me. I have to keep up my loyal façade for as long as necessary to help you guys. If I stand up to him like your crazy sister, I'll be locked up in here with all of you. So I'm here to help you, on one condition."

"Of course there's a catch," Wylie groaned. *Are there any good people on this island?*

"I want to go with you," Tinka replied.

"What?" Micah asked.

"I want to go with you. I want to start over on the mainland."

Phinn had betrayed them both. Wylie had wasted months of her life on him, but Tinka had wasted years. It made complete sense that she would want a different future for herself. Who were they to deprive her of that chance?

"Don't you think my dad's too old for you now?" Micah blurted.

"I don't care about your dad," Tinka replied. "I care you about you."

"Guys, how about we table this discussion for when we're not held prisoner on the part of the island where a bunch of people were kidnapped, never to be heard from again," Wylie said. "Tinka, we've got a deal. If you get us out of here, we'll take you with us."

The keys to the cages were never out of Phinn's possession, so Tinka had to pick the lock to Wylie's cell with her knife.

"Come on," she mumbled as she lodged the blade into the keyhole. "I've been practicing for three days to get this right." Her hands trembled and she dropped the knife. She fell to her knees and fumbled through the sand to find it. She picked it up and tried again.

"Slow down," Wylie advised.

Tinka gingerly placed the knife back in the hole. She calmly adjusted it until she heard a click and the lock opened.

"Do you still have that pepper spray?" Tinka asked.

Wylie nodded. So Tinka had let her hold on to it on purpose.

"Good," Tinka replied. "You were smart not to try to use it sooner."

Tinka picked the lock for Micah's cell next. The keys to the handcuffs were kept in the wooden box with Hopper's calling card written on it. Tinka freed Wylie and Micah from their cuffs, and the three of them ran across the way to Joshua's cell.

"Are you coming with us?" Wylie asked her brother.

"What's the point? I'll just be going from one jail cell to another."

"It might be a few years of hell, but then you have the rest of your life to look forward to. There's Abigail. There's college. There's maybe even the White House. Please. I won't leave you here," Wylie said.

Joshua fought off a lump in his throat as he considered his options.

"Okay. Let me out. I want to go home," he replied.

"How do we know we can trust him?" Tinka asked. "How do we know he's not gonna go running to Phinn the second we leave?"

Wylie looked at her brother in the moonlight. His face was covered in dirt and grime. He looked like he'd lost a few pounds. A lot had gone wrong between them, but she didn't think he'd sell them out to Phinn. She squeezed the compass to remind herself of the days when the Daltons were a package deal.

"We can trust him," she said.

The four of them stayed in step with each other as they ran to the fence. Tinka thought they had a better chance of reaching the docks on foot, since they'd be much easier to spot while flying.

"Phinn's got his little army of insomniacs on guard in the sky. We need to get a head start before they see us. Once they do, that's when we fly. We should take separate routes and meet at the docks," she said, handing them each a *parvaz*.

Tinka held open the fence and they all quietly crept through. Running was no easy task after being in a cell for three days with no opportunity to exercise.

"Let's go!" Tinka said, tearing down the dark trail as quickly as she could. Wylie and her brothers turned to follow, but they were all startled by a scream.

"*Phinn!*"

They looked up to find Patrick hovering above them.

"*Phinn!* They're running away!" he shouted.

Wylie could see the spark of flashlights and candles flicker in the bungalows. Patrick had screamed loud enough to wake up the entire island.

"*Run!*" Tinka yelled.

No matter how fast their legs could carry them, they couldn't outrun someone amped up on *parvaz*. Micah and Tinka each popped a flower and Wylie moved to do the same, but it slipped through her fingers and fell on the ground. She would have had to crawl on her hands and knees to find it, so she kept running. Patrick flew inches above her and tugged at Wylie's shirt, but she pried free of his grip and kept moving. Joshua was a few feet ahead of her.

"Take the *parvaẓ*!" Wylie called to her brother, not wanting him to know she'd lost hers. Joshua swallowed the flower and careened above her. The wind picked up around them and Wylie knew that meant there were more people flying after them. She glanced over her shoulder as she kept sprinting and noticed Nadia holding Patrick back, trying to give Wylie a head start. It was about a three-mile run from the Forbidden Side to the beach. About half the distance she ran on the basketball court during a game. She could make it there. Wylie looked up at the sky to see if she could spot Tinka or her brothers, but instead she saw Phinn speeding through the air, his focus locked on her. He grasped at her hair, just inches away from catching her, but Wylie ran off the trail into the trees and bamboo. The thick of the jungle would slow her down, but it would also make it harder for Phinn to grab her.

"You can't outrun me, Wylie!" Phinn yelled above her.

I can try, she told herself. Phinn followed her into the brush and yanked her shirt, causing her to fall. Just as he landed behind her, she remembered the *parvaẓ* flowers she'd kept in her pocket. They were long dead, but maybe they could help her fly for a few yards. Phinn grabbed her leg and she kicked him hard in the stomach. He keeled over in pain as she popped a handful of dried-up petals into her mouth and swallowed them whole. She floated slowly at first, then picked up speed. This would be her last flight, she realized.

As she flew through the sky, she tried to find her brothers, but they were nowhere in sight. She arrived at the docks, but if she landed on a boat and tried to sail away,

Phinn would easily capture her. The effects of the *parvaz* carried her well past the dock and into the middle of the ocean.

"Wylie! Stop flying away!" Phinn yelled. He grasped at her feet in midair and managed to hold on to her ankle. He pulled her toward him, and for a brief moment they were floating in the sky, face to face. Wylie dug into her pocket for the pepper spray. Her palms were sweating and she worried if she didn't move quickly, Phinn would wrestle it from her grip.

"Let me go!" she screamed as she pointed the canister at his face and sprayed the liquid straight in his eyes.

Phinn howled in agony, clasping his hands over his eyes. Free from his grip, Wylie kept flying into the night, but she suddenly felt her stomach lurch. She was falling. The dried flower had lasted only a few minutes. The water splashed loudly as she plunged into the ocean. The waves were rough, but she kept her head above the water. Phinn called out to her from above.

"You'll drown!" he shouted.

"No, I won't. I know how to swim," Wylie called back.

Wylie gulped air and immersed herself in the water. She swam under the surface as long as she could, then came up for a breath. Phinn was still wheeling around in the air, trying to find her through his blind haze. She dipped beneath the waves and kept swimming till her lungs felt like they were going to burst. Phinn's voice was fainter now as he called out her name. He would have to give up eventually before the effects of the flower wore off and he plummeted into open water and drowned. Wylie was a strong swimmer. By the time he could get on a boat to find her, it would be like searching for a grain of salt in a sandbox. She kept swimming and coming up for air till she could barely make out the island anymore.

The only light came from the moon and the stars. The water looked black, and Wylie didn't know if there were sharks or any other sea creatures she had to worry about. She couldn't see Phinn anywhere, but now he was the least of her problems. She was in the middle of the ocean with no life raft or vest. It would be at least six hours before the sun came up, and there was no way she could tread water for that long. Her eyelids drooped as she fought to stay awake. The water seemed to get colder and colder as she swam away from the island, and she didn't know how long she had before hypothermia would set in. She had thought Minor Island would extend her life by decades, and here she was about to die at the age of seventeen. *Please let my brothers fare better than I did tonight*, she thought. *Please let them be safe*.

Though her arms and legs were exhausted and it was nearly impossible to catch her breath, Wylie kept swimming. The movement helped keep her awake and would only take her farther away from Phinn and everyone else on the island. With the light of the moon, her eyes focused on what looked like a rock a few yards away. Or maybe a few miles. The ocean could be deceptive when it came to distance, and it was very likely her vision was playing tricks on her. She kicked and plowed her arms through the waves, but swallowed a mouthful of water. Wylie choked as her nose and eyes stung from the salt. It was hard to tread water and cough it up at the same time, but Wylie was now close enough to see the rock wasn't a figment of her imagination. It was high enough to protect her from the tide. A few more strokes and she could finally get some rest.

As soon as her fingertips met cold stone, Wylie let out a cry. It took all the strength she had left to lift her body out of the water and climb to the top of the rock. She could rest here until morning, and with any luck, wouldn't freeze to death. She tried to catch her breath, but the thought of her brothers still trapped on the island made her hyperventilate.

A sharp pain sprang from her thigh and Wylie reached into her pocket to find the source. She pulled out the compass Joshua had given her on her birthday only to discover the glass was now broken and had cut into her flesh. Her body shook with heavy sobs as she thought of the words to her dad's favorite Simon and Garfunkel song. The melody slowed down her heart rate like a lullaby. She was a rock, she told herself. She was an island.

✦ ✦ ✦ ✦ ✦ ✦

"ARE YOU ALIVE? CAN YOU HEAR ME?"

Wylie's eyes blinked open. A thick fog covered the horizon as the night sky gave way to gray. A boat was floating a few feet from where she'd fallen asleep. This had to be a dream. All she could think was how sad and alone she would feel once she woke up from it and remembered she was in the middle of a vast ocean, all by herself.

"Grab on to the rope. I'll pull you up," a voice said.

Wylie looked up to find a man's face staring down at her.

He had a mane of thick curly hair and a beard that was long enough to be braided.

"I'm not dreaming?" she asked.

"No. I'm going to help you." She dipped herself into the cold water and floated toward the rope. Every muscle screamed in pain as she tried to climb up it.

"I can't," she yelled to him.

"I've got you," he said, using all his strength to pull her up. She was halfway up the boat when she noticed his hands. The nails were grimy and overgrown, but that wasn't what horrified her. On his right hand, there were three small stumps where his fingers should have been.

Hopper.

"Get away from me!" Wylie cried. She let go of the rope and flung herself into the ocean. The water smacked her limbs, and the salt in her open wounds felt like a thousand tiny needles pricking her skin.

"What are you doing?" Hopper yelled. He jumped over the side of the boat and into the water. Wylie tried to swim away, but her aching muscles betrayed her. Hopper grabbed her arm and Wylie flailed and kicked as hard as she could. She got in one good punch, but it wasn't enough to knock him out.

Then Wylie felt her head strike the rock that had briefly saved her life.

"Now you've done it," was the last thing she heard Hopper say as she lost consciousness.

lost and found

all Wylie could see when she opened her eyes was white. For a moment she thought she was crawling toward the pearly gates, but if this was heaven, she wouldn't be in such excruciating pain. Her vision slowly came into focus and she realized she was staring at the white baseboards of a boat. Her clothes were dripping from spending the night in the ocean. She tried to use her hands to stand up, but she couldn't move them. They were tied with a rope behind her back. A drop of blood fell from her head and splattered on the wood floor. A hand rested on her shoulder as someone placed a washcloth against her temple.

A guy's voice reverberated through her head, but she couldn't make out exactly what he was saying over the ringing in her eardrums.

Wylie tried to lift her head and look up. The tears that were forming made it difficult to focus. She blinked a few times, but it wasn't helping. She knew she had to get away.

Hopper was dangerous. He had practically knocked her out in the water, and now he'd tied her up. The longer she stayed here, the less chance she had of surviving.

"Wylie, it's okay," a girl's voice said. A few more blinks and then Wylie's eyes finally focused.

Lola was kneeling in front of her.

Hopper lingered next to Lola, his mutilated hand on her shoulder. Behind them, Wylie saw multiple new faces staring back at her with concern. She was too disoriented to count, but somehow she knew the number would add up to twelve. A girl stood next to Lola, her wrists decked out in friendship bracelets. She had to be Charlotte.

All the kids staring back at her held weapons in their hands: arrows, daggers, and spears. The smell of kelp and fish was so strong, it made her queasy. The waves rocked the boat back and forth violently, only worsening the nausea.

"We're not going to hurt you," Lola promised.

"Why am I tied up?" Wylie asked, her voice raspy.

"We didn't want you to run away."

"If you hadn't freaked out on me, then you wouldn't have hurt yourself," Hopper said without an ounce of sympathy.

"She was scared," Lola reminded him. "Phinn's got a talent for keeping people terrified."

"Can someone please tell me what's going on?" Wylie begged. She gestured to Hopper. "Is he holding us hostage?"

The kids erupted with laughter, but Hopper didn't seem to find the question funny. He shook his head and clenched his jaw. There was so much hair and scruff on his face that he was unrecognizable from his photograph, but Wylie still found herself struck by his eyes. They had a twinkle to them and didn't look like they belonged to a maniac at all.

"Wylie and I need a few minutes alone together," Lola said. "If I untie you, will you promise not to do anything stupid? There's nothing but ocean out there. If you jump overboard, you'll drown."

Wylie nodded. Lola gave a look to Hopper. "You can untie her."

"Are you sure?" Hopper asked. "She's got a hell of a left hook. My jaw is still killing me."

"I'm sure."

Hopper used a knife to cut through the rope, freeing Wylie's wrists.

"Put your arm around me," he said.

Wylie did as she was told and Hopper helped prop her up to her feet. Every joint was sore from the hours of swimming, but she managed to stay upright. The lost kids backed off as Lola and Hopper moved Wylie down a staircase and into the cabin of the boat. The room, much too cramped for more than a dozen people to share, was filled with sleeping bags.

"We usually sleep seven down here and seven up top. We trade off so no one has to freeze their butts off every night," Lola explained.

Hopper left to give them privacy, as Wylie slowly changed out of her wet clothes and wrapped herself in a blanket. After wearing the same outfit for four days straight, she dreaded getting dressed again once her clothes were dry. After Wylie was covered up, Hopper returned with a mug of hot soup.

"It's from a can," he said apologetically.

"It's okay," Wylie replied. "Anything will taste good right now."

The steam from the soup curled its way up to the ceiling. She quietly blew on it, keeping her eyes glued on Lola as they sat on the sleeping bags.

"I thought I'd never see you again," Wylie said.

"I wish I could have told you I was okay," Lola replied, looking down at her hands. "Maz . . . how is he?"

"Not good," Wylie admitted.

Lola nodded but didn't say a word. Hopper gently scratched the top of her head with his good hand.

"You're not the one to blame for his pain," he assured her, but she started to cry anyway. He used a towel to wipe the tears rolling down her cheeks.

Wylie had a long list of questions, but right now Lola seemed too fragile to answer them. So she decided to spill her guts first. As she listened to herself speak, it felt as though she was relaying the details of someone else's life. Just your typical, run-of-the-mill love story: Boy meets girl. Boy takes girl to a mystery island. Boy turns out to have a lifelong vendetta against girl's father. Boy holds girl captive. Boy loses girl. Lola's face didn't register shock when Wylie revealed her dad's true identity. Maybe she had learned the truth already.

"I don't know what happened to my brothers," Wylie said. "Maybe they got away, or maybe Phinn's holding them hostage again."

"Don't worry about that now. You're safe here. Phinn can't get to you," Lola said.

I don't care about Phinn, Wylie wanted to snap back. *I just want my brothers to be okay.* But it wasn't Lola's fault they were safe on this boat while Micah and Joshua were somewhere else, possibly in danger. There was no sense in making her feel guilty when she'd endured her own share of traumatic events these past few weeks.

"How did you end up here? Everyone thinks you were kidnapped by Hopper," Wylie said. "But I was never convinced."

"Smart girl," Hopper mumbled, a wry smile on his face.

"I knew Phinn would blame him," Lola said. "Just like he blamed him for everything else. Prom, for example. Hopper didn't have anything to do with that. It was just Phinn trying to keep us afraid." She stood up and moved around the tiny cabin, tidying up the piles of towels and clothing that were crumpled up in every corner.

"Sweet Honey Stew," Lola continued. "That's how I discovered Phinn's secret. You said that day your dad had taught you how to make it. Well, it was a dish my tribe used to cook. It was Gregory's favorite. I would whip it up for him in secret sometimes, because Phinn was never fond of it."

"What happened when you left the garden?" Wylie asked, even though she dreaded the answer.

"I went to find Phinn. I tracked him down to the docks fixing one of the boats. 'They're Gregory's kids, aren't they?' I asked as soon as I saw him. He denied it the whole time, but I didn't believe him. I said that I would tell you, I would tell everyone. That the entire island would know that he was nothing but a liar and a manipulator. And he . . ." Lola trailed off, seemingly haunted by what had happened next.

"He gagged her and tied her up," Hopper said matter-of-factly. "And then he set sail and put her on a dinghy in the middle of the ocean."

Lola managed a wan smile. "He said it wouldn't seem right to let me drown, so he left my fate to the ocean. At least I managed to bite him before he got the gag all the way on."

"She'd been drifting in the water a few hours when we found her," Hopper went on.

"Hopper saved my life," Lola explained. "Just like he saved yours."

Wylie thought back to that day. She had left the kitchen and found Phinn in the clinic getting bandaged—he'd said it was a cut, but it must have been the wound from Lola's bite. She'd packed them a picnic basket and they'd gone out to the beach together. They waded out into the ocean and she gave him a swimming lesson. The entire time, he knew how he'd spent his afternoon. He'd left her best friend to die and he'd let Wylie grovel and apologize to him for putting a few measly nails in the floorboards.

"You're not a bad person, are you?" Wylie said to Hopper.

"I guess it depends who you ask," he replied.

"Tell her," Lola urged. "Tell her what we all did to you."

"I don't much like to relive it," Hopper said. He took a

scroll from his back pocket and handed it to Wylie. "And anyway, I'm better on paper."

Wylie unrolled it and began to read.

Prison changed me. Prison changes lots of people. I'm not unique in that way. In fact, I was one of the lucky ones. Most people go to jail and mourn the seconds and hours and days that pass them by. Some are locked up in their youth and don't get their freedom back until they're old and gray, but I was held prisoner on an island where no one ages. Even if I had been in captivity for decades, I wouldn't have looked a day over seventeen upon my release. I got off easy. I lost a few fingers, some of my sanity, and a lot of my dignity, but technically, I didn't lose a day of my life. That's the silver lining when you're doing time in a place where "time" doesn't exist. Now that I'm gone, I know there are theories and stories about what exactly happened to me. I know there are people out there terrified of me. I could go down in history as the bad guy. But even if I'm the only one who ever reads this, at least I'll feel like I've had a chance to tell my story.

I was lonely and vulnerable when Phinn found me. I was unloved. I had no parents or siblings or family. All my childhood, I'd been shuffled from one foster home to another. I don't blame myself for buying the bill of goods Phinn sold me. Why wouldn't someone like me want to go to an island where no one grows old and where parents don't exist? Minor Island was everything I thought it would be and more. I spent my days taking parvaz and flying above the palm trees. I ate better than I'd ever eaten before in my life. I had a roommate named Maz who was more generous than any foster family I'd ever lived with. I'd brought my guitar from the mainland and spent my evenings serenading all the night owls in the Clearing. They even threw me a party in my honor to welcome me to the island. The early days were some of the best days of my life.

Maybe if I didn't have such a problem with authority, it would have lasted longer. Phinn was charming and funny. He was the kind of person who made you feel better about yourself, simply because he chose to associate with you. But pretty soon I realized we weren't just there to be Phinn's friends. We were there to be his disciples. He wasn't just some kid running the island.

He was a god and we were supposed to treat him as such. I don't do well with hero worship. I didn't like that there were rules and laws we had to follow, but that those same rules didn't seem to apply to Phinn. Back home, I was always suspicious of the government, but all I wanted now was some sort of democracy. A chance to vote on decisions and maybe even give someone else a shot at running the island. The more I talked to other residents, the more it seemed like they felt the same way. They had me fooled.

Phinn and a few of his cohorts grabbed me in my bungalow in the dead of night. I was guilty of treason, they told me. They dragged me out of my room and I assumed I would be taken to a boat and sent back to the mainland. According to the Minor Island handbook, exile was the punishment for treason. But that's not where they took me. I was brought to a secluded part of the island, swallowed up by the jungle. I'd been told these parts were prone to quicksand. My heart began to race as I became convinced they were going to let me sink to my death. But that would have been too easy. I spotted a lone cage. They threw me inside, handcuffed me, and locked me in. I'd gotten into a lot of trouble on the mainland, but I'd never once been arrested for anything. Now I was in solitary confinement.

I'm not sure exactly how much time passed or how long I was there. Months, I think. It's hard to say. I suppose I should have been flattered to be the first recruit to warrant his very own prison cell. I was a trendsetter. Before long, other cages popped up with other prisoners. Some were accused of sympathizing with me. Some were just tossed in for disrespecting Phinn. I feel guilty admitting it, but I was desperate for the company. The worst day in prison was when I lost my fingers. Phinn knew playing guitar was my only form of therapy and he wanted to take it away from me. It could have been worse. It could have been my entire hand. It was Tinka who did the deed. If she hadn't been so nervous, it would have been swift and relatively painless. Instead, it took a while. The things we do for love. I hope he at least let her stay in his bungalow that night.

And then one day, they let me go. They waited until I was mentally, emotionally, and physically shattered. At the time, I wasn't sure why Phinn didn't take me out

in the middle of the Clearing and just have
me hanged in front of everyone. Now I
know. I was much more useful to him alive.
If he could keep everyone terrified that I
might come back and exact my revenge,
then they'd depend on him even more. Or
maybe he was just too much of a chicken
to actually kill me. Instead, he took me out
on his boat and sent me off on a raft in the
middle of the ocean with enough water to
last me a few days.

It was a miracle I survived. All thanks to
William and Margaret Regel, a retired
couple who'd always dreamed of living
out the rest of their days together on a
sailboat. They were a week into their new
life when they found me. I was skin and
bones, I could barely speak, I was afraid of
everything and everyone. They took me back
to the mainland, made sure I got the medical
attention I needed, and even gave me a
little bit of money. I had no place to live,
and William offered me one of his old boats
that was taking up space in the Connecticut
harbor. One day, I'll bring them to the island
as a show of my gratitude. It was Margaret
who encouraged me to write down my story,
even though the version I had told her was a
complete lie.

If you're reading this, I don't want you to feel sorry for me. I want you to join me. I have a plan. I'm going to exact revenge on my captor. I'm going to take away everything that means anything to him. I'm going to take his land and put him behind bars and do everything to him that he did to me. I will stock up on supplies and weapons. I will take William's boat and I will go back to the island. I will wait patiently. There's enough room on this boat for Charlotte and Sebastian and Jersey and everyone Phinn has locked up. I'll make it look like a kidnapping. Phinn will use it to his advantage, I'm certain of that. He will make everyone think I might come back again and kidnap more people. And while he keeps them all terrified, he'll give us time to prepare.

We will take back the island. And we will make Phinn suffer.

There were fourteen signatures at the bottom of the paper. Hopper's and all the lost kids in faded ink, and then Lola's name, more visible than the others.

"I'm sorry for what you've been through," Wylie said.

"I'm not looking for your pity," Hopper replied.

Wylie didn't know what else to say. She did pity him. She couldn't help it. But she could tell Hopper pitied her, too. The judgment in his gaze made her feel small and foolish, but then again, weren't they all guilty of falling in love with Phinn?

"We can't take you home, Wylie," Lola told her.

"I could never go home without my brothers," Wylie replied.

"Good, because you're going to help us take Phinn down." Wylie had never heard this tone in Lola's voice before. This was no longer the same girl who loved tending to her garden and daydreaming about life on the mainland. Phinn had left that girl in the ocean.

"I just want to get my brothers and go home."

"That's awfully selfish," Hopper said.

"I don't think you understand, Wylie," Lola interjected. "You are Phinn's biggest weakness. You're his Achilles heel. We're outnumbered. Yesterday, we didn't think we could beat him. Today we have a secret weapon. Today we have *you*."

Hopper handed Wylie a pen. "What do you say?" he asked. "Will you help us give that bastard everything he's got coming to him?"

The boat creaked loudly. Wylie could hear the pounding of feet from the deck. It sounded like the lost kids were jogging in place or doing jumping jacks. She unrolled Hopper's manifesto and read through all their signatures:

Hopper, Sebastian, Charlotte, Fiona, Jersey, Danny, Elizabeth, Kia, Benjamin, Zoe, Riley, Grace, Thomas, Lola.

The light switch was still on. The one her mom had warned her about that day on the fire escape. Even after all the terrible things Phinn had done, she wasn't sure if she would ever be able to turn it off completely.

Welcome to adulthood, Wylie thought.

"How soon would we go back?" she asked.

"As soon as we're ready," Lola replied. "You'll have to be patient."

Wylie pressed the tip of the pen against the paper and signed her name. Lola gave her a satisfied smile. Waiting out their return would be long and excruciating, but Wylie knew it would be worth it in the end. And until they turned the boat around and sailed back in the direction of the island, there were three lines from Hopper's manifesto Wylie would hold in her memory:

I'm going to exact revenge on my captor. I'm going to take away everything that means anything to him. I'm going to take his land and put him behind bars and do everything to him that he did to me.

Wylie would keep repeating those words in her head until she meant them.

ACKNOWLEDGMENTS

No disrespect to any of the other pages in this book, but the below is the most important thing I've ever had to write. There are so many people to thank who made this novel possible. Friendly warning, it's about to get super warm and fuzzy.

A huge thank-you to Tom Jacobson for being the first person to suggest I write this idea as a novel. You shepherded this project from day one and helped me with it every step of the way. None of this would have been possible without you. You have been a wonderful mentor to me and I'm eternally grateful.

A very special thank-you to Jessica Regel at Foundry Literary & Media for taking a first-time novelist under her wing when I'd only written a few chapters of this book. You held my hand through this entire process and I could not have finished the book without you. Your ideas, advice, and encouragement were invaluable. You are a real-life fairy godmother and it's an honor to work with you.

I hit the editor jackpot with Kendra Levin at Viking Children's Books. Kendra, you were a true partner and collaborator throughout every stage of this novel. Thank you for all of your insightful notes and ideas. Most of all, thank you for your patience and all the phone hours you spent helping me refine and revise this story. You gave me perspective when I had none. You are a gem of a person. Thank you to everyone else at Viking who helped make this dream a reality.

A special thank-you to Blye Faust and Wendy Rhoads for being early supporters of this book and early supporters of my career. You are among the first people to believe in me as a writer. Thank you for everything you've taught me.

To Eric Brooks, thank you for all of the career (and legal) advice throughout the years. You've been a calm and supportive presence at every crossroad. To Dana Spector for believing in this project and for your patience as it underwent months of rewrites. Thank you as well to Lynn Fimberg, Matt Ochacher, Michael Pelmont, and David Rubin for the endless support and guidance. I am very lucky to be working with all of you.

To Nathan Zolezzi and Michael Grant for the early reads and the very generous and helpful feedback.

To Susan Levine for #1 Listening and #2 Years of advice.

To Georgi Schafer, Edward Schafer, Jennifer and Chris Krisiewicz. I'm so lucky to call you my family. Thank you for all of your love and support.

They say it takes a village and I agree if that village equals a really good group of girlfriends. A special shout-out to my besties Alison Asaro and Kayoko Akabori for celebrating the victories with me along the way and for all the pep talks in between.

Thank you additionally to my favorite book club ladies: Alison Asaro (yeah, you just got thanked *twice*), Agnes

Chu, Anne Trench, Daya Berger, Emily Brough, Gabrielle Ebert, Jen Kleiner, Jihan Crowther, Karin Nelson, Lani D-Barrett, Toby Lowenfels, and Valentina Garcia-Loste for reminding me that books (and mimosas) are my first love.

For me, the relationship between the Dalton siblings is the heartbeat of this story. Thank you to my sister Samira Saedi Abrams and my brother Kia Saedi for being my best friends and biggest inspirations. You have endured many of my career twists and turns and you've never stopped encouraging me. You are the most generous, compassionate, and funny people I know. If I ever move to a magical island, I'm taking you both with me. Thank you also to Jacob Abrams for being the older brother I've always wanted. You're totally invited to the island, too. I love you guys.

To my kind and curious nephew and nieces, Mazin, Ella, Keira, and Cameron. I hope once you're old enough to read this book you will permanently refer to me as your "cool aunt."

A very special thank-you to my incredible parents, Ali and Shoreh Saedi. You changed your entire lives so your kids could have better opportunities and no form of gratitude will ever be enough. Your love and support mean the world to me. Thank you for never asking me if I had a backup plan, for always believing in me, and for making me feel like I was meant to be a writer. Thank you also for reading the book in its earliest incarnation when you had a million other things keeping you busy. You are the kind of parents a kid wants to make proud. I love you so much.

Is it weird to thank your dog in acknowledgments?

What if your dog is an adorable pug named Mabel who sat on your lap during the writing of this book? Okay, in that case—thank you, Mabel, for filling my days with so much joy.

Most importantly, thank you to my loving husband, Bryon Schafer. If it weren't for your confidence in me, I would never have had the guts to quit my day job. Thank you for never rolling your eyes during my frequent bouts of self-doubt, for reminding me to laugh at myself, and for your unwavering support. Also, thanks for marrying me, because a) companionship and b) I had the idea for this story on our honeymoon. You are the best life partner a girl could ask for. Everything is better with you by my side, and there's no one I'd rather grow old with. I love you.

Read the first chapter of

The Lost Kids,

the sequel to *Never Ever*!

"phinn, are you listening? Where's Wylie Dalton?"

Dead.

Sleeping at the bottom of the ocean.

Permanently trapped in the folds of my mind.

Tucked away in the corner of my heart.

All of the above.

"You have a chance to do the right thing here. Answer the question."

A fan buzzed overhead. The steady beeping of the heart monitor made Phinn insane. He missed the *pop-pop* of *parvaz* flowers and the *whir* of teenagers flying above him. He missed the melodies of the island. Hell, he missed blue sky.

"Where's Wylie Dalton?"

The question had haunted Phinn from the moment he heard Wylie plummet into the ocean, and now it was being asked of him with about as much urgency as someone looking for a set of missing keys. All he wanted was to see Wylie again, to hold her and tell her that the moment he'd met her, he'd given up on making her part of his intricate revenge plot.

Phinn's plan had always been to befriend Joshua. The son in trouble with the law seemed the most vulnerable of the Dalton siblings. But all that changed when Wylie came into Phinn's line of sight. She'd been on the dance floor, surrounded by friends, but had somehow created the illusion that she was alone. From where Phinn had sat that night, he'd barely been able to make out the emerald shade of her irises, but he'd seen a trace of pain behind her eyes. On that rooftop in Brooklyn, he'd forgotten about her dad and all the reasons he'd manipulated a run-in with the Dalton kids. Their future didn't feel premeditated anymore. It felt inevitable.

"If I knew where she was, don't you think I would have found her?" Phinn finally responded.

"What did you do to her?"

I lied to her. I broke her heart into a million pieces. I held her captive.

"Nothing. I didn't do anything to her. I want to go home."

"I'm afraid that's not going to happen."

Phinn did the math. He'd been here for seven days. That meant two hundred and eighty-eight more days to spare before he'd turn eighteen.

"How old were you when your parents died?"

"What do you have on that little clipboard?" Phinn asked. "A list of every upsetting question you could ask me?"

"This will go a lot more easily if you cooperate."

"Five. I was five when my parents died."

"And how did they die?"

He'd thought that it was just an elaborate game of hide-and-seek, that, when he found them, they were only pretending to be asleep. He'd yanked his mother's hair, screaming at her to wake up. He'd scraped her skin with his fingernails as Lola's family pulled him away.

Phinn looked into the eyes of his interrogator and waited until he was certain he wouldn't cry.

"They killed themselves."

sleepless nights

the water was still for once. Lying on the floorboards of the boat, Wylie felt almost as if she was back on dry land. After three weeks trapped on this vessel, she was finally getting used to the cold dankness. The surrounding abyss of ocean no longer left her overwhelmed. The days of motion sickness slowly retreated into the past. Despite all she had grown accustomed to, sleepless nights continued to torture her, and tonight was no exception. It didn't matter that every joint and limb was weak from hours of exercise—Wylie's mind refused to slow down. She spent every night searching for constellations and counting stars, but nothing seemed to lull her to sleep.

It had been twenty-one days since she'd last seen her brothers. The Daltons had never spent that much time apart. Here, on this boat, she had no parents and no siblings. She was an orphan. The lost kids were her only family now. She sat up and looked at all the sleeping bodies sprawled in every direction. Charlotte snored loudly next to her, as she did most nights. Wylie tried to shut out thoughts of smothering her with a blanket. It wasn't Charlotte's fault that she could fall asleep anywhere she laid her head down.

"I love sleeping," Charlotte explained to her. "Every night when we go to bed, we wake up one day closer to taking the island back. One day closer to going home."

Home. Wylie wasn't sure where that was anymore. The lost kids meant the island, but Wylie had no desire to live there without her brothers. She wondered if Micah and Joshua had made it back to their Manhattan brownstone. For all she knew, they were sitting on the fire escape together right now, wondering if they'd ever see their sister again. If she closed her eyes long enough, she could make believe she was back in her old bed, wrapped in worn-out flannel sheets. What she would give to wake up in the morning and brush her teeth in a normal sink and take a hot shower in an actual bathtub.

The snores were even louder now. Wylie gently tapped Charlotte's shoulder.

"Charlotte," she whispered. "You're snoring."

Charlotte groaned and turned on her side. The rumbling subsided for a few minutes, until it started back up again. After three weeks of insomnia, Wylie wasn't sure what tormented her more: sleep deprivation or Phinn.

She'd finally conquered it last night as she'd let her mind drift off to the party at Vanessa's and remembered what it felt like to see Phinn across the rooftop. She'd recalled how everyone else melted away except for them. Before the memories could turn dark, before she could remind herself that Phinn was a monster, she'd fallen asleep. But tonight, the very thought of him made her restless mind even more alert.

Wylie stretched out her legs and quietly pulled herself to her feet. She grabbed the thin blanket that barely kept her warm and wrapped it around her shoulders. She'd perfected the art of moving without disturbing others in their sleep. Her feet knew every floorboard to avoid and every sleeping body to step over in the pitch dark. All they had to do was follow the soft sounds of guitar strumming to the bow of the boat.

"Couldn't sleep again?" Hopper asked as she tiptoed toward his regular spot.

"Nope."

"What about last night? You were sleeping like a baby."

"Charlotte must've been snoring less."

"No way. I bet they could hear her all the way on the island."

"Mind if I hang out here for a while?" Wylie asked, lying down before he answered.

"Not in the slightest."

Hopper hadn't always been this nice to her. During her first few days on the boat, he'd mostly ignored her or given one-word responses to every question she'd asked him. And he'd never asked any questions in return. *He'd be terrible on a date,* Wylie had thought.

"He doesn't like most humans," Lola explained at the time. "Don't waste your time trying to win him over."

Perhaps it was boredom that made Wylie determined to be his friend—or maybe she needed a challenge. After their daily training sessions on the boat, the lost kids spent the rest of the day fishing and sharpening their spears. Most of them filled the hours rehashing every bad thing Phinn had done to them. Wylie grew bored with the same conversations, so she turned her attention to Hopper. It was like her secret game: *Person who doesn't like most humans, I will make you like me.*

It wasn't an easy pastime. In the beginning, all of Wylie's sarcastic quips and witty jokes had gone over like lead balloons. Hopper would respond with a blank stare, mutter an excuse under his breath, and walk off to another corner of the boat. *Try to find something you have in common*, Wylie told herself. Their mutual hatred of Phinn seemed like an obvious starting point, but Hopper never engaged in her verbal tirades against her ex. Wylie got the sense that he wasn't quite convinced she was over him. And then, when Wylie mustered the courage to ask if she could pass the evenings with him while he played guitar, Hopper said he preferred to be alone.

Finally, Wylie remembered his manifesto. There was no email on this boat and no texting, but Hopper himself had admitted he communicated best on paper. So Wylie wrote her own manifesto. She told her story, in her own words, and confessed how stupid she felt about having fallen for Phinn.

She folded the sheet of paper into a rectangle and slipped it under the strings of Hopper's guitar. He never mentioned reading it, but the following day, he meandered over to her as she tried in vain to fish for her dinner. They both knew she never caught anything.

"If you can't sleep tonight, you can come hang out with me." He said it casually, as though the ocean hadn't shifted from the invitation.

Now, every night since his overture, she snuck over to his tiny corner of the boat and listened to him clumsily play guitar. Thanks to Tinka, he'd lost three of the fingers on his right hand and was still teaching himself to use his right hand to press down on the frets. The chord changes were slow and unsteady, but Wylie hummed along to distract him when he got frustrated.

"Maybe she has a deviated septum," Wylie said.

"Who?" Hopper asked.

"Charlotte, obviously. What if we pinned her down, plied her with vodka, and did surgery to fix the thing? You hold her arms and I'll go in with a knife."

Hopper's face broke into a smile at the suggestion. It felt like such a victory when Wylie could get him to shift from his usual scowl.

"You're such a weirdo," Hopper said.

"A weirdo you're stuck on a boat with."

"I know. I should have left you on that rock."

Wylie tugged one of his curls playfully. She hadn't expected to get used to his appearance. Phinn was chiseled and clean cut, but Hopper was neither of those things, though it was hard to know what his face really looked like under his beard. Back in New York, he'd look like a homeless person. Most days, he smelled like one, too. Good hygiene wasn't really an option on a small boat filled with a dozen sweaty kids.

"I would give anything to go to sleep," Wylie replied.

"How about when we go back to the island, after we do the whole, you know, overthrowing Phinn bit, we'll go to the Forbidden Side and pick a bunch of *rahat* flowers and sleep for days."

Wylie felt like an imposter whenever Hopper talked about Minor Island. He always made references to plants or landmarks she wasn't familiar with, but she hadn't lived there nearly as long as he had. She felt like one of those people who called themselves New Yorkers after spending only a year in the city.

"No one ever told me about *rahat* flowers," Wylie admitted.

"Good. I like getting to be the one to tell you about stuff. They're red, almost burgundy. They're twice as big as *parvaz*, but they don't make any sound when they grow. Phinn never liked people taking them. But they made me feel . . . invincible. Aldo and Patrick gave them to me to help with anxiety, but if you take enough, they make you sleep for hours."

Wylie remembered spying the plant he was describing through the bars of her cage, just out of reach. Lola had mentioned there were herbs that were native to the Forbidden Side, but she'd never mentioned *rahat* flowers.

Wylie wondered what else about the island she'd never get a chance to discover.

"I could have used a few of those when Phinn had me locked up," Wylie said.

"I used to beg him for them, especially after they chopped off my fingers, but he wouldn't allow it."

"Well, he won't get a say now."

Aside from the guitar, Hopper's favorite pastime was fantasizing about life on Minor Island without Phinn, and Wylie always indulged him. They talked about how they'd get rid of all the cages on the Forbidden Side. Hopper promised he would personally nail down the floorboards to the panic room and would never make anyone hide out in the dark. The girls would no longer be herded into the clinic, forced to take birth control. Everyone could use their preferred form of contraception.

"Condoms are kind of a drag though, you know," Hopper joked.

"It's a good thing no one in their right mind would have sex with you," Wylie replied.

The conversation turned, as it nearly always did, to Wylie's thoughts about her brothers. Tonight, Hopper struggled with a few minor chords on the guitar and told her not to worry so much about them. Wylie rolled her eyes. She was starting to grow frustrated with only children who told her not to be so concerned about Micah and Joshua.

"If they're not on the island, I'll sail to New York and bring them back," Hopper promised.

Wylie closed her eyes and listened to a melody slowly forming on the guitar. Hopper said it was out of tune, but she didn't know the difference. The thoughts in her mind slowly swirled and the rooftop in Brooklyn came into view.

Don't think about Phinn, she told herself as she saw his face, and drifted into sleep.